S0-BOF-631

New Lines from the Old Line State

An Anthology of Maryland Writers

Edited by Allyson E. Peltier

Published in the United States by MWA Books, a division of the
Maryland Writers' Association
PO Box 142
Annapolis, Maryland 21404
www.marylandwriters.org

Permissions acknowledgements appear on page 227

ISBN-13: 978-0-9820032-0-6

Printed in the United States of America

Cover photo by Sonia L. Linebaugh
Cover and interior design by Lauren Manoy

10 9 8 7 6 5 4 3 2 1

First Edition

NEW LINES

FROM THE

OLD LINE STATE

An Anthology of Maryland Writers

EDITED BY ALLYSON E. PELTIER

A MARYLAND WRITERS' ASSOCIATION BOOK

TABLE OF
Contents

FICTION

POETRY

MEMOIR

INTRODUCTION

J UST SOUTH OF THE MASON-DIXON LINE BUT NOT QUITE Southern, a person needs to spend a day in Maryland to even begin to understand what "Mid-Atlantic" means. There is an indefinable "something" here that makes living in Maryland distinctly different than living in the Northeast or in the South; it straddles both regions but can be claimed by neither. Moreover, each city and county has its own character that further flavors the language and imagery of its artists. The Chesapeake. The ocean. Blue crabs. Old Bay. That "Bal'mer" accent, hon. Lush, early springs to hot, sauna-like summers to long, beautiful autumns and mild winters. Harbors filled with boats. Rolling hills dotted with farms. Cicadas. Cherry blossoms.

When the opportunity arose to edit the first-ever Maryland Writers' Association anthology, I was thrilled to get involved. How else but with an anthology does an editor get to collaborate with such an eclectic collection of writers working in such a variety of genres? So it was with great joy—and not a little trepidation—that I took on the task of editing and generally ushering this collection into existence.

I wondered, having recently relocated from New York City—the heart of publishing and home to some of the world's best writers—what kind of community I would find in Maryland. It was with immense pleasure that I discovered a thriving literary and artistic community in the "Old Line State," and how the work here is colored by the region in a delightfully unique, unexpected way.

In fact, Maryland has a literary legacy stretching as far back as America's written history goes. Maryland saw one of the New World's first printing presses—the first south of Boston—in the mid-1600s. And it was the brilliant bombardment of Baltimore's Fort McHenry that became fodder for Francis Scott Key's poem, "The Star-Spangled Banner." Maryland's cities and shores have inspired such literary greats as Edgar Allan Poe (how many states can boast a sports team named for a poem?) and Gertrude Stein, as well as more contemporary writers such as Madison Smartt Bell and Laura Lippman. Maryland, the Old Line State, nicknamed (so the story goes) by General George Washington in honor of the Maryland Line regiment, which served with distinction in the Revolutionary War. The Free State, with its streets still named after founding Calvert family members and the green-coated Rangers who patrolled the western front against the colony's enemies. So much history here, still present everywhere you look.

Today Maryland boasts a population that cuts a wide swath through the tapestry of ethnic, cultural, and religious backgrounds. From Charm City to Ocean City, from the Eastern Shore to the panhandle, Maryland's small size belies its great character and rich legacy. I hope you will enjoy and celebrate the artistic vision of these Marylanders as they take us from Baltimore, to Virginia, to California, to India, and beyond to worlds and realities as yet unmapped. Fantasy, mystery, poetry of longing and hope...*New Lines from the Old Line State* has it all.

Many thanks to all the volunteers who helped make this anthology happen, especially Gary Lester, Lauren Eisenberg, and Angela Render, without whom I could not have coordinated the huge undertaking that has become *New Lines from the Old Line State* and MWA Books. Thanks also to: John Machate for doing double-duty on chores so I could meet my deadlines; my intern, Benjamin White, for his invaluable assistance; Nicole Schultheis and Sherri Woosley for their fundraising efforts; Sonia Linebaugh for the use of her beautiful photograph on our cover; Lauren Manoy for her design wizardry and advice; the MWA Board for launching this project in the first place and continuing to support it; and all the authors for their various contributions, not the least of which is the incredible work showcased in this book.

—Ally E. Peltier, July 2008
Columbia, Maryland

FICTION

CICADAS

Eric D. Goodman

So, he was going to do it. They were going to do it. A few months of bliss together and they were ready to devote themselves entirely to one another forever. They had no idea what was coming.

I returned to northern Virginia that year, the year the cicadas returned. It was the summer of 2004, and my friend Skip was tying the knot. Leona was the most wonderful woman he had ever gotten to know. They were intimate, in love, soul mates. So alike, they looked and acted like twin copies of the same person, male and female.

So I returned to Virginia for their wedding—one I never expected to see, Skip not seeming the marrying type. I arrived a day early for the rehearsal. I drove into the wooded hills, my windows rolled down to enjoy the warm summer air cooled only by my speed. The uncanny noise started soft and dull, nearly unnoticeable. But it grew louder and fuller, an incessant screeching.

By the time I'd reached my destination it was unearthly, a crescendo from nature, unnatural. It was an eerie alien landscape, a scene from an old 1950s bug-eyed monster movie with sound effects so bizarre they couldn't possibly be real. But this sound was real. It was nearly off-putting enough to make me turn around and return to the comfort of my home, where I'd postponed a romantic rendezvous of my own.

Skip and Leona had heard whispers. Older friends and relatives, those experienced in life, had warned them that the cicadas were coming this year. But that didn't deter them. An outdoor wedding was what they wanted and an outdoor wedding was what they would have.

Looking at them in the park under the warmth of the afternoon sun and the spell of love, it seemed they were younger than they had been. Skip was more naïve now, the day before his wedding, than he had been years ago when we were still in high school, back when he was devising the best strategy for asking a girl to the prom without risking rejection. When he found a taker after two strikes, he was convinced he was in love. That affair had lasted five weeks and ended in emotional disaster.

But this one had already endured more than three months. They were so in love that they barely noticed the strange insects all around them, Skip in his T-shirt with the imprint of a tux, and she in her matching wedding tee. But they were too inexperienced to understand such a commitment, unaware of the cycle. They didn't remember the last time the cicadas had come.

Clint sat at one of the aluminum picnic benches under the pavilion, drinking a beer. As one of the groomsmen, he was wearing his tux. He'd forgotten this was an informal rehearsal. He slammed his fist against the table, the momentary look of anger on his face lifting as he flung something from his hand and then wiped away the remains. He stood and walked toward the trash barrel, then saw me approaching. He glanced back toward Skip and his bride to be. "Stu's here."

The cicadas had come seventeen years ago as well. And at that time, too, I was arriving in northern Virginia—that time, for the first time, to live. Halfway through high school, in 1987, I came to the school that would send me out into the world.

I met Skip and Clint that year, the year of the cicadas. It was during that year, shortly after I came to know him, that Clint married his own first true love, Amanda. His was an indoor wedding —Clint was no fan of insects—though the buzzing of the cicadas could be heard through the manmade boundaries of the divine structure. Clint had dropped out of high school with only a year left so he could do the honorable thing, the thing that he wanted to do not just because he had gotten Amanda pregnant but because he loved her. I envied him at the time and wished I could be so bold, parting with convention and leaving the tortures of public school to get a beautiful girl pregnant and marry her.

I had a run at it. It was during those noisy days of cicada love songs that I found my own first true love—a love that ended as the cicadas were dying off at the summer's end. I courted her alongside the cicadas, serenaded her with their voices instead of my own, and mated with her alongside them during camping trips. Before their eggs were falling from tree branches and delivering offspring to burrow into the earth for another seventeen years, our own relationship had dried up, crushed like the insect husks covering the sidewalks.

I learned a lot about love that summer. Clint did, too. So did Skip.

Now, at the wedding rehearsal, the groom gave me an emotional hug and Leona gave me an obligatory one. "You had us a little worried there for a minute," Skip said.

"Am I ever late?" I asked.

Clint scoffed. "But are you ever early?" His handshake pulled me into a bear hug.

"Let's get going," Skip said, anxious for the rehearsal, excited to get to tomorrow's real thing.

What Skip and Leona still didn't know—not yet—was what I didn't know the last time the cicadas had emerged: that romance is like the cycle of a cicada. There are a few weeks, perhaps a couple of months, of excited buzz—liveliness, romance, excitement, attraction, mating—and then comes a seventeen-year sleep; a lapse into monotony and routine that can't live up to the promise of the noisy romance at the start.

2

A LOT HAD changed since high school, but the fact that we were friends had not. We all lived in different places—me north, Clint west, and Skip in Virginia—but we had managed to keep our friendship. A few times every year we met up in one place or another: sometimes a weekend at one of our houses, other times at a cabin in the woods or mountains or just a hotel room with a couple of beds and a sleeper sofa.

The last time we got together, Skip had arranged the gathering. A cabin in the Smokies for three days provided just the isolation Skip desired to break the news.

We spent our days hiking and our nights playing cards. We liked to do things like that, things that involved activity but no intense concentration. We played hearts and spades and seven-up. An occasional hand of poker, the winner with the most chips—potato chips, pretzels, or tortillas—chose who went on the next beer run.

"Remember back in high school?" Clint said as he finished dealing and picked up his hand, spreading it into a fan and ordering his cards. "We used to play every day." Skip and I smiled and nodded. We had this conversation most times we played cards, every three to four months. "Those were the days," Clint said, taking a swig of beer from a longneck and discarding the bottle.

We'd spent many a lunch break playing cards back in high school. We'd eat our cafeteria lunches, then clear our trays and pull out the deck. As adults, Clint never let us forget it. He had an excited memory of his youth, in part because it was lost prematurely in the webbing of his complicated marriage. When loosened by whiskey he sometimes admitted regrets: that he wished he'd finished high school and gone to college and not gotten married so young. He'd had a good shot at a football scholarship. He could have been a success, something he didn't feel he was to his own wife and three kids. "Yes, those were the days," he sighed.

Playing cards was one of our favorite things to do because it gave us an excuse to talk. Cards, hiking, fishing, eating, drinking—they were all excuses that allowed us to talk without admitting that talking was what we wanted to do. We couldn't talk about serious things without pretending the talk was a by-product of partaking in some other action. Playing cards was a husk.

By the time Skip won the next hand we were out of beer. Clint threw his cards down. "Get the hell out!" he yelled angrily, thrashing his strong arm violently through the air in pursuit of a fly that had been buzzing around our table.

"You get the hell out!" Skip said, then grinned. "And get us some more beer."

Clint glared at him with mock irritation. "I'm going. You sissies practice so you'll be ready when I get back and really start playing." We laughed as he picked up his keys and left the cabin. Skip collected the cards.

"Hey, Stu." Skip looked at me with eyes that wanted to tell me something big, something monumental. Probably something stupid, I figured, but in his mind this was pivotal. Each eye twinkled on an axis of destiny. "I have something to ask you."

I looked at him with leery anticipation. What's he want now? Help with his resume? A reference? A loan to start another business? Most of the business plans he or I had been involved with were crushed dead at our feet within months of energized excitement. Maybe love advice? That's what it looked like, seeping from him. I'd had enough lovers to offer plenty of that. His eyes asked permission. "So ask," I said.

"Will you be my best man?"

I laughed. He was a boy catching his first insect of the season, offering her a comfortable place inside a glass jar, cushioned with dry grass, knife-jabbed holes in the metal lid and a stick inside for comfort. But Skip was offering this new lover more than the comfort of a stick; he offered her his freedom, his very life. He wanted to protect her within his glass jar and he wanted to be protected within hers.

"Seriously, man," he said. He tried not to show he was hurt by my dismissive laugh.

"You don't want to get married," I advised without seeking permission from his eyes. "That's crazy."

"I love Leona," he insisted. "Of course I want to marry her."

"I love women, too," I rebutted. "But you don't see me dragging any of them to the altar."

"You just haven't found the right one."

I laughed again, this time a little harder. "If there was a right one I've certainly had her." There had been quite a few right ones, which was exactly why I wasn't stupid enough to commit.

"So, what's it gonna be?" he asked. He had opened his protective layer of bark and I'd jabbed him. Now he was putting up the tough front. "Are you gonna be my best man or what?"

I considered. "If I'm the best man you can find." This pleased him. I was happy to be my friend's best man. I just wished I could convince him that this whole marriage thing wasn't the best idea.

Or maybe it was, for him. I suppose there's something to be said for the soul mate, whether self-created or truly destined. Maybe Skip could dig the comfort of having someone to burrow through the years with in the same way I could dig picking up anyone who put off the right pheromones at the right time without feeling the heavy weight of a marriage contract. But the feeling that Skip wasn't making the right decision, that Clint hadn't made the right decision seventeen years ago, echoed in my head.

If it was a soul mate or life partner Skip was looking for, Leona was probably the right one. But didn't he realize that their love was temporary and that in a month or two their buzzing romance would lie dead at their feet? The remains would burrow underground and remain dormant for years. And the two of them would be much happier and more alive if they shed the exoskeleton of their relationship when the newness ended and pursued happiness with fresh mates.

3

WE WERE NEVER the rowdiest bunch on the block. Skip, Clint and I had our fun, but it usually consisted of eating and drinking, going for a nature walk or catching a movie, playing cards and talking. We talked about movies we'd seen or books we'd read, if not recently, then back in high school. And we talked about our lives, at the moment, in the past and in the future. Our fun no longer included challenging each other with corny pick-up lines to use on women at singles bars. That had subdued when Clint married Amanda, and it ended entirely when Skip announced his engagement.

For Skip's bachelor's party we rented a hotel suite with a pool-side patio and went crazy with drinks, conversation, music and cards. Our friend, Dana, was a professional dee-jay and provided us with music of yesteryear and today.

It was three weeks until the big day, and the cicadas were out in full force, even at night. Dana had recorded them at ninety decibels earlier in the day. That's about how many lovers I'd enjoyed since the last time the cicadas came. But this night, the dancing girls we'd hired for the party left after only an hour—and spent only the last twenty minutes of it unclothed—so it looked liked the after-party would not be one of amorous love. Brotherly love would have to do.

The party ended around two in the morning as our scattered collection of friends and acquaintances left Skip, Clint and me alone. It was like one of our regular weekend getaways. Only a few weeks after this one, Skip was inheriting a potential pest.

Clint swatted at the cicadas. "Six weeks of this bullshit?" He swore at them, was angered by them.

"Leave the poor things alone," I said.

"These poor things are all going to be dead in a month anyway," he said.

Clint had become my opposite in many ways. In high school we had been alike; over the years that distanced us with space and time we had become counter to one another. For every movie he purchased, I bought a hardcover novel. For every healthy meal I ordered, he super-sized it. For every woman contenting me, he lingered on his discontent with Amanda. For each cicada he killed, I transplanted one from harm's way.

"Movie or a card game?" Skip asked.

"How about a quick game and then a movie?" Clint suggested.

"Fine." I sat at the outside table overlooking the moonlit swimming pool. Clint shuffled, I cut.

"Here, you deal." He handed the deck to Skip. With his hands free, Clint swatted at the cicadas. "Can't you damn bugs shut up?"

A half-bottle of Southern Comfort and five cans of beer remained. I poured us each a shot. "To women," I said. Clint chuckled humorlessly.

"No," Skip amended as he raised his glass. "To true love."

"Gimme a break," Clint said. We shot back the sweet drinks.

Skip finished his shot, but he wasn't finished on the subject. "Since meeting Leona, I've learned what true love is." We fanned our cards as Skip enlightened us. "True love is when you love someone so much that you don't need them as much as you need them to need you."

Clint spit out a sunflower seed. "True love is a crock of shit. I learned that the hard way." He laid down a heart. "By getting married." He jabbed Skip in the side playfully and then took a swig of beer.

"Don't you love Amanda?" Skip asked. "I mean, you bitch a lot about her, but you love her. She was one of the hottest girls in high school. You're lucky!"

"Lucky?" He considered. "Yes, I love her. But it's a different kind of love. It's… I don't know. Just be sure you know what you're doing, Skip. Know for sure she's the right one, that this is the right time." A hum filled the air when our conversation hit a pause.

I snapped a club into the center of the table. "Love's a cicada cycle."

"Oh, that's deep," Skip said with a windy sound that conveyed annoyance above amusement.

"No, really. The high of romance, then years and years of mundane routine. That's why I'm single."

"So you think it's better to never have it than to have it and lose it?"

"No," I said. "I get the exciting part. But when the excitement fades, detach. Find someone else and the buzz begins again. Single life offers all the buzz without the mess."

Clint came to his lifestyle's defense. "There's a lot to be said for family life, though. I love my kids more than you can imagine, Stu. I'm not saying it's the most exciting life, and sometimes I want to break out and be a kid again. But I wouldn't trade my family for the world." He took a drink of his beer and crushed the empty can. "I love them too much. It's not the exciting love of a first date. But it's a stronger bond than a single person could understand." He threw the can toward the trash.

"See?" Skip said. "The truth comes out. The glory days are fun to reminisce over, but they weren't really better. Love is better."

"Hey, I dig love," I said. "But give me budding romance and keep the ho-hum love of wilted flowers."

Skip put down his spades and won the game. "How about that movie?" He changed the subject from love to its opposite. "*Saving Private Ryan* or *Apocalypse Now*?"

"This is a bachelor party," I said. "It can't be a war movie. We need a sex comedy."

"Yes it can," Skip argued. "I'm blowing away my loneliness."

"Yuck," Clint reacted to the phrase. "*Apocalypse Now*."

"No," I disagreed. "*Saving Private Ryan*."

"*Full Metal Jacket* it is, then." Skip said.

The soundtrack of the war movie did battle with the cicadas outside, and their combination brought a thought: Not just love, but war.

Wars followed the cicada cycle: a nervous excitement, guns, tanks, testosterone, bombs and missiles, and then, after the hideous noise...silence. The cicadas ceased, like so many fallen soldiers on the shores of Normandy, in the sands of the Middle East and on the wrong side of the demilitarization zone. Now, as we watched our movie, our country was at war with Iraq, still lingering in Afghanistan, and fighting that elusive enemy known as terrorism. Two cycles before, we were fighting in Vietnam. The last time the cicadas had come, we saw only minor conflicts in the Persian Gulf. Sometimes these things skipped a generation.

Like love and war, death also followed the cycle of the cicada. During the last cycle, my grandfather died. During this one, an uncle passed away. Whose soul would they sing for the next time around? My father's? My own?

4

CLINT IS AN especially forceful nose-blower. He's been known to blow holes in tissue paper. It's usually best if he does his business behind the closed door of a stall, behind the second closed door of a bathroom. But he never does, of course. Clint likes to make a show of things, likes to display his force, his dirty mucus, his mundane life, his miserable marriage, his poor parenting and his misbehaving kids. Clint's example helped form my own list of things to avoid, I realized for the first time at Skip's wedding. It wasn't coincidence that we'd become opposites, pawns at the far ends of a chess board. I like to keep my affairs secret; I blow my nose in private, and increasingly so as old age brings about stronger and more defined allergies. Allergies are just one of the weaknesses that come with age, position and place. It's only one of the insecurities of security.

There must have been three hundred guests at the wedding, not including the cicadas. Clint and Amanda were there, but Clint was more focused on the other women in attendance. Amanda noticed it more with acknowledgement than anger. He looked, but he didn't touch. It's okay to imagine strangling your kids, as long as you don't really do it, Amanda had once said. She knew her husband was true to her and loyal to their family.

By now Clint had expanded his arsenal. His hand was no longer enough to combat the annoying foe. Decked out in his tux and tails, he carried a black fly-swatter with him and used it violently.

There were others present that I knew but didn't know. People I remembered from high school, but didn't really remember. Faces familiar but without names. Names that, when introduced, I'd heard before but didn't remember, or remembered incorrectly, faces and names skewed, not matching my memory of them. The Rubik's Cube I never quite had the patience to solve beyond one side, phantoms from yearbooks, manifested but deformed.

It was a nice service, a beautiful wedding. The shade trees stood alive with the cicada noises we had all become accustomed to. The screeching radiated from the branches, providing an applause so loud that it competed even with Dana's music at the outdoor reception that followed in the same location.

I could barely hear the song end beneath the drone of the insects; that was my cue. I tapped my knife against my glass and stood. "Ladies and gentlemen, friends, family and guests." All eyes came my way. "Now's the part where I say something nice for the lovely couple." I looked at Skip and Leona. They looked lovelier than the newlyweds on the top of their cake, happier than a pair of cicadas newly emerged from the earth. "We have a lot of guests here from all over the country. But if you listen, you'll hear that there are quite a few uninvited guests, too." I paused to let the song of the cicadas illustrate the point.

Skip and Leona looked concerned that I might ruin their day.

"Seventeen years ago I came to Virginia for the first time—that's when I met Skip—and we've been the best of friends ever since. Now, with the return of the cicadas, I've returned to Virginia to visit Skip and share in his celebration of love with Leona." I strained to say the thing that I knew I needed to say. I strained to mean it, to believe it could be so for someone, if not for me. I looked directly at the happy Skip and Leona. "I hope that seventeen years from now, when the cicadas sing their love songs again, I have the chance to return and visit the two of you, still happy, still together, and still in love."

It was a decent toast; at least the audience seemed to like it as they all raised their glasses with me in honor of the newlyweds. But as I finished my Champagne and returned to my seat, as the music resumed with a soft tune and Skip and Leona took to the floor and initiated the dancing, as I listened to the cicadas sing their own song, I wondered. Skip and Leona would have a delightful few weeks. But then, when the romance faded into mundane affection, and then into dormant co-existence, would they remain happy? When the cicadas stopped their buzz and fell dead, would their love do the same? Would Skip and Leona survive the silence?

After a bit of dancing, Skip and Leona approached me. "You had us a little worried for a minute," Skip said, gleaming.

I laughed. "Have I ever shamed you in public?"

Skip smiled. "I won't answer that now. This is a happy occasion."

Clint and Amanda joined in. "It'll get even better," Amanda said. "It changes, romantic love. It gets deeper, more meaningful."

"Now we just have to do something about Stu," Clint said.

"Me? I can take care of myself." There were plenty of girls at the wedding to choose from, and more back home—some yet unmet.

"Sure," Leona said. "But there's someone out there who can take care of you better than you can. It's just a matter of time."

"Right." Amanda smiled. "After all, Stu, you can't live like that forever."

5

THE DAY AFTER the wedding, the happy couple flew south for their honeymoon and it was time for us—the guests—to scatter. I drove north.

The cicadas were dying already. The sound was still there, but it wasn't as loud as it had been. It didn't take long for me to exhaust my supply of wiper fluid; cicada splatters decorated my windshield. A few even entered my car, one of them smacking me in the face with more force than I would have expected from such a small creature.

The lush, green trees surrounding the road were freckled with brown spots where the moisture of life had been sucked dry by the hungry insects. The trees stood tall and proud, but blemished, diseased, broken down by too much excitement. Huge blotches of leaves were left dry and without purpose, except that of drifting groundward to decay. Much as my life had been sucked dry by my playboy ways and left meaningless except for the excitement I allowed to feed upon me as I fed upon it.

Part of me wanted to join the cicadas in the earth, to sample the quiet life of mundane normalcy. To slow down and not be in such a hurry for the next squeeze, the next thrill. To join Skip and Clint in the good life. Was I going nowhere fast, fleeing the inevitable green lawn and white, picket fence? But as roadside trees gave way to concrete and buildings—as I came closer to my apartment in the city—I stomped out the thought as best I could. Better wait and see how the good life held up for my friends.

We would see one another in a few months. We would see how Skip was feeling then. The cicadas would be dead by then. They were dying already.

BIG, HOPEFUL LOOPS

Juliet M. Johnson

I MET HIM IN A CAFÉ, IN THE BACK ROOM, WHERE THERE WAS AN artist's opening, wine and cheese, free drinks and meats. He was there because it was raining. I was there because I was hungry and broke.

The wheel of cheese looked disheveled by the time I got to it. It was no longer round, or even any shape at all. White, but beaten up. It looked like the neighborhood where I grew up. Or maybe not the neighborhood, but how I felt in the neighborhood where I grew up. Beaten and ignored.

I saw his finger first. His finger touching the white linen tablecloth. The rain was hitting the window outside in the alley behind the café, where the ambulances screamed by on their way through the shortcut to the hospital. Someone was always on the verge of dying, sirens screaming, white and red ambulances shooting past the windows of the café, facing the brick wall of the opposite building.

His finger rested on the tablecloth like it had just made a long journey. It was his index finger, the pointer one, an Indian chief awaiting its squaw. A grape rolled off the tray of cheese and his finger curled around it. I looked up his arm. He was talking to someone else, an artist maybe, someone with a beret. The grape was cradled in his finger. He hadn't even looked at it. He had just known it was coming and caught it without looking. I watched it go to his plate. His mouth moved. His glasses were thick with meaning. He must be a genius, I thought, looking like that. Catching a grape without looking. Talking to an artist, in the rain, on a Thursday.

I loaded up my circle paper plate, which was thicker than my sweater, with lots of orange fruit, melon, crackers, flat foods, gooey foods. Got a glass of coarse red wine, hot as blood. I took a sip, slipping past him, looking out over the top of my paper cup, but he still had not looked at me. I noticed the finger on the grape. He was fiddling with it. Stroking its soft, green head.

I slid into a booth least populated by artist sycophants. There were two at the end of the booth, but they were both gasping over the painting nearest them. I hadn't even looked at the art.

I thought about his finger, lazy on a newspaper on a Sunday morning. I thought about his hand on my head, like the green grape. I thought about his fist curled around a pen, writing his death notices in sloping handwriting. I thought about his finger on a trigger. I thought about a gun pointed at his wife. I thought about her scream. I thought about his relieved, drooling laugh.

When I looked up he was looking at me. Sort of the way you'd gaze at a mime with no money in his hat. He seemed drained, like the woman with the beret, who was leaving to talk to someone else, had unplugged all his energy. He looked like he knew what I was thinking.

As he moved nearer, the women at the end of my booth left, and I started to dread his footsteps. Oh no, I thought. Conversation. But he set his plate down and then walked away, someplace else. His footsteps sounded like little bursts of sobs. I turned.

His finger was next to me again. There, on the red table-cloth. Tapping. I stared at the nail. He had faked me out.

"This seat taken?"

I looked up, hollow-eyed. He had a regular face, like the kind on a cereal box. Someone you could trust when hitchhiking, unless it was past two A.M., when you can't trust anyone. I wondered what he looked like past two A.M.

I mumbled, moving over. I looked at his deserted plate at the end of the table. He reached across and got it.

"What do you think of it?" He motioned vaguely.

"What?"

"The art."

"I don't know." I didn't feel like sounding smart, or making something up. I looked up at the painting nearest me, but it just looked like wallpaper. "I can't tell."

"You can't tell what it is, or you can't tell what you feel?"

He picked up his grape and put it between his lips. I suddenly felt his tongue on my face. His teeth on my eyelid. He was eating me.

I was blank. Watching his teeth.

"What?" He said.

I couldn't speak.

"That's too big a question I think, for a Thursday."

He laughed. "You can't tell things on Thursdays?"

"I'm pretty sure things don't get understood until at least Friday or Saturday. Thursdays are for hunting and gathering." I felt my amusing glands emptying of their power. I wished my plate was empty so I could get more food. I needed an activity. I shoved some cheese mixed with fruit into my mouth. I didn't normally like to mix my food. But there wasn't time to organize.

I thought he was looking at me, so I tried to look peaceful chewing. When I looked up he was looking out the window at the rain. A silent ambulance passed, its red lights flashing the emergency without the sound. We both watched the quiet red.

"Maybe that was a deaf person," I said, spitting cheese.

He looked at me, oddly.

I imitated the flashing siren in a gesture. "No sound…"

He nodded, suddenly, getting it.

"Oh, do you have deaf relatives or something? Maybe that's offensive."

"Finish chewing," he said.

I swallowed my crackers whole. It scratched all the way down. "Oh, sorry. Is that offensive?"

"No, I just can't understand you."

We were silent. I was instantly regretting my whole persona. Why had I let him talk to the real me? The one who ate and drank with other people was way more entertaining. He was getting the dregs of a Thursday night when nothing particularly mind-shattering had happened to me. I hadn't overheard a great story that I could retell, embellished, as my own. I hadn't formulated some clever scam for bilking money out of people. I hadn't participated in any group consciousness. It was over, it was all bad, bad, like my clothes, and my food choices, and where I lived, and my relationships…

"You're married," I said, wiping my mouth on my napkin, indicating the ring. The ring was only two fingers away from The Finger, the one that had led to this whole conversation. I wondered how the Ring Finger felt about the Index Finger. I thought the Index Finger was ultimately more attractive. The leader. The flexible leader.

He glanced at his ring finger. I noticed the index finger shake a bit. My heart melted at the shake.

"I like pathetic shaking in a person. I like when people are weak. It turns me on." I drank a whole lot of wine after that one. He was looking at me, but not stunned, more perplexed. I drained my cup. "Whew, that's over. Want some wine? I'm getting some more." I stood up. "I haven't eaten all day."

"Maybe I should get it." He started to get up. I let him get the wine. Maybe it'd make him feel more like a man, if picking up two paper cups and pouring wine from a plastic jug could make you feel like a man. I always thought women were the serving ones, but whatever. He returned pretty quickly. Sat back down. I noticed, when he handed me back my cup, which went straight to my mouth, that he brought his finger back with him.

I drank a long swallow. Then I handed him a pen.

"What's your handwriting look like?"

He sat a moment, then slowly looked through his pockets, picking out an envelope, flattening it and turning it over. He took the pen cap off. He held the pen poised. His lovely index finger was helping out all along. What a trooper.

"What should I write?" He asked. "I mean, I realize we aren't going to have a conversation on any realistic kind of level."

"That's a relief." I glanced around the room. "Virtue" was written on the wall. "What's virtue? The artist's name?" He pointed at Virtue. The tall woman with the beret.

"Which virtue is she?"

"I think maybe it's Chastity. Her artwork is certainly chaste." "Chastity isn't a virtue. Charity is, though." I shoveled some more cheese into my mouth.

"Gluttony is ranking high up there," he said pointedly.

"I haven't even gotten started. Did you see that cheese wheel?" I realized I had no chance with this man, so I was pulling out all the stops now.

"Maybe you're hungry for something else."

I thought maybe if he put his hand on my hair I'd stop all the chatter. But his hand was firmly on the pen. He wrote "Chastity" down on the envelope. Then he wrote "Sonny Bono." Then, "Cher." I admired that. At least he knew where Chastity came from.

"Are there any other virtues that are the children of famous people?"

He squeezed up his eyebrows, as if thinking hard about that one.

"I think people shy away from the virtues because they're so hard to live up to," I concluded. "Not that you see many sins running around. No kids named Wrath. Or Greed."

"Greed O'Malley. I like that. It's to the point."

We had a real camaraderie going now. I felt like we had been in camp for years, each summer looking forward to seeing each other again. Our little table was our encampment, and nobody would disturb us.

Two ladies sat immediately at the end of the booth, shattering my illusion.

He saw my distress at their appearance.

"Infiltrators," I whispered.

He spoke slowly to me, as if sensing that I could barely hear him from way out in his world. "Do you want to go somewhere for coffee?"

I looked at him weirdly. Motioned at the cheese plate and the wine in front of us.

He spoke again. "This isn't coffee."

"It's free. They have coffee over there. I haven't gotten to it yet." I pointed at it.

He looked.

"Actually, I don't even drink coffee. If you said, 'wanna go somewhere for a cinnamon roll', or 'wanna go shopping for a new DVD player' I might consider it."

He doodled on the paper, looking up at me with confusion. I liked that look. It was a look I was familiar with. I slid down in the booth until my hair was piled on the shelf behind me, and my chin was to my chest.

"I'm not good at talking to anyone." I said finally. "I'm much better at watching."

He stopped doodling. He stuck his big fat hand out, the finger waving at me happily. The Finger.

"I'm Frank," he said, frankly.

"All the good ones are named Frank," I mumbled, eyeing his

hand. "Where's that been?"

"Everywhere."

I looked at my hands. "Mine, too. I'm almost ashamed of the places I've put these."

"Let's take them somewhere else."

He was crushing up his trash. I focused on his hands. They were strong as little tractors. I felt my face curling up at the edges from the humidity, and fear.

"Okay," I nodded.

On the trolley, I studied the envelope. I had his handwriting on the envelope. His letters connected and yet they didn't, really. His Gs had big loops in them. Big, hopeful loops. I felt his leg beside me. I could feel his heat through his thin pants. I looked at my feet lifted and passing over the rolling concrete of the road. I could only look from my knees down. I saw my bare legs, my feet in sandals and the rolling concrete. The concrete had a curb, and other people's feet on it. Lots of grass growing up through the cracks. Some trash. Mostly blank grey. Moving.

"I never take the trolley," he said, from somewhere above and to the side. His voice was sifting in through the hair covering my ear, and the air, and I liked that. His voice was going right inside my body.

I tilted my head a little bit. His profile was aimed out at the street, higher than me, at the tops of buildings and the sky. One big claw was holding on to the hand railing. He looked down suddenly and I felt like vaulting off the moving trolley. His look was too close. He smiled, perplexed. "It's so unnecessary," he said promptly.

I didn't know what we were talking about. The trolley, the hands, the movement of the wooden machine, the benches, the man in a uniform standing at the steering wheel even though the thing was on tracks and wasn't going anywhere not already pre-destined, dinging the bell…

I looked back at his handwriting. The small As looked squashed. Trampled on.

"I once got this hand in a pretty bad accident. For about four months I had to write with my left hand, and I am not a lefty." He put his hand into my vision, showing me, a big flat white pancake hand.

"Maybe you shouldn't play favorites," I said.

"What?" The dinging bell had drowned me out.

I looked up at him, the giant mountain, precariously.

"Maybe if you didn't play favorites your left would write better for you."

"My left would right better?"

"You know. Write. Not right."

"You think I'm wrong?"

"Write."

It was a glamorous day. I imagined the city when it had horse carts pulling vegetables around. When kids carried guns to go hunting. I imagined the weather felt the same then. Then motor cars came, and women's skirts got short, and the whole world got sidetracked looking for a better deal.

"I like the trolley because you have to hold on," I said finally.

He reached down and held onto my hand. A hot little planet catapulting into my atmosphere.

We got licorice at the corner store. Some little black kids were on the stoop fighting over a can of Coke. We started walking down a big hill.

"Did you know the artist?" I said.

He shook his head. Held his hand out, as if looking for rain.

"Is it going to rain again?" I asked.

He studied me carefully. "I don't know."

In the park we stopped at the birdbath, which was filled with water from the earlier deluge. The park looked as though it had been abandoned quickly by children and nannies, some toys strewn around, the empty playground equipment mewing mournfully the loss of the clambering, sweating children.

The birdbath was a circle of peeling paint and leaves, full to the top with fresh water. Frank felt the water with a finger. He moved one leaf. His finger surfed on the surface.

I touched the leaf floating near the edge. My sweater started to hang in the water. He pulled it back.

He put his other fingers on the surface, just on the top, not pushing into the water.

I laid my palm flat on the water, feeling the floating feeling, the top layer.

I watched some drips drop onto my shoe straps. I saw some bird footprints on the ground where wet birds had hopped away after showering.

Halfway across the park, still walking, he looped his arm through mine. I looked up at the sky and it seemed to gasp a huge, relieved cloud-filled gasp. Finally, it said.

The next time I saw Frank we were on the bus.

"I don't think we can get married right away," I said, on the bus.

"Why not?" He asked, just as soberly.

"I don't like the way you treat your r's." I showed him the much-mutilated envelope. "It's like they're ignored or something. You just pass right over them."

"Some things you have to pass over in order to get to the good stuff," he advised. I hated when he adopted that teacher mode.

"You can't pass over letters," I admonished him. "They form everything."

He was studying the map. "You know if you stay on the bus long enough it loops right back to where you started." He pointed at us, on the blue line.

"I'm just glad we're on the blue line," I whispered, suddenly afraid. "The red line is certain death."

A man beside Frank got up for his stop, abandoning his seat. Frank ushered me into the open space. The seat was still hot from the other guy's butt. I wondered what the guy had been thinking about that made his butt so hot. I suddenly didn't want some other guy's butt heat on my butt. I looked up at Frank worriedly but he was smiling out the window at the brick buildings. His absent smile looked like an Oxford student crossing the wet green grass on a crisp fall day in England. It had a nice sweater in it, and perhaps a purple cotton scarf. I might've relaxed, if that had been something I was able to do.

A few stops later he sat next to me.

His finger felt the material of my coat.

"Do you think you'll be married forever?" I asked after six more stops. We were somewhere very far away.

"That's generally what you do it for," he said, practically.

I sighed. Two more stops went by.

"Can we still take different modes of transportation together, never getting to any real destination?"

"We can do anything you want to do." He spread his arms back against the seats, his coat gaping open. He looked like a starfish missing a leg.

"Frank," I said into the payphone. "My car broke down."

I watched the traffic in the street. My car sat idling at a no stopping zone.

I imagined him in a sweater, in the library of his mansion, pulling the pipe out of his mouth. "It did?" His metallic phone voice said back to me.

I faced the building, scratching the brick with my extra quarter. Drawing lines into the red. "No," I said, finally.

"Are you okay?" He said after I said nothing else.

"You just wanted to call me?" He echoed my thoughts.

I nodded into the phone. Very effective.

I heard him sigh. I listened to the noise on my end, and the quiet on his end.

"What happens at your house this time of night?" I said, dawdling.

"Night? Afternoon, my dear. It's four o'clock."

"Whatever."

"Umm…well, one daughter is at dance class. The other is napping on the couch…" I instantly liked the other daughter better. "I'm not usually home. I just happened to have a physical today and didn't go back in to work afterwards."

"What'd they say at your physical?"

"They said I should stop taking public transportation."

I looked at the wall where I had etched "Frank's wife sucks" in white with the quarter. I looked at George Washington on the quarter and wondered if he was mad that he was on such a low sum of money. Then I wondered if that was George Washington's real hair.

"Oh."

"My wife is at work. She works at a shelter."

"I actually didn't call to talk about your wife." I said, matter-of-factly.

"Oh."

Long pause. I looked at some people passing my car, ready to leap over and beat the shit out of them if they tried to get in or steal it.

"You don't really need my help," he said, finally, with a long sigh. The kind of sigh you have after eating a lot of warm food.

"It's not that I don't need it–I want it."

I waited, then hung up.

We sat by the indoor pool, the shouts of the million nine-year-old relaying swim-teamers and their coaches echoing off the community center's walls. He was in a dripping bathing suit. Barefoot, on the bench. I sat next to him in my coat over a dry pink bikini. He had his elbows on his knees and we were both looking at his feet.

"I've never seen them before," I said, glancing at the dripping water between the bench slats.

"Yes," he said.

"They're so…innocent. I hope you don't speak harshly in front of them."

A pack of nubile fifteen-year-olds passed us. I felt overdressed.

"I don't speak harshly in front of anyone," he said, quietly, as if to prove his point.

My foot was twitching. Maybe it wanted to get out and meet Frank's feet.

"Well, look, we can't just keep meeting in weird places. There's no point to it."

"What point did you want?"

"I wanted a place where our points could run free. Where my feet were allowed to mingle naked with your feet. Not with this wardrobe, and your whole other life thing draped around the room like a shroud," I said.

"What makes you think you're ready for me?"

I looked at him sitting there, dripping.

"I'm kind of cold," he added, and I noticed goosebumps.

"Get back in the water."

"Are you going to get out of your coat?"

"I didn't get a locker. Besides, showing more skin is hardly going to help at this point in our relationship."

He stood up. "We're having a relationship?"

I gestured at his body. "You're practically nude in front of me."

"We're in a public place. There're kids here," he motioned around.

"It's not ideal. But it's happening. It's only a matter of time."

"Everyone's almost nude here."

"Well some of these people take their nudity home and share it with others who know them well," I said, exasperated.

"What do you want?"

I didn't say anything. That wasn't something one said.

He knelt in front of me. He put both hands on either side of my head. He kissed me, his full mouth on my scrawny one. I tried to remember how to kiss back. Then it got fun, like an otter rolling down a wet slide.

When he pulled away I wanted him to come back. I wanted to take a cab to where he had taken me. I wanted to get out and buy a little house and bake brownies and wait there until he came back. I tried to look him in the eye and pass all this information to him via mind-meld, but he just knelt there, remaining separate, still separate in a whole body not mine, one that required shaving, and fatherhood.

"Can I see you again?" he asked, his blue eyes kind.

He placed his hand on my cheek, cementing the deal.

We sat at the bus stop. It was freezing. I clutched my coat around me. He sat very close beside me. The weather didn't seem to bother him. He looked like he was on a fishing expedition, happily sunning himself, the Old Man and the Sea.

"It's just that I'm not like this," I said.

"What are you like?"

"It's fucking freezing out here."

He put his warm hand into my pocket.

"I'm not tragic enough to be following you around, meeting on pieces of wood. I'm not black and white. You aren't Ingrid Bergman."

"You're plenty tragic."

We watched the traffic go by. I leaned on his shoulder a bit. Quiet.

"How did it get like this? I mean, it used to be me in my life. Now if a day goes by that I don't see you, it feels wasted."

"But there are so many days that I don't see you," he said, surprised.

"I know. Do the math."

He thought hard about it, touched.

I fidgeted. "Why does it get like that? I'm fine alone, and then there's you, and then suddenly I'm not fine alone. There's you, now."

"You weren't fine alone."

"I was great."

"No one's fine alone."

"I was pretty great."

He kissed me again, and my heart fell to its knees. My heart, on a street corner, in tattered clothes, held out a little cardboard sign: "Will Work For Frank." My heart, the good one, the full one. Bucketsful of Frank, its autobiography.

"Don't do that," I finally said, mouth free.

"You wanted me to," he squeezed my hand.

"That doesn't matter," I said.

Frank looked sorry the next time I saw him, on a big red bus. The kind pretending that it was from England when really it was from someplace in Illinois. We rode on the top even though it was November and it was freezing, and the sky above us looked evil.

When the bus took corners, it heaved like a fat woman with huge breasts, threatening to spill us out the top. I clutched on to Frank, his new beige trench coat with the soft lining on the inside. Obviously an early Christmas present. Something substantial from someone substantial.

I looped my strongest finger through a buttonhole and watched the streetlights rushing by, the trees, the blur of human faces, American with a British feel.

Frank looked French, his hair a halo of wind frenzy, his eyes grey and withdrawn, the bus a circus ride beneath us.

"This is definitely the sexy ride," I said finally, mostly to my shirt sleeve, which was wiping my cold, wet nose. I wanted to say, "It's like riding a giant undulating French woman," but I didn't want him to know my mind worked that way.

He was staring out at the streets, at the foreigners, at our life, passing by at a hundred miles an hour.

Desperately, I took out the tattered envelope with the fractions of sentences on it. "Your o's," I said, yelling. "Look at your o's," waving the paper in front of him like an excellent report card.

But he was gone. My Frank, the one I traveled with, the one who knew nothing of me and took nothing from me. The possibility of Frank, he was dwindling. I could feel it slipping away, the perception I had had, falling around me like dead flies.

The bus stopped at a light.

"We don't have to stop here!" I shrieked, but a bird flew over my head, shrieking louder. Frank looked at my shoes.

His eyes made short sputtering trips up to my belt. To my nose, like he was building blocks, but not looking at what he was building, instead composing music in his head. His eyes flickered at mine but what I saw in them was broken.

"Where are we going, Frank?" I finally said to him, after three more blocks.

I watched his lips, pink. They turned grey as he tightened them across his teeth, and then they parted and the great whites showed through.

"I think we're getting off soon," he said.

Frank sat on the curb with me. The curb was grey and used, like an old felt hat from the '20s. I felt dizzy, a sailor fresh from sea, unused to the stilted land.

"It's not that you're different," he said.

I looked at his hands folded thoughtfully in his lap, like a teacher.

"It's that there's too much of you," he finished. His index finger twitched with accomplishment. He had obviously been working on that statement.

I scoffed at his absurdity.

We sat there a while longer.

"Coward," I said, finally. I wanted to get up. "And not even Noël Coward. Regular Coward."

His finger twitched again. I decided never to look him in the face again. Never to look any man in the face again. Fingers were bad enough.

"I just needed a little movement. You were so good at it for awhile," I said, my voice warbly and depressing me.

He hesitated. Cleared his throat. He suddenly put his face down on his knees, and then turned it, so he was looking in my eyes.

I felt my knees turn soft like warm Thanksgiving gravy. His eyes sang to me.

After a moment, his index finger touched my calf and ran all the way up to my gravy knee. He felt the edge of my skirt.

His eyes looped around my head and pulled me in until I couldn't breathe.

"Eventually we would've run out," he said.

There was a pause, the kind long enough to enter a house, take off a raincoat, and hang it up on a strong wooden wall rack while checking your reflection in an old-fashioned mirror.

Then his fingers were gone.

SHANTI'S CHOICE

Lalita Noronha

Today she feels it, deep within her bones, a restless foreboding, a premonition she cannot shake. Shanti wipes her face with the edge of her sari. She has the day's washing and cooking and cleaning to tackle before Mrs. Seth, her employer, returns home from her weekend in Mumbai. Her chores stare at her like sullen children forbidden to play outside.

Shanti was sure she had gotten past it. Gone was the turmoil and turbulence, churning in and out with the tide, subsiding, roiling up again. Now, her days were filled with the solace of routine. And then, last night as she slept, a makara, a water-monster, rose in a tidal wave and there he was, riding on its scaly crocodile tail. He swam to shore, walked toward her in the clear light and stood in the doorway gazing at her, saying nothing. He was older now, sober, clean-shaven, the scar on his jaw alive like a row of red ants.

Her voice quavered. "What do you want?"

"Shanti?" he'd whispered hoarsely, and it was his voice, an echo across the chasm of time that sliced through her sleep. She'd sat up, trembling, rubbed her arms and feet and reached for her shawl. Did she have a fever? Her teeth were chattering; her eyes burned. There was no one in the doorway. She'd tiptoed to the earthen chatty, ladled out some cool water in a cup, and stood by the window, sipping. It felt good going down her dry throat. Outside, it was pitch black, not even the faint glow of a star. What time was it? Tiptoeing back, she lay down and pulled the sheet over her head as if to cover her dreams.

Why had he come to her after so many years? Was it some sort of omen? Had something terrible happened to him? And if so, why should it concern her? She lived in a little apartment now with running water and electricity, far from their village, where one night nearly twenty years ago he'd stormed out of their one-room home in a drunken fury, leaving her with their two little girls, Jaya and Seema. She had followed him into the street, purple crescents under her eyes, begging him to stay. Wait, wait, husband, wait, don't go. Please don't go. Next time, I'll give you a son. I will; I promise. But he'd cursed at her, shaken off her cries and tottered away. She'd stared at his retreating back until the road was empty and the sun had dipped behind the hills. Perhaps he would return, tomorrow. She had waited three days, then thirty, then three hundred, and then she stopped counting because forever was too long to count.

She'd picked up her shattered life. The girls began attending the convent school run by the Sisters of the Holy Cross—those kind, white-skinned women, who dressed like crows and lived in a house with no men. They didn't ask Shanti for school fees and even gave her free cooking oil and rice. Meanwhile, all around, rich influential people fleeing the city's grime and pollution had started moving closer to her village, building big houses with verandas among the mango groves. When the Seths moved into the mansion on the hill and began looking for a servant, Shanti asked the Sisters to recommend her. It was a perfect arrangement. Mrs. Seth even let the girls do their homework in the kitchen after school and play in confined areas of the house.

Shanti brushes off her thoughts and hurries into the washroom. She begins to sort through the laundry—Mr. Seth's shirts, Arun's little overalls, Mrs. Seth's lacy underwear. She picks up a black lace bra and puts it against her chest. Doesn't that hard, curved wire hurt? Every time Mrs. Seth goes to Mumbai, she brings back a mountain of skimpy clothes that barely cover anything. What purpose do they serve? She wonders if Jaya, who now lives and works in Mumbai, also wears such strange-looking garments.

Jaya is a bartender in a fancy hotel, a good daughter who faithfully sends money home every month; were it not for her, Seema's hope chest would be filled with air. But something about that girl has changed. She seems more distant, her eyes veiled and lusterless. Shanti does not understand this. What kind of girl doesn't practice a smile in the mirror for her husband-to-be, doesn't carve a heart in a tree, doesn't look at a full moon, and feel warmth between her legs? What kind of girl is apathetic about marriage and motherhood, oblivious of village gossip and innuendo? And from where does she get so much money? Some nights Shanti struggles, unable to decipher a pattern from all the mismatched, jagged-edged pieces of her life as if someone has tricked her and jumbled up different puzzles from worlds she's never been to and will probably never see.

Shanti feeds Arun his mid-morning snack. Heaviness, a sodden blanket, weighs her shoulders down. Something is not right today. This is why she has sent Seema to the bazaar, although she'd rather have gone herself. It is her only opportunity to laugh, trade stories and drink gossip-sweetened chai with her friends Most of the vendors have known her for years; their language is unspoken—as immune to the passage of time and inflation as they are to houseflies buzzing around their produce. Shanti knows that if a vendor quotes thirty rupees to a bystander, she can assume at least a third less.

And, of course, there is Shiva, who always slices a guava or a papaya with his penknife the minute she appears and lays it on a clean napkin for her.

"It's beautiful; really, really sweet today," he'll say, offering her a piece of fruit, and she'll remind him that he says that almost every day. "But it is true, every day. Some things are always true, day after day, no?"

Such foolishness! She knows she lingers at his fruit stand longer than necessary. She knows he is looking for a wife since his own died a year ago. But she is nearly forty with two unmarried daughters, and no spare money for fantasies. And what would people say? She still wears the red kumkum powder in the parting of her hair because she is not a widow yet. If a man deserts his wife, it doesn't mean he's dead. Maybe it is her fault after all—giving birth to two girls in a row.

Shanti wipes Arun's little face and waits for him to swallow the last bite of *puri*. "Let's go, *beta*," she says, lifting him off the chair. "Time for your nap."

Arun protests. "No, no."

"No? No? Yes, yes."

Arun pouts. "I want milk. And cookies."

Shanti picks up his cup and grabs his hand. "You can have that in bed. Come on, *beta*, it's getting late."

She sets the milk and two cookies on the nightstand, draws the shades to darken the room and turns the ceiling fan on low. She puts the cup to his lips. "Okay, drink fast." He bites into the cookie and takes another gulp, alternating cookies and milk. "All gone," Shanti says. "I'll sit with you a few minutes, if you close your eyes."

"I want my mama," the boy whimpers.

"Close your eyes, *beta*. She's coming home today."

She settles herself comfortably on the floor beside the bed and begins rubbing the child's back, thinking: strange how Mrs. Seth always plans her weekends in Mumbai when her husband leaves on business trips. Mumbai must be a carnival city. She'd heard it was a new India filled with rich, beautiful people. No wonder her Jaya went there. Perhaps Seema should go too—find a good job and fatten up her own dowry. Then again, Seema isn't as smart and bold as her sister. The city might swallow her whole like a python.

Last night's dream resurfaces again. Why had her husband come to her? She recalls the story of Shaibya, a pious woman, whose sinful husband was reincarnated several times—as a dog, jackal, wolf, crow and peacock. Shaibya, herself, remained faithful to him, recognized him in each incarnation, and helped him attain Nirvana. In his final incarnation as a man, they were reunited and lived happily on earth until it was time to ascend beyond the moon. Shanti shakes her head wishing the story away. Am I to follow in Shaibya's footsteps? Am I to keep watch over him?

Her head throbs and the room swoons about her. As soon as Arun dozes off, she tells herself, I'll go to Mrs. Seth's bathroom and take two Anacin from the medicine cabinet as Mrs. Seth does. She begins to hum a lullaby as Arun's eyelids droop. Quietly, she rises from the floor and ambles along the long hallway to the master bedroom suite. It is Monday, her day to change the bed linens. She gazes at the carved, teak bed frame, fit for a maharaja. Then, slowly, she begins to strip off the sheets and pillowcases and tuck in fresh linen, smoothing and folding and plumping pillows. For a moment she lays her cheek on the silken patchwork quilt sewn from remnants of Mrs. Seth's saris—why, just gathering these rich fabrics in her arms makes her feel wealthy! What must it feel like to lie in such a bed? The only bed she's known is the floor where, like most servants, beddings are rolled and stacked like cards in a corner of the room.

She steps into the bathroom. Everything is clean and

shining as she'd left it—the brass-knobbed faucet, the sink and toilet, the cream tiled floor. She peers at herself in the large mirror over the sink. She looks pale this morning, her almond-shaped eyes large and liquid, her cheek bones more pronounced. Timidly, she half-smiles into the mirror. It occurs to her suddenly that she is still beautiful. Might that be what Shiva sees?

Such foolishness! The fever must be getting to her brain.

Opening the medicine cabinet, she is taken aback by a spectacular array of bottles and tubes. On the lowest shelf are medium-sized bottles—a creamy pink liquid, cough syrup, eucalyptus oil, Tiger Balm, a thermometer, Band-Aids, and tubes of creams. She recognizes the red bottle of mercurochrome that Mrs. Seth dabbed on Arun's boo-boos, the calamine lotion for mosquito bites, *hajmollah* for indigestion. Vicks she can smell without opening the jar. On the middle shelf are several like-sized bottles—green with white pills, white bottles with green pills, capsules, blue tablets, small pills packed in round, sundial containers. She cannot read English labels; she can only recognize some alphabets from Arun's baby book: the cross, X; the zigzag, Z; the circle, O; the one like a snake, S; the upside down cone, A.

She reaches for a green bottle. Yes, this must be what Mrs. Seth gave her when she felt feverish last month. She taps two tablets out, cups her palm to her mouth, and swallows quickly, finishing it off with handfuls of water. As soon as Seema returns from the bazaar, Shanti will cook the evening meal. She'll knead the dough for *rotis*, but she'll roll them out later, closer to Mrs. Seth's arrival time. If only she didn't feel so weak. She taps out four more pills and swallows them; perhaps she'll feel better quicker. As they glide down her throat, she returns to the bedroom. For one moment, just one, she thinks she will lie down on this gorgeous bed and pretend she's a queen.

Ahead is a large, enclosed garden, under a peach and purple sky. Along the garden walls grapevines drip red and black grapes. To one side are groves of fruit-laden trees, orange-tinted mangoes, apples, pomegranates, big prickly jackfruit, persimmon, all ripe and abundant. In another corner is a flower garden with pendulous lilac blossoms, nasturtiums, yellow roses, and wild orchids growing profusely in graceful arches. There's a candlelit pond in the middle with lotus flowers in bloom and a reflection of the moon in the water.

Shanti enters the garden on a white horse with a gold saddle. She is young and beautiful, dressed in a magnificent white sari, her long, black hair flowing down her back in waves, her feet encased in soft, em- broidered sandals. The garden is full of angels all with beautiful faces, too—there by the pond is her mother, her grandmother, her aunts, the women at the village well, the still-born sister she never knew; they are all there, arms outstretched, smiling, beckoning, calling her to a table laden with food. She dismounts. If she eats this heavenly food, if she joins the consortium of angels, she knows she must stay here forever. The angels fill their plates with dewdrops and mist and mounds of whipped clouds, and sit by the edge of the pond to eat. Shanti surveys the garden, the food and flowers, keenly aware of a strange sensation. What is it? A full moon has risen, raining moonbeams that settle like sheared lace over the garden path. Shanti looks to her left, then right, and straight ahead, searching for something she cannot name. Something is missing.

And then, she knows. She does not see him. He'd come to her last night riding on the makara's tail. He'd stood in her doorway; she'd heard him call her name. And then, he'd dissolved in the moonlight. Her eyes scan the garden. There is a riffling behind the jasmine vine, but it's only a little hummingbird. No, he isn't here. And then it occurs to her. Her father isn't here either nor her uncles, her brother, the village priest, the husbands of her angel-friends. No men. There are no men here in paradise. Not a single one. And yet the angels are content without them. How could that be?

The angels wave in unison, bidding her join them. Oh, how she longs to! But a gnawing sense of loneliness begins to seep in, a hollow- ness. Something isn't right. Slowly, she runs her life backwards like a film reel, pausing at each frame, past her girlhood, past her birth, to a dark, hollow, womblike space. And then forward to other times, to that same dark, timeless womb, where two baby girls await birth. And now her eyes search frantically, not for her father or husband or any man, but for two missing angels—her daughters. But they are nowhere. Not in the fruit orchard, not by the pond.

Tears slide down her cheek. In the whispering breeze, she hears a faint call but the voice isn't in the garden. It is muffled, an echo from behind the garden wall, from somewhere below, far, far away. Shanti walks to the wall and peers over it. Coal black. An abyss of darkness. Not a star. Not a sound except the flutter of her heart. She gazes longingly at her mother, who is radiant in a sky-blue sari with silver raindrops. Gone are her creased eyes, her bruised lips, her broken arm. Gone are the marks of her painful destiny—an arranged child-marriage, separation from her mother before she'd even got her periods, the beatings following Shanti's birth. Her life on earth seems to have been erased; perhaps even the memory of it, and all that remains is one shining moment in the present, and then another and another. Shanti closes her eyes. She longs to be like her mother, free of sorrow. She longs to stay here. Yes, she will stay here. She will go now and fill her plate with dewdrops.

But there is that call again, a half-familiar voice. And then another voice, a softer, hesitant whisper, almost a sob. Imagination; she is imagining things. She holds her breath, waiting. This time it's a little louder. There is no mistake. She hears it clearly. She knows these voices. She loves these voices. They come in waves of broken breaths now, in sing-song magnetic chants that are drawing her away from the garden. She listens over and over, feeling her body dissolve until only her heart remains, beating. And in this one isolated moment, she knows what her heart wants. Scanning the angel faces one last time, and not finding what she is looking for, she climbs the wall and jumps into the great, big, black beyond. Free falling.

A faint perfume wafts past her nostrils. Her eyes flicker open. She is startled by the soft, silky coverlet about her arms and feet. She finds her wrist in the hands of a man in a white coat, a Y-shaped black rope around his neck. Jaya is bent over her. Seema's tear-streaked lips touch her cheek. Mrs. Seth's worried face blurs in the background.

"Where am I?" Shanti whispers.

Jaya strokes her damp forehead. "You're home, Amma."

"Where was I?"

Jaya kisses her forehead. "Somewhere far away."

Shanti eyes fill with tears. She closes her palms over the hands of her girls. For now, here is where she wants to be. This, here, is her Eden.

THE LOST DAUGHTER CAPER

Austin S. Camacho

"I CAN'T LET YOU LIVE AFTER GOING IN THAT SAFE."
Jeff Aaron held the small revolver steadily at his side. "I've never killed anyone before, but, you know, I don't think it will be as difficult as I expected." Jeff's face glowed with anticipation, but he was not an experienced assassin. That gave the woman facing him a chance.

Felicity O'Brien stood cornered on the balcony of her own apartment. Her long evening gown and high heels felt inappropriate for facing a crazed gunman. She backed slowly into the evening gloom, her face displaying the expected degree of fear while her mind searched her available options, looking for an escape. In the end, there seemed to be only one.

Letting her facial expression slip to total horror, Felicity took one too many steps back. She let out a short shriek, her arms windmilling wildly as she leaned backward. With a flurry of swishing taffeta, her body flipped over the balcony and into the darkness, leaving the gunman standing alone.

Jeff was briefly paralyzed with indecision. Had she really fallen to her death? Should he run? He had never done anything like this before. He had better take a look to be sure.

His stomach lurching in anticipation, Jeff slowly stepped to the rail. He swallowed hard, and then looked down. It took him a moment to realize that nothing lay on the pavement five stories below. The redhead had disappeared. Panic gripped his heart. He pocketed his thirty-eight quickly and bolted for the elevator.

Felicity O'Brien had fallen past the balcony below her own and desperately reached out to grasp the rail of the next one. She gritted her teeth against the sudden stop, which threatened to tear her shoulders out. She could take time for only two deep breaths before hauling herself up to the safety of the narrow balcony. Her shoulders and fingers ached, but they would have to wait. She told herself it should be no big deal. She had practiced this kind of deadfall maneuver countless times. After all, you cannot depend on your natural gifts if you want to remain the reigning cat burglar in your adopted country.

Thankfully, no one was home at the apartment Felicity had unexpectedly dropped in on, so she needed no explanatory story. Less than four minutes later she reached the ground floor and had her black Porsche 911 moving down the wide Houston street toward the city's heart. Her assailant had lost her, at least for the moment. She needed a safe place to think, so she sought the anonymity of a very public place. A few minutes later she was considering her situation over a hot cup of coffee in a small diner.

Felicity could never live in this big, brassy town. Houston reminded her of Las Vegas on a bad night. She had only rented an apartment so she could stay around long enough to ease herself into Houston high society. She planned to case the area, pick out a couple of good scores, and move on. She had not figured, however, on having her life threatened.

Had she been careless? How did Aaron know she'd robbed his house? They had only met once. He couldn't have spotted her as a thief in that brief encounter. And even if he did, what would possess him to try to kill her? Why not just call the police? Well, she would simply have to have a second cup of coffee and think it through one more time.

Felicity had found her niche in life early. She had extraordinary night vision, a photographic memory, nerves of steel, an excellent sense of timing and a native instinct that always seemed to steer her clear of danger. Obviously, she was meant to be a thief. Although born in Ireland, she traveled the world over, applying her skills in a different city every few weeks. As was her pattern, she arrived in Houston alone and within days had eased smoothly into the social lives of the well-to-do.

She remembered meeting Jeff Aaron and his wife, Linda, at a cocktail party at their home. Jeff was a tall, handsome blonde with deep blue eyes and that perfect tan that only comes from a booth. He had made his considerable fortune as a financial advisor. He smiled too much. Yet, something in his eyes told Felicity that he had the capacity to be ruthless. He leaned against the oversized brick fireplace in his den and talked freely about his past, his future, and his plans. Jeff Aaron was his favorite subject.

Linda had made an impression on Felicity because the women seemed to be complete opposites. Felicity was tall and shapely, while Linda Aaron was no more than five feet two with a small bust and hips. Felicity's wavy red hair hung nearly to her waist; Linda's was mousy brown with an occasional grey strand, and cropped short. While Felicity's eyes were a piercing green, Linda's matched her hair. Linda seemed to overdo her makeup. Felicity hardly wore any.

"So you're Bill Collier's date tonight," Linda had said, smiling up into Felicity's eyes. "He usually sticks with the local talent. You're obviously new here."

"Does it show?" Felicity asked, sipping her brandy. "I've recently come into some money and decided to move up in the world. Billy's helping me find a good home around here. I've got to get out of that dinky apartment soon."

"Don't feel bad," Linda said. "Your skin is kind of fair. You'll fit in better when you've picked up a good, solid tan. And don't worry about fitting in here. With Bill as your ticket you'll be a 'good ol' girl' in no time. Jeff and I, we had to fight to be accepted here."

"Really?" Felicity doubted this woman had any trouble fighting for what she wanted. "So what's the secret of your success?"

"Conformity," Linda said. "All you need is the tan, and to play tennis, and ride horses, and learn those insipid dances, and don't have a family because kids get in the way of your trips to Club Med."

Felicity sensed resentment there, and she recognized the feeling. After all, she had never been much of a conformist herself.

A little later during the party, Felicity slipped away from the polite conversation to visit the restroom. On her way, she found the basement door, which led to the security system downstairs. She opened the burglar alarm control box and quickly surveyed its contents. She could see connections for six separate systems. Photo relay alarms with infrared pulsed beams. Ultrasonic motion sensors as backup. Not bad. She inserted her own plug-in power module and closed the box.

She was back upstairs and in the conversation in time to

hear about the hosts' three-week vacation, coming up in a few days. She had never been missed. She hoped it would be as easy to escape her boorish date at the end of the evening.

FELICITY SMILED AT the waitress when her pie arrived. Her mind kept wandering back to that night just three days ago. She had parked four blocks away from Jeff and Linda's spacious ranch home and walked past sculptured hedges and lawns right up to the front door. After all, sneaking around made people suspicious. She wore a black stretch top and pants, with her hair tied back in a green ribbon. In her shoulder bag she carried a wireless radio remote control.

People used RF remotes all the time, to raise their garage doors, or to turn off appliances and lights at a distance. Felicity had simply adapted the device to her needs. With the touch of a button she turned off all the burglar alarms and security systems in the Aaron home. It took her less than a minute to pick the lock.

Once inside, Felicity applied her own systematic search technique. The layout of the house was recorded in her memory. She started in the huge master bedroom. The most obvious place to begin was a walk-in closet. Jeff's closet was spartan and yielded nothing of interest. She expected better luck in Linda's.

Closing the closet door tightly, Felicity turned on the light. Linda's wardrobe was vast and expensive. Her tastes tended toward the conservative, but Felicity noticed one rack of dresses that seemed too young for Linda. Pushing them aside revealed a row of wig heads on a low shelf. Moving the plastic heads revealed the door to a safe.

Felicity loved combination locks. The miniature stethoscope she kept in her bag allowed her to hear the tumblers. She probably opened the steel door faster than its owner did using the combination. Then she stretched a gloved hand inside, expecting to find jewelry or cash. Instead she encountered a stack of poorly posed snapshots.

Puzzled, she stared at one closely. It was a shot of a girl, whose age Felicity guessed at fifteen or sixteen years. An older man stood with his arm around her. Perhaps an uncle. The girl had long blonde hair and freckles, and a shiny clean face that was eerily familiar. This had to be Jeff and Linda Aaron's daughter. Her resemblance to Linda was uncanny. She was smiling in that way teenagers do when they are being teased. On the back of the photo, someone had written "Juliet and Uncle Sid" in pencil.

Curious, Felicity reached farther into the safe, this time retrieving a stack of cassettes. Each was labeled with the name Juliet and an accompanying number. Correspondence?

Felicity was only puzzled because she remembered Linda telling her at the party that she and Jeff would never consider disrupting their perfect life with a child. But why hide a child they obviously cared about so much? Could fitting in be this important to anyone? These pictures must be precious, or they would not be stored in a safe. The tapes were bound to be recorded letters home from, well, wherever one stashed a child.

Well, it really did not matter to Felicity. Behind the tapes she found what she was really looking for. Linda was partial to pearl necklaces, and Felicity loved her for that. She found several strings of pearls, perfectly shaped, carefully matched, easily fenced, and almost impossible to trace. There was also a nice little plastic packet of investment grade diamonds and twenty thousand dollars cash. A good night's work.

From here there was no art to Felicity's business. It was simply a matter of leaving things as she found them and removing her plug-in module from the security controls. She was soon cruising toward her temporary home and a hot shower.

She always felt a bit of a letdown after a successful caper. Hers was a lonely life, despite the glamour and wealth she had amassed in so few years. Texas was getting old. She would probably only hang around for another week or so before shipping the car and flying back to her home in L.A. Or New York. Or maybe Paris. Right then her immediate future held only an empty apartment and a glass of Bailey's Irish Creme. Or so she thought.

Felicity paid for her order and left a hefty tip as she rose to leave the diner. She knew she had to get to a motel. Returning to her apartment would be suicide. Her entire take from this city's rich but unwilling contributors was locked in her car's trunk, to be shipped with it to her next stop. She was sure she had left no clues to her identity at the scene of these crimes. She was quite surprised when Jeff had appeared at her door minutes ago. He was smiling and pleasant, but she knew it was false. A warning buzzer had gone off in her head, alerting her to danger. That was why she had led him over to the balcony during their conversation. And she had been wise to hang her purse over her shoulder. One minute they were discussing social life in the New South, the next he was waving a gun in her face.

She was sure Jeff was capable of using his weapon, but he was no cowboy, or self-defense nut. So, he must be a criminal himself. She had no other reasonable explanation for why he would come after her personally instead of going to the police. And only someone else in her business could have told him which of his recent house guests was a professional thief. That would mean excellent underworld connections. He was dangerous, and the only way to escape the danger for good was to find out just what he was hiding.

She would have to get back into the house.

Felicity checked into the first motel she came to. Her lack of luggage made her more aware of how vulnerable her position was. She had made her dramatic exit from the apartment in a full, ankle length dress. She was hardly dressed for a break-in. Nor did she have time to arrange a sophisticated scheme for entry. She knew Jeff would not kill for the money or jewelry she took. She must have seen something she should not have, and whatever it was could be moved at any time. Her mind returned to the hidden pictures and it occurred to her that the answer to her puzzle had been right in front of her face. If she could get in tonight, she could find what she needed to protect herself.

Cheap stores seem to stay open later. In two stops Felicity was able to buy an expendable set of work clothes: black leotards and tights, gloves, socks and sneakers. She then drove to the Aarons' neighborhood, parked in a secluded place, and went to sleep in her car.

Felicity awoke at three-thirty in the morning. She stretched, frowning at what she was about to do. It was all she could come up with, but it stunk. She squirmed into her work clothes in the back seat of her Porsche. Her hair was piled and pinned on top of her head and covered with a black silk scarf. She retrieved her black bag from the trunk. It contained all the tools she would need.

The night was a deep black, dripping ink onto the suburban streets. Felicity moved from one splashed shadow to another, invisible in the gloom. A quick running circuit of the Aarons' contemporary home revealed only one car. That meant one of them was probably out for the evening. She sure hoped it was Jeff. In the back yard she pulled a black nylon line from her bag. A blackened steel grapnel hook hung at one end. She spun it three times above her head and then flipped it to the roof. It caught the end of the large brick chimney.

Might he be waiting for her? After all, Jeff knew who she was now, and that she had broken into his home. Anything was possible, but Felicity would gamble all her chips on her judgment of his arrogance. He would never expect her to return so quickly. And if she was wrong? Well, Felicity was a risk taker by nature.

"Now the fun begins," she whispered. With rubber soles braced against the white brick wall, Felicity hauled herself up, hand over hand. She moved like a silent spider on her slender web line, slowly yet with smooth, steady progress. Once at the top she squirmed over the eaves. She carefully moved upward on fingers and toes, toward the center ridge.

Her breath caught in her throat as a shingle slid loose under her foot. She watched it fall in apparent slow motion, to crash like a damaged UFO onto the lawn below. Like a modern day gargoyle, Felicity hung frozen on the roof for five full minutes.

She heard no sound from inside the house. Her heart eventually slowed to its normal pace. She pulled herself through the darkness to the chimney, looked down into the square brick tube and sighed.

Felicity felt she was beyond this sort of thing professionally, but this was an emergency. She dropped the nylon line down the flue, its hook still secure on the edge. With infinite care, she slid into the funnel feet first and slowly lowered herself down. Her breath bounced back into her face in the narrow space, carrying soot and the gagging smell of creosote. She knew how many people killed themselves doing this every Christmas season, but she shut that thought from her mind. They were idiots. She was a professional.

After several interminable minutes, Felicity's feet swung forward into thin air. Seconds later she was in the den on all fours. With eyes, ears and instincts, she probed the house for any sense of movement. She knew that motion sensors covered the rooms adjacent to all doors and electric eyes covered all the windows. Luckily, it had never occurred to Jeff that anyone would suddenly appear in the den.

Church mouse quiet, Felicity stalked across the carpet in a crouch, stopping at the master bedroom. The door stood half open. Someone lay there in the darkness. Felicity released her held breath when she realized the figure was too small to be Jeff. She crept to the bed as silently as a cheetah stalking an antelope. As she moved she pulled a cotton pad from her bag.

It must have been the acrid stench of the soot that awakened Linda Aaron. She spun to stare at the blackened face of her assailant. Felicity shined her pencil torch into Linda's eyes while rushing across the room. Linda's mouth opened just as the cotton pad covered her face, stifling her scream. One deep breath sapped much of her resistance. A second breath, and a third, and she was out cold. Felicity dropped the ether pad and pulled a vial of nose plugs from her bag. She shoved one into Linda's left nostril. The anesthetic-soaked plug would keep her out for hours. Felicity smiled. She would have all the time she needed.

In seconds she had the safe open again and was tossing things on the floor. She had no use for the pictures, each showing a different uncle, but she did need the cassettes. And when she took the cash on her last visit she had noticed film canisters behind it. They would contain the negatives, and they were what she really needed. Almost as an afterthought, she picked up one wig, then closed the closet door and continued through the house.

She knew Jeff must have an office in the house, and it took her little time to find it. She turned on his home computer, and looked through his software while it booted up. She found precious little in the way of accounting records, certainly not enough business to support the Aarons' lifestyle. But, of course, Felicity knew they had other sources of income. She did find a disk containing a long list of names and addresses in various cities. A client list, perhaps. She could use a copy of this one. Before leaving, she typed a message on the monitor screen.

MEET ME AT THE CIVIC CENTER
CONFERENCE ROOM B, AT 4 PM
TO DISCUSS TERMS OF TRUCE
NO GUNS

The Civic Center in Houston is the Albert Thomas Convention and Exhibition Center, right in the center of town. Before getting there, Felicity had to leave the Aarons' home by the back door and return to her motel. Arriving before sunrise, she treated herself to a long hot shower, a soak in a perfumed tub, and a four hour nap. By noon she had purchased new clothes for her meeting. Then she had to affect a convincing accent and concoct a believable story in order to book the conference room "for her civic group" on such short notice.

Felicity was standing at the far end of the conference room when the Aarons walked in. She wore a brick red business suit, the skirt hitting at the knee. It complemented the brighter red of her hair. Despite her long night and busy morning she looked bright and chipper, much better than either of the Aarons. Linda in particular had lost her healthy glow, and dark circles showed under her eyes.

"What's the matter, Linda?" Felicity asked as the other two sat at the conference table. "You're looking poorly, dear. I know you got plenty of sleep."

"I take it you're responsible for that," Jeff snapped. "I pulled that drugged thing out of her nose this morning after looking for you all night. Now what's this all about?"

"You know what it's about. It's about blackmail."

"I don't know what you're talking about," Jeff said, following Felicity with his eyes as she paced slowly around the room.

"Don't insult me. You had to have some criminal contacts to find out what I do for a living. And if you were legit, you'd have called the police about your loss, not come after me with a gun."

"Doesn't prove anything," Jeff said, crossing his arms. "I can still go to the police."

"Be serious. I figured it was blackmail when I thought about the pictures. At first I figured you had a daughter hidden away, until I looked at the pictures more closely. Besides, a child would be hard to control, wouldn't she?"

"Jeff, make her stop," Linda whined.

"I won't stop. I almost didn't recognize you, but once I realized that was your face under the blonde wig it all became clear. I guess you figured out that important people cheat on their wives often enough these days that it's hardly enough to blackmail with.

But pederasty, sex with a minor, now that's an act even today's politicians would want to keep quiet. You must be quite an actress."

"I'll have you killed," Linda said through clenched teeth.

"Oh, I doubt it. You see I've got it all. With your slight figure and height, you have no trouble passing yourself off as a girl in her early teens. As I saw last night, you have quite a youthful face without all the makeup. Young-looking clothes and a blonde wig complete the picture. You seduce your targets during your little vacations every year. And your sick husband even manages to actually get the acts on tape, doesn't he?"

"Where are my tapes?" Jeff was calmer now.

"Later. To top it off, you usually get a picture of her with her latest catch. You must set it up very carefully. I noticed that each picture features a different older man. Quite a list. I left you the pictures and took the negatives. Of course, after the fact, the girl disappears from the face of the earth, since she never really existed to begin with. You make the contact, and the money comes rolling in."

"It is a neat business," Jeff said, "and you seem to have it all in a tidy little package. It's quite profitable."

"It must be. Nobody seems to know you in the financial community in this town. Just a cover, I guess, for your real business."

"It's not bad," Linda put in. "I work maybe four weeks out of the year, and we live very well." She seemed to switch tactics, to a more conciliatory tone. Jeff picked up on it and followed her lead.

"We could cut you in on it, Ms. O'Brien," he said. "My associates tell me you're a professional. We could count on your silence for a fee, I suspect."

"Thanks, but I don't want any part of your sleazy business. I don't earn every dollar I get, but I do work for it, and I don't trade on other people's vices. I just want out of this. Now, here's the setup. If anything happens to me, three different attorneys will post sample negatives and tapes to the police with your names and address. They're in sealed packages to be opened only in case of my having an untimely accident. You back off and I back off. Nobody gets hurt. Deal?"

"What happens to us?" Linda asked. "Without those negatives and tapes…"

"Ask your husband. He'll tell you the marks don't know

you've been taken. As long as they think you've got that evidence they'll keep paying. Now, what about it?"

The couple looked at one another. After a pause, Linda nodded slowly. Jeff rose and extended his hand to Felicity.

"I believe you have us at a disadvantage. I suppose we can do business your way. Sorry about the gun bit earlier. I panicked. Shall we say we have…an arrangement?"

"Yes, we shall, but you'll understand if I don't want to shake your hand on it."

Dusk found Felicity O'Brien driving her Porsche 911 straight into the sunset on Route 10. The complex vocal artistry of Clannad filled the car. She liked night driving and she intended to stay behind the wheel until dawn. There was a special solitude in pushing a vehicle at high speed through the blackness of a long, southwestern road. She had decided to drive on to her Los Angeles place, stopping at a roadside motel when necessary to freshen up.

She understood Jeff Aaron well enough to know he would come after her eventually. Knowing her life was on the line made it easy to lie to them. Besides, even jewel and art thieves like her looked down on blackmailers, regarding them as the dirtiest of criminals.

She was prepared to be careful for a while. It should not be necessary for long. After all, some of Jeff and Linda's "clients" were prominent, and therefore powerful, men. Felicity had not trusted the cassette tapes and negatives to any lawyer, but rather to the United States Postal Service. Those items, along with the Aarons' location, would arrive at the home of each of their blackmail victims in a couple of days. Very soon their unearned payments would stop arriving, and by then Jeff might realize he was minus one computer disk. He might even put two and two together and realize Felicity had a copy of his list of victims. But it might not take that long for one of his targets to see to it that Jeff and Linda Aaron were the ones who had an untimely accident.

With a sly smile, she settled back to enjoy the drive.

CLEAR LAKE

Mary Stojak

THE LIGHTS OUTLINING THE FERRIS WHEEL BURN WHITE in the twilight, twilight that paints the carnival scarlet against the lengthening shadows. I've been dreaming about the last time I was here with my father.

We'd taken a holiday with Mom, fishing every day off a rented pontoon boat in the middle of the lake, eating baloney and pickle sandwiches, drinking Cokes from red cans that darkened in the sun. In the evenings, my father would drive me to the carnival, where we would park our Buick at the end of a long line of Chevys and Fords and walk across the August grass to the rides.

That last night, I insisted on riding the Ferris wheel even though I knew he was afraid of heights. High above the cooling earth, I waited for that time when our cradle would be at its highest point, looking over the rippling lake and the white clapboard cabins arranged around the shore. My father's hands had tightened on the crossbar. His gaze never met mine as we rode home to the vodka over ice he demanded on our arrival.

I didn't tell him why I wanted to ride the Ferris wheel and he didn't ask. I was thirteen that year, in the third year of what he called my "education."

Rolling down the car window, I breathe in the sultry air that pours into the car. I've never told anyone except Mom about what my father did to me. Instead, when the topic of my father would come up, I've always changed the subject, sometimes talking about how the climate is warming, how strange it would be to have palm trees in Chicago. My father did the same on the Ferris wheel when we were high above the maples and poplars; he talked about the night sky, the globular star cluster in Hercules and Orion's belt. That restraint I always felt when I was with him had eased that night, expanding like the nebulas, releasing me to float away.

A silhouette of a man appears against the sunset. When he stoops, one of the sideshow hawkers appears framed by the window. Why had I imagined it might be my father's face? He died of a heart attack almost a year ago.

"Something wrong, lady?"

"Nothing. It's nothing." I floor the gas pedal, spewing a wave of dry grass in my wake.

The gravel road from the fairgrounds turns smooth before I come to the end, easing into the "u" I make onto the road that embraces the lake. In the rearview mirror, the pink sweater that Tom gave me for my birthday is hanging on the hook above the door, and I can still see the bright arc of the Ferris wheel above the shadows of the trees.

Dumpy cottages with multi-paned windows and bungalows with decks blink by, tiki torches lighting the decks where the now-popular martini parties are in full swing. I wish I was with them, walking around the tanned women in strapless dresses, men in their crisp shirts.

When I left Chicago a week ago, I told my husband Tom that I needed some time alone. Driving across Illinois and into Iowa, I thought about turning back, wondering if he was seeing someone else. I even pulled off the highway once, intending to circle back around to the north-bound ramp, until I thought about how pointless it would be to confront him, to try to start again.

Before I left, he asked me if I was happy. We'd been at a faculty party when he'd started discussing some new computer technology that I didn't understand. I'd drifted away, circulating among the crowd, stopping to chat when people's eyes met mine. I might have talked too long to the new professor or Tom might have been wondering why I don't want to use the money that my father left me. I never answered him when he asked me why I didn't want to pay off the mortgage, didn't want to have a baby.

A Camry pulls out in front of me, and I slow in the growing darkness. The profiles in the car turn to and fro as if they're engaged in some animated conversation. Their movements are smooth; sometimes, one head dips gently toward the other as if in confidence. The conversation won't be about love or children's morals. Tomatoes. People here always seem to be talking about the huge, sweet tomatoes that you can buy at the Iowa roadside stands.

THAT NIGHT ON the porch of my cabin, I'm reading. Beyond the screens, the night is impenetrable, except for the broken light reflecting off the lake; invisible wildlife sings as it did the last night I saw my father alive. Instead of keeping silent that night, my anger had poured out. I hadn't listened to Mom's apologies.

Five years ago when I took her home from the hospital to die, she wanted to talk about my father, how he hadn't meant to hurt me, and I felt that old anger again. I couldn't stop thinking about the expression on her face when I'd first told her how he'd touched me.

The book I'm reading is hers, one that I pulled from a box I didn't open until two weeks ago. When I touch the yellowed paper, I feel her warm hand holding mine the first day I went to school, feel her cool hand just before she died. The sleuth has just been threatened and the second murder committed when I drink the last of my Chardonnay and go back inside.

THE MORNING IS fresh after last night's rain. The fishermen have returned and the children are anxious to go into the water, throwing stones at the waves, when I decide to walk west to town.

Small shops with shingled roofs stretch out over the sidewalk and line the town's street. Rafts shaped like sharks and dolphins, candy-colored blow-up balls, and those long foam sticks in apple green and hot pink fill the windows. The toys are dazzling compared to the red lifesaver my mother bought me the first year we came to Clear Lake.

Couples stroll around me, licking twirled ice cream cones while their children dart in and out of the stores. Across the street, a small totem pole stands outside a shop, the same shop that my father loved so much.

Inside, rubber knives and tomahawks fill plastic bins and feathers sprout from headbands and headdresses hanging from the walls. Farther back, the beaded leather goods that I collected when I was small hang in rows on long silver arms. A herringbone pattern that reminds me of a belt my father bought on one of our vacations catches my eye. He wore it until the beads started to come off, long ago, long before my parents divorced, long before I buried him next to Mom outside of Ames. I finger the smooth beads, shining drops of turquoise and red.

A whining woman and her son are going through the other belts.

"What about this one?" The woman holds up a belt with "Clear Lake" lettered in crimson.

"Mom, I told you. I'm not going to wear it. It's too dumb."

"What about the one she's holding?" his mother asks as she smiles at me. "Do you know what that pattern means?"

"I always thought they were arrowheads when my father had one." I offer the belt to the boy.

"See, Mom? Old people wear these." He shuffles past, his body swinging side to side.

After selecting a change purse with red ideograms that look like flowers, I go to the counter and discover that the belt is still hanging over my arm.

My father didn't seem that old when we went to his funeral. I'd focused as long as I could on a brass handle of the casket before my eyes drifted up to his body. Hard planes marked his face even in death. When tears came to my eyes, Tom seemed to think I missed him, regretted staying away for so long.

The smell of grilled beef draws me out of the shop. Two doors down there's a sidewalk café with white metal tables topped by red and white umbrellas. Most of the seats are filled; none of the people look familiar. As I choose an empty table off to the side, I hear someone asking if the tomatoes are Big Boys or another variety.

At a table in the far corner, girls in black t-shirts with "Dracula" written across the front are clustered around an older man. They must be part of the company from the play I saw last weekend with the Petersons, the family in the rented cabin next to mine.

When I bite into my burger, it's so juicy that a thin stream runs down my chin. I don't think I've ever tasted anything so good.

"Do I know you?"

I chew my hamburger slowly and swallow. The man from the Dracula group is standing by my table. I wipe my chin with a small napkin before I answer, "I don't think so."

"I noticed you were looking at us. Thought I might know

you from the university."

"I'm not from Iowa." I want to take another bite, taste the tomato.

"No?"

"I thought that the girls might have been in the play last weekend." The smell of my burger curls up, wrapping itself around me, burning wood and sweet onion. I remember Tom standing by the grill, flipping burgers with a long-handled spatula, his teaching assistant's long red hair brushing his bare arm when she whispered in his ear.

The man laughs. "Go ahead, take another bite," he says and pulls out a chair. "Do you mind if I sit down?"

The burger has cooled when I bite into it again.

"Dracula. It's been a big hit with the kids. Are you here alone?" His brown eyes seem friendly enough, not asking too much.

I don't answer; my mouth is still full.

"I noticed your rings." His eyes twinkle, flashes of life crossing the warm darkness.

I just nod and chew.

"Well, it was nice to meet you," he says as he rises from his chair.

As I finish my burger, the man returns. "Did you know this is where Buddy Holly died? I can show you where his plane crashed outside of town," he says. "It wouldn't take long; it's just a couple of miles away."

"Sure, why not," I reply, thinking of the red-haired girl.

HEAPS OF SWOLLEN white clouds have filled the blue landscape, changing the sky into a mountain range that blocks the August sun. I wonder if it's cooler now outside the air-conditioned jeep, or if the clouds will make the day even hotter.

Will—that's his name—drones on about his classes at the university, wondering how they might be different from the undergraduate classes I teach in art history.

When we pull over, I see the path by the fence that holds back a crowd of corn, dark green tongues lapping over tall rods. Humid air surrounds the stalks of corn, hot like my father's body; I think I hear his voice calling my name from the rustling leaves.

Up ahead, the stainless steel guitar of the shrine shines

darkly against a low wall of plants. Beside the cut-out guitar held up by pipes, "Peggy Sue," "Donna," and "Chantilly Lace" are etched onto three discs.

"It's not much, I know." Will leans forward to look at the plastic-covered pictures of the dead musicians.

"These weren't here when I came before." My father is standing by the barbwire fence decorated with bouquets of flowers. "There were four trees, one for each person who died, and there were flowers." The dying or dead flowers in the hot sun surround my father, gladiolas on long stems are stuck into mayonnaise jars, plastic bouquets of white carnations and dusty red roses are tied to the barbed wire.

"Some people say they feel something weird here. I've never felt anything." Will takes a baseball cap from his back pocket and eases it over his curls. "Why didn't you tell me you've been here before?"

Dark planes seem to mark Will's face. I ask him if we can go.

When Will asks where I'm staying, I tell him and he says that he'll pick me up at ten after the play. My body nods as I let go of that last thread—a hope that I can be like everyone else. He waves as he drives away without saying goodbye, says he'll see me later.

My cabin, shaded now from the afternoon sun by the tall oak trees, looks out of place in this new world I've chosen. The kids outside are yelling and splashing in the water, not knowing who I am.

I settle back into the naked wicker chair on the porch with a glass of wine, picking up Mom's book again. The wine bottle is almost empty when I read the last page. The light has faded. Children play cards on the other porches and the woods wait for the darkness. When a soft mist turns to heavy rain, I go inside to lie on my unmade bed.

I sit upright, remembering Mom—how I blamed her, how I watched in silence as she wasted away. I see her face, sunken eyes that are still bright blue. Tears run down into the half moons under eyes. They spill down her swollen cheeks when she tells me she loves me. In the dim light, I try to slow my pulse, listening to the rain dripping off the eaves. The dog at the cabin next door is yapping at something in the woods. Mrs. Peterson shushes him and speaks softly.

What is Tom doing in Chicago? Will his arm be slung across the back of the sofa, imagining that I'm there? I haven't called him today as I promised two days ago.

"You were supposed to call at six." His voice sounds fuzzy on my cell phone.

"Is it too late?"

"I waited over two hours for your call." His voice is still blurred. He's become sleep deprived, waking each night when I jerk awake beside him from my dreams. I hear someone in the background and the noise is muffled as I imagine him covering the phone with his hand.

"I'm sorry," I tell him. That's what I always say.

"Is that all?"

The words won't come.

The line crackles and goes dead.

The bare hangers rattle in the closet when I pull my clothes free. Amber light from the lamp sends small echoes of fire up the cedar paneling as I pack. The twilight outside wraps itself around the cabin like one of Mom's cottage quilts.

After I clean out the refrigerator, I dress in my blue linen outfit, the one Tom likes best. I don't leave when I'm ready to go. I sit at the white table suddenly tired. The numbers on the kitchen clock only read nine o'clock. The second hand ticks off the seconds, another round makes the minute hand edge forward; thirty turns of the second hand will only move the minute hand to six. I turn off the lights.

The Ferris wheel is dark when I arrive at the fairgrounds. The fair is closed on Mondays. I wonder if the carnival people are sitting around their TVs, sipping beers, commenting on the rubes that buy yellow tickets for the rides. Looking out across the empty parking lot, the only hint that they're here is the light coming from their RVs, parked near the rides. I cradle my pink sweater before I stuff it in the tailpipe.

I'm so tired, I can barely turn the key. The sun is setting behind the Ferris wheel, orange turning to scarlet. The car hums a strange song under its breath and I feel my father's hand on my knee. He whispers in my ear. I close my eyes and will him away. Tom is sitting next to me now, raising his eyebrows, putting his hand on my shoulder, singing "Michelle" along with a Beatles' CD, kissing me on our first date as we wait for a red light to turn green in the busy streets of Chicago.

Our Lady of the Helicopter

Frank S. Joseph

L OOKING OUT THE PLEXI AT THE CARS BELOW, I SEE HOW it will end. One day, diving toward the freeway, a million mouths agape as I flutter down, a broke-wing moth on her last trip. The chopper goes chugga-chugga-sput and my fate rises up to meet me.

Two-vehicle pileup on the 405 at Harbor Boulevard, looks like it could be a fairly bad one, let me check the scanner. Garden Grove is on its way over. Looks like they're going to need an ambulance. Bring me down a little closer, Chuck, let's see if we can scope this thing out for the folks in KAKX-land.

Like them down there, bending and creasing their metal forms into one another 24/7, death is never far. I signed up knowing it. Part of the job. Thirteen years up here, first for Metro Traffic as a kid out of Pomona, broadcast major, later for Skywatch, now this. Loving every minute. The head boss big sky lady of L.A. Chopper queen.

Take her down a little closer, Chuck. Can you get a shot of that now, Arvin? Folks, my man the intrepid Arvin is a camera-wielding fool. The Man with the Cam, eh, Arv? What do you see down there? Oh folks, this looks like a bad one. Going to need the paramedics too. Anyone call Long Beach yet? This looks like more than Garden Grove can handle. Anyone got ambulances on the way yet, Chuck? What are you picking up on the radio?

I love the feel of it, a thickness to the air when you head into trouble, ten cars and a jackknifed semi on the Santa Monica Freeway, and right over the trouble spot a column of more viscous air in which my beast may hover. The prop wash is an oily fluid only I can see, spreading extreme unction on motorists, a blessing of the helicopter goddess.

They look up. They see me. What salvation they have, I give.

Closer, Chuck, closer. Folks, as you can see on your TVs, we're just, oh, 500 feet above this accident on the 405. We're near the Harbor Boulevard exit in the southbound lanes. It's only two vehicles but it's a bad one all right. That's a silver 2006 Lincoln Navigator down there, must've just rolled off the line at the Rouge plant, except it's on its side and you are looking right down into the driver's window. A Bel Air daddy, driving where he oughtn't, looking for what he shouldn't. Wish he had that window open. Damn air conditioning. Keep trying to get us a better look at him, Arv. Check that: bring me in on the other vehicle for a moment. Looks like a stake truck full of cantaloupes and Mexicans, probably on a run down from Bakersfield. Folks lying all over the road. It's ugly, all right. Can you get us in just a little closer, Chuck?

Near thing once. Chuck sliced through a power line in the Valley. I was trying to get him too close that time, too. Cable could have wrapped around our prop but instead it went onto the ground with a hot sizzle. Chuck managed to keep it revving and we went up instead of down, to heaven. Made the front page of the *Herald-Examiner*. *Times* gave it a ride, too, but on Metro, the phonies. Things haven't been the same since the *Examiner* folded. But there's still KAKX.

We've got a few cops down there now. Good thing. The jam-up is back to Warner Avenue. You don't want to be getting on at the Warner southbound right now, folks. This tie-up is two miles long already and growing every moment. Can't beat the system on the L.A. freeways. You get a couple million cars barreling along at seventy-five every minute of the day and night, things don't always go according to plan. Am I telling it like it is, Arv?

Thirteen years up here, building ratings. You see my face on billboards everywhere you drive. For Freeway Traffic Checks, Look Up—To KAKX. God, I loved that at first, kids stopping me on the street for autographs, getting a good table at Spago. That was all it was about. But now I see the thing that's more important. This is a calling. I heal.

They're going to have to use the shoulder to bring in the rescue equipment. The traffic lanes are frozen solid. Ordinary rush hour, the 405 carries 23,300 cars an hour. Some perspective, folks: we have an accident every one minute and five seconds in the State of California, an injury every one minute and 49 seconds, a traffic death every two hours and 28 minutes. A lot of them right out here on the 405.

I know much more. I am very busy with my reading. Traffic statistics, sure, lots more besides. NTHSA reports, the Insurance Institute for Highway Safety, municipal statutes, the criminal code. They have to throw me out of the County Clerk's office at closing time. Dead air is the enemy.

There was this monster pile-up on the Ventura Freeway in '96, dozens of cars, five or six dead, emergency equipment coming from as far as Downey. Had to go to the public library for that one. I'm so glad. Bending over the microfilm shadows, I saw beauty.

I pulled the KAKX film at midnight, just to see what we did with it. We were contemptible. It was just after we got the chopper. The first one up here was this dude with spiky hair, looked like Bart Simpson. No grand sweep of twisted metal, just Mister Hair Gel with his helmet off, yakking away. The second the footage began to roll, I knew he didn't get it. He didn't have my vision.

Radio says the troops are on their way. We should spot them any second. Arv, give me a long shot back north. Now crank it out as far as she'll go. You can see those flashers back a mile or two, can't you, folks? Arvin can pick out a bug on a windshield with our new HDCam. Eighty grand, but worth it. That's your eighty thousand dollars, folks.

They offered me the Hollywood beat one time. Said with my looks I'd be perfect, interviewing Cruise and Cage, camera wouldn't know where to turn first. "No" was easy. Standing in front of the Chinese Theater with a mike in my hand, short skirts and goose pimples, waiting all night for the dork to come out? I'd rather be up here, bringing understanding, flying until forever ends.

The sun's in my eyes. Let's see if we can come back in from the southwest, Chuck, give the folks a better look at the Navigator. The cops are trying to let the emergency vehicles in now. Get on the radio and tell them the shoulder is clear except for, there's a Dodge Caravan down there. She's looking for daylight. What a jerk. You in the Caravan, this is Myra in the KAKX chopper, yeah, look up. There are people dying a quarter-mile in front of you. Would you please move your kid taxi back into traffic and let the emergency vehicles through? That's better. When the freeways freeze, folks, everyone watches KAKX.

I would do it all if it were possible—talk the talk, aim the cam, fly the helicopter. I could. I am oriented in three dimensions. Up and down are easy, free. I see vectors as we fly. Even Chuck doesn't see what I see, the path that leads us to the next hover, a channel cut through a yellow sky.

They're in. You see that one jumping out of the ambulance? Tight on him please, Arv. He's helping one of the Mexicans now. See the paramedic, folks? He's working on the guy's shirt, ripping it open. The guy's unconscious, clearly. Oh, yeah, look at them pulling out the defibber. We're going to see a rescue now, folks, this is what it's all about, this is why you've sent me up here. You're about to see one man save another man's life, give the greatest gift one person can give. See the paddles on the guy's chest? Now watch this. There! And another, and another. Did you see it, folks, how he twitched? The guy's okay. I think he'll be okay. That would not have been possible fifty years ago. Thank God for television.

I would heal them, too, wish them back to life, but that is not the power I've been given. No. I help the dead to share their deaths, and that's holy, or so it seems to me. Let others mourn.

Folks, if you have a choice, I suggest almost anything but the southbound 405 right now. I see a backup for three, four, five miles and it's getting longer by the second. The Navigator is on its side across two lanes of traffic and the truck, well, let's just say no one's going to drive it again for a long time. We've got cantaloupes everywhere and the cops still haven't figured out what to do with the cars. Drivers are getting through on the two inner high-speed lanes only; the other lanes are blocked. And, wouldn't you know it, the ones getting through are rubbernecking at three miles an hour. It's going to be a long afternoon.

When I stop this, what? Pointing to a blue screen and pretending it's a low-pressure zone coming in off the Pacific? Commercials for Lou Ehlers Cadillac? Maybe they'll ask me to be an assignment editor, telling me I've got the grit and the guts. I do, but that's not the point. This is what I was meant to do. No one can replace me. No one would dare try.

Chuck, bring her up to a thousand. Let's get a long shot of the backup. Arv, pan back north. Look at that, jillions of cars, nobody moving. Keep me at this altitude for a few moments, Chuck, until something starts happening again. Patience, folks. We'll have more good film in a sec.

I could do radio perhaps. Not an American company but some foreign outfit that hasn't lost its edge yet, a BBC posting to Penang or Rangoon. On radio, they can't judge you on whether or not you've lost your looks. Or I could just get out, say the hell with it, marry rich and settle in Palos Verdes Estates like June did. Have kids, June says. It's like no other experience in the world, she says, speaking with certainty.

What, we're off air? Hey, come on, Harry, this thing isn't cleaned up, far from it. The ambulances haven't even taken anyone off the street yet. I know it's a little slow right now, but Jesus. The damn Navigator, the son-of-a-bitch is still trapped inside.

Oh shit. I hate this.

Arv, for God's sake, isn't there anything down there to give Harry?

Put me live again, Harry. Screw your five minutes on the eleven o'clock news, I want to be live, right now, do you hear me? Look, they got the Jaws of Life coming, it'll be here in five max. Come on, Harry, put me back on right now. You cocksucker.

Under the truck! Isn't there someone trapped under the truck? Oh, come on, Chuck, take us down so Arv can get the shot. Right there, dammit, don't you see him? Those are legs, aren't they? Bring it down. Bring it down to two hundred if you have to.

The poor man, it's his moment. Grant it to him. Don't be afraid. Nothing can harm us.

Harry, make you a deal. When they get that can half-open, you put me back on, okay? Who gives a shit about Wheel of Fortune? Just put me back on for the Jaws. Just two, three minutes is all I'm asking. I'll give you the heads-up, you'll even have a couple minutes to make ready for the feed. Come on, Harry, promise me. Of course if it's good film, but it will be. You know it will. It always is.

This is how it ends. This is the only death I fear.

Don't lose them, Arv, don't lose them. Come on, Chuck, damn it, we're supposed to be friends. What's with you guys? Get me that shot. Do whatever you've got to do. We'll be on again soon. I'll make certain of it.

No. No jasmine tea on the patio, looking out over the Pacific. My course is clear. We're going down.

The Last Drummer

Gary L. Lester

The great bird settled into a comfortable rhythm high above the earth. Whether it was by instinct or by intelligence, it was in the air long before dawn. As it wheeled around in the sky, dawn began to break, sending rosy streams of light onto the wakening world. The creature felt the warmth of the light. It turned so its whole body could feel it.

As it looked down with its keen vision, it could see many small creatures scurrying about. It could easily swoop down and claim any one of them for a morning snack, yet it was content to drift. It watched the ground as darkness gave way in a series of ever-shortening shadows.

As it flew, the bird felt an itchy, prickly spot on its wings. When it craned its neck to look, it panicked. It saw a line of smoke emanating from its feathers. It shrieked. As it reached its beak around to bite at the irritation, the creature turned from a flying object into a falling one.

Again, the bird panicked. It beat its wings to recover altitude. The force that the bird used sent sound waves like that of thunder. The reverberations echoed from the slowly brightening earth. The cliffs and valleys of the surrounding countryside fell silent at the sound. Other birds and creatures dared not move, hearing such a cry from the great predator above.

A farmer who had risen early to tend to his cattle was startled by the bird's first cry. He waited at the fence to listen. Soon other cries emanated from the bird, along with the percussive force of its beating wings. The farmer quickly ran inside.

Waking his wife, he told her she must tend to the cattle this morning and have their grandchildren help. With a worried look, she rose and began to dress. The farmer ran into the family room and grabbed his drum.

The drum was an old barrel-style instrument with a worn leather skin stretched tightly across the top. A series of bright silver tacks held the leather in place. There were numerous dents and chips in the wood.

The farmer ran from his house and found a spot in the back yard. He sat down and began to play. The wife listened. She knew he had always had a gift with the drum. He was always asked to play at the high ceremonies. Even when they were younger, he would just play different rhythms and patterns—but not this. She'd never heard this rhythm before. Whether it was the cold morning or the seriousness of her husband, a chill ran through her, and she sought to busy herself with chores.

Far above the Earth, the bird heard the drum, its repetitious pattern momentarily distracting. The bird searched for the source of the sound. It changed its course and flew in that direction.

Something about the drumming was familiar. As it circled, a memory slowly emerged. Then, without warning, it remembered. It remembered. The ancient rhythm resounded in the bird's entire being. Yet the sound was different. The drumming was not as loud as it once was.

The bird was older than any living thing had a right to be. It was painful to fly. It was painful not to fly. Its skin was old and cracked like leather left in the sun too long. The hollow spines of its feathers were brittle. Just flying taxed all its reserved strength.

It didn't eat as much as it used to. Prey would out-run the bird. Or out-maneuver it. It was only able to feed on weaker or dying creatures. And now the smoldering from its skin haunted it. The trail of smoke grew larger as the bird flew on.

It was time. In the very core of its being the great creature knew it was time. It floated along looking for the perfect location. Although other parts were rapidly failing the bird, the eyes had not lost their sharpness. They spotted the wheat fields from miles away.

The drummer became aware of a presence. Without missing a beat, he raised his eyes from the drum. The images of his ancestors appeared, surrounding him. His father stood in front of him.

"My son, where are the others?"

"I am all there is."

"That cannot be. Where are your sons?"

"They have left for the lights of the city."

"If we cannot save her, we will die. Perhaps all of mankind will die. There must be somebody."

"There is my granddaughter."

"No. That is forbidden."

The drummer returned his attention to his drum. "So be it."

The bird let out a long and mournful cry. Yet, in the cry, defiance was evident.

Slowly, the wings began to beat with powerful strokes that propelled the bird upward. Each stroke was more powerful than the last. With each pull rolled the sound of thunder. After the seventh stroke, the outstretched wings froze in place. The bird could hear the thunder reverberating from the world far below.

Gravity finally defeated the upward motion of the bird. Gradually, the predator keeled over and started downward. Its body had frozen into a perfect dive position, gaining speed on its downward journey.

The air flowing across the bird's wings and body had caused the smoldering areas to heat up. The bird heard the crackle of flickering flames, a sound that disappeared almost as quickly as it had come: The bird lost its hearing.

The ground came rushing to meet the bird. It was still able to see, and its mind still functioned. It did not feel the rhythm of the drum as before. The drumbeat was everything to the creature. Would it survive this time?

"It is time," the farmer's father shouted. "Play louder."

The drummer nodded, his fingers already numb from the pounding. Two of his ancestors knelt on either side of him. They lifted the drum and held it just above the ground. The earth no longer muffled the volume of the drum.

The bird plummeted into the wheat field chest-first. The dried brown stalks of wheat did nothing to cushion its fall. Even with the ferocious impact, the bird maintained consciousness, helplessly watching as the flames from its body set the surrounding wheat on fire. Had the bird been able to smell, the pungent aroma of burning flesh would have overwhelmed it. The old, dried-out skin and brittle feathers slowly peeled and fell off the ruined hulk. The flames spread in a circle around the doomed animal.

At last giving in, the bird laid down it head. Mercifully, the nerves stopped functioning, not allowing the pain to pass. The flames consumed all.

Then, with agonizing slowness, feeling began to return the very tips of the wings. A warm sensation started to spread inward. Whether it took an hour or a week, the bird did not comprehend, only knowing that it was happening. The warmth spread to the legs and tail. Soon the bird began to feel, once again, the beating of its heart. Strength began to fill in where once there was weakness.

The bird instinctively shook it wings. Bits of skin and feathers fell away. Again, the creature shook like a wet dog; burning embers and charred skin flew in all directions. It calmly looked around and saw flames and smoldering ashes.

The bird slowly stood. Then, suddenly, it emitted a loud cry and leapt into the air. The body of the bird changed from a glowing, orange-red to a metallic grey. The bird flew with a renewed freedom. No longer was it burdened with an aged, decrepit body; it was reborn. It wheeled and danced in the sky.

The bird once again became aware. The instinctual cycle had ended, returning the bird to its own whims. Time once again had meaning. The drum continued. The bird remembered the drumming from other times. It was louder before, with many rhythms and drum sounds weaving together into one great heartbeat. Now, the bird heard but one drummer. One lonely drummer.

The bird flew lower towards the drumbeat. The drummer never looked up, continuing to concentrate on his playing. He grew tired, but he dared not stop. The drummer's wife and grandchildren surrounded him and watched the bird.

The bird remembered when there were many drummers. Without the drumming, the cycle would not begin. The bird honored the drummer. The drummer honored the bird. The bird flew lower yet, in a tight circle descending slowly over the family. As it got lower, the drummer's wife became more and more apprehensive and drew the children nearer.

Finally, the bird landed. Ever-so-gently for so large a creature, it settled on the farmer's house. The roof beams creaked and the little house swayed slightly. The bird folded it wings and looked around. The drummer's wife began to sob, clutching her grandchildren by the shoulders. The drummer continued. The bird gazed intently at the family, tilting and turning its head to examine them through both eyes.

The drummer looked up. The bird locked eyes with the drummer and held his gaze for an eternity. Finally, the bird reached around its back with its beak and, after much fuss, pulled out a feather.

Turning once again to look at the drummer, the bird released the feather. As it fluttered to the ground, the granddaughter ran to catch it. The drummer's wife tried to stop her, but it was too late. The girl ran to the house and caught the feather just before it hit the ground.

Looking up, the young girl saw the bird gazing intently at her. She smiled. Never had she seen anything so large, let alone a bird. The wings gleamed and shimmered in the sunlight.

Suddenly, the bird stretched open its wings and screeched. The sound was deafening, exploding the window just below the bird's feet. The bird leapt into the air, passing closely over the little girl. The wind from its wings pushed her toward her grandfather. She never removed her eyes from the reborn creature. She felt something akin to worship.

The bird circled again, this time gaining altitude. The drumming kept on. The bird flew on. It became smaller and smaller, a tiny dot over the mountains.

The drummer looked up to see his ancestors beginning to fade.

"The Thunderbird chose my granddaughter. She chose the Thunderbird. Is this still forbidden?"

"My son, you must do what the bird commands. So be it."

The father faded.

Still drumming, the old man told his grandson to build a fire in the center of the yard. The boy gathered broken sticks and other wood and soon built a roaring fire.

Finally, when the flames leapt high, the old man stopped drumming. He reached to his side and pulled out his knife. He cut the head on his drum, then turned the instrument on its side and stood up. With one step he stomped on the drum and crushed it, gently placing its remains in the fire.

The granddaughter wept. Smiling, the farmer held her chin and looked deep into her eyes. "Tomorrow," he told her, "We will begin making new drums, and I will teach you how to play."

THE LAST GOOD DAY

Sonia L. Linebaugh

"Meteorologist Dan Shaw predicts sunshine with a high of sixty degrees," said Joe, with the phone still in his hand. "Do you hear that? Do you hear Dan shouting? Motorcycle. Motorcycle. Motorcycle." He grinned at Justine.

"No, thanks," she replied to his implied invitation. "This might be the last good day I have to work in the garden."

"That's why I have to ride—it might be the last good day."

"Enjoy yourself. I'll save the mowing for you."

When Joe rumbled out on the Harley, Justine was already loaded down by the long-handled pruner and a bucket of hand tools. He waggled an arm and Justine waggled her whole body in return.

Great day for a ride, she thought without regret as she waded into branches of the butterfly bush under a blue sky with the least nip in the wind. Grappling with the dying abundance of the summer would hopefully transform her mental debris into the seed of a story.

The bush, a volunteer, sprawled across pavers half buried in groundcover that started out as a handful of clippings from Natalie. Justine thought about her former neighbor as she lopped at the branches, the pruner braced at a low angle with her foot, the blade notched over each branch in turn as she pulled long and slow on the rope. Her thumbs pinged with pains embedded from years past when hand clippers were her only cutting tool. Was there some story in the memory of pain? Something to do with Natalie, who had disappeared into her daughter's car after that debilitating stroke? She had lain there helpless until Fred from across the road noticed the piled up newspapers. Does life always come to loss?

Branches piled up. Justine bent over them, wrapped her arms as far around as she could reach, and started dragging. She had perfected her technique over the years: a larger branch on the bottom served as a sledge for the others.

She thought again of Natalie, who had been the livewire of every neighborhood party for so many years. Maybe her antics were a cover up for loneliness. Justine yanked the branches through a tight spot near the back of the house, knocking over the trash can and the recycling bin. She skirted the wood pile. A few logs fell as the bundle lost its cohesion. No matter, Joe would take care of it later.

The story would open with the soft thud of a log on matted grass, the soft thud of Natalie's body as she fell to the floor in the bedroom doorway, no, the kitchen doorway. Wasn't there a cocktail involved? A hayburner—Natalie loved those. She'd have to find out how it's made.

She dragged and coaxed the branches behind the shed, out of sight of the house. Joe would mulch them one of these days. Would Natalie be mulched? Buried and returned to the earth? Cremated and flung into the garden? No, she wasn't dead yet. They would have heard.

She looked at her arms, regretting the long-sleeved shirt left behind on the breakfast chair. Scratches and bruises would be evidence of her labors. The women in her yoga class would look at her with pity as if Joe were to blame. That was never Joe's style. No, she couldn't think of a single instance when Joe had left marks of aggression. Signs of loving maybe—a chafed chin back when he first started his beard and kissing played a big part of their lives. Or rug burn on her lower back in the days before the kids, when the living room rug and so many other spots had been blessed by their embraces. She smiled standing there behind the shed with scratches and aching arms.

Hours passed. Branches piled up. Logs tumbled from the wood pile. Trash and recycling described a trail from house to shed. Justine thought of Natalie as she mowed down the zebra grass that had jumped across the road when neighbor Paul tried to eradicate it. It would return in abundance come spring. Natalie had spent the last twenty years eradicating the pain of her first marriage. The story began forming itself in Justine's mind. *Emotions cut back. Emotions resurging in the abundance of spring. A new love? Did Natalie ever find her new love? She tried. Maybe Philippe? It was an open secret that*

Annie Elian was in love with the Frenchman, boy really, barely into his twenties. In the story, Natalie would find moments of happiness in his smile. In his bed? Hmm.

She untangled the dried heritage tomato plants from their cages and heaped them on the compost pile that never got turned. Her son Danny had set up the compost for her, but he lived in town now with his latest girlfriend. No time for mom and dad these days. What was the compost word: aerobic? Anaerobic? She replanted the bulbs another neighbor, Leah, had given into her care the year she moved away. She wondered where Leah had gotten to after her stint with the Peace Corps in Morocco. She pictured her wandering behind a veil, a veil of tears. A great story, but not one she could tell.

Leah. Natalie. Philippe. Fred. Annie. Her mind wandered the neighborhood thinking how to twist raw material into a story worth telling. Joe—would he make the cast? Joe. Abruptly, the old fear intruded. Joe cut and bleeding, smashed and bleeding on the roadway. When they called to tell her that Joe had run into the bridge abutment at Solomons, she would keep cutting away the errant branches and dead plants of the summer past. That's what she would do.

And then she would go into the house and start drawing on the walls. She would shove the dining room table out of the way to draw the butterfly bush on the wall; then climb a ladder into the loft to start vines that would wander down the walls all the way into the basement. She would cover her bleeding insides with drawings of zebra grass and words telling the story of Joe and how he had rescued her from the wreck of her childhood. This was the story she would write, the story of her first good day and her last.

It was edging darkness, but still there was no phone call.

Justine's thoughts cleared and she headed for the kitchen. She had her head in the refrigerator when the distinctive stutter of the Harley preceded Joe into the yard. She breathed in and breathed out. Her shoulders dropped and softened. Joe pushed open the back door with his elbow, flipped his visor and asked, "Hey, Just, how about crabs for supper?"

He posed it as a question, but she'd lived with him a long time. "Just so," she answered in their secret code. "Stopped by John's truck, did you?"

"Yep. Might be the last crabs of the season." He was pleased with himself, glad she wouldn't complain about this year's high cost of crabs.

"Great. I'll make a salad. I think we have a couple of beers. How was the ride?"

"Best of the year. I went down Sands Road where there are so many trees. It was chilly in the woodsy patches and warm in the sun." He wanted her to be there. "The leaves smelled like autumn to-day—all damp earth and dry wood. You would have liked the colors, all those browns and tans and oranges that you favor." He described it as if he were the artist in the family. She'd taught him well.

As he stripped off chaps and leathers, he went on, as always, about the freedom and joys of riding the Harley. She didn't listen so much to his words as to the flow of his voice. His happiness compounded her own. She forgot her earlier worries.

Joe set the table with the morning paper, wooden cutting boards, two bottles of beer and a roll of paper towels. Justine added forks and bowls of salad greens, with olives, cauliflower, chunks of cheese and homemade dressing. They got to work.

"How many times have we done this?" Justine asked. "Whacked crabs with a mallet, pried them open, sucked their meat? How many times have we rolled up the detritus of shells and guts in newspaper and tossed it into the trash can for the critters to knock over and scatter across the yard?" She had a prick of conscience as she pictured the trash she'd scattered that afternoon.

No matter. She plunged on, "Life is like playing scales on the piano, C-D-E-F-G-A-B-C, a progression of notes, repeated and repeated and repeated."

Joe followed her lead. They'd played this duet before. "Like the piano, life has a limited number of keys, but think of all the tunes that can be played. Life doesn't stop at scales."

"But, in the end, it's the same eight notes. Look at the garden. There might be a symphony in there, but if I don't cut back the trees and bushes, and pull the weeds, it will turn to chaos. Nature will repeat its oldest habits. That dratted ivy will swallow the house in ten years if we don't keep re-orchestrating. And inside the house, there's nothing but dust..." she acknowledged Joe's raised his eyebrows with bark of laughter and added, "... occasionally. But, whether I clean today, or let it go for a month, the pattern remains the same: dust settles, I dust; dust settles, I dust."

Joe had heard this before, but she plunged on, "The garden is a mess. The house is a mess. *Life* is a mess. No matter what decisions we make, the reality is the same. It doesn't make any difference if we change our cleaning day or our gardening schedule. The course of our lives is not changed because we made this decision or that. Even when we change houses or states—and we have plenty of experience with that—the situation is the same: dust and dusting, weeds and weeding. We always arrive back at the natural state of things—at *our* natural state."

"So our natural state is covered in dust and ivy?" he taunted. "I disagree. Our natural state is to be players. Life is a stage play, an illusion. We are actors, playing our roles. I play a role on the stage *and* sit in the audience, *and* move the sets, *and* shine the spotlights. But when I get on the bike, everything looks different. There's a great role."

"Okay, Joe, putting aside the fact that you are avoiding the issue of dust, do you think you can write the role so the actors never age? Or are we, each one, growing old in our role as though it were our life?"

"Yes, yes. We live our role as if we mean it. We laugh as if we've got it. Cry as if our hearts were broken. Clap as if we loved every moment. Especially on the Harley."

She laughed, but she wasn't quite done. "We do, Joe, we do love every moment. But not the dust. In an ideal world, there would be no dust. I don't mind the weeds so much as the dust."

"Just-So, maybe you ought to leave dust-consciousness behind."

"Yeah, yeah, if I am not conscious of it, it doesn't exist. Tell that to the dust motes. Or the weeds."

Joe gave in one iota. "Okay, let's say that at some level, dust, weeds, warts, and mosquitoes do exist. We are courageous just for showing up in a world full of dust and weeds."

Laughing, Justine stood up. "I'm courageous enough to carry the bowls back to the kitchen. You can have the courage to clean up the crab shells, and, oh, better wear gloves when you take them out. You'll find a mess by the trash can." She made a little half-apology with her upper face. "Let's have another beer and leave the dust to increase and multiply and possess the earth."

They woke to a morning already soaked in rain, but it didn't matter because the sparks of a story spun brightly in Justine's head—it was not, after all, the story of Natalie.

It was a story of the last good day, a day like yesterday, a day set in the garden among plants beloved not only for themselves but also as a kind of botanical collection, each labeled in memory of a beloved neighbor. A day in which her players would live as if they hadn't yet read the tragic scene to come. She, the writer-creator who speaks her creatures into existence and devours them with the same fierce tender love, she would write all the roles and see how they played out.

A story of the last good day and the day after.

At the breakfast table, she dashed the opening lines on a three-by-five card while Joe attacked Sunday's Sudoku squares without her. She was headed to the monthly writers' breakfast and excited to have some ideas to bat around.

"Bet you can't finish the Sudoku before I get home," she challenged.

"Bet I can't," he laughed. "But mowing won't be my excuse. It looks like a messy morning. Give me a ring when you get there."

"I'll be fine," she assured him. "I'm okay."

"I know." His smile didn't have any reservations. "It's just the weather. I'll feel better if you call."

She drove out into the grey fog. It felt like another good day. Anticipation of the writers' breakfast gave her incentive to develop the story. On the highway, rain and yellow leaves flew across the windshield in competition. Thoughts of paint and canvas added compost to her thoughts. *The last good day would be followed by a day like today when the rain and the yellow leaves blew in equal measure across the story's stage. The last good day would be fecund with the earthy smells and textures of the garden. News of her beloved's death in a motorcycle accident would bring her life to an end and a tragic beginning. A tragedy and a love story.* She drove and thought of his body splattered across the highway. She drove and thought of losing herself, no, not herself, the protagonist—Judy—*Judy, losing herself in the garden, sinking down into the debris of the dying season. Or drawing her loss up into a monument of grief on the rough walls of the cottage they'd shared for so many years.*

The grey fog deepened. Justine passed the light at House

Road, the cemetery at All Souls. Thoughts flew at her with the speed of the storm. The grief of Joe's death swept into the car, into her mind. No, not Joe—Jim—Jim and Judy. The high school went by, then a roadside stand boarded up till the next season, her grief boarded up inside. The strip mall at came and went…

Oh shit, she thought. I missed the diner. I can't see out the damn window in all this rain. Now I'll have to—oh, shit, where am I? Okay, I'm okay. Mills Highway. I know where I am—I just have to stay in this lane and…

"Idiot!" she yelled, "What are you doing, changing lanes without a signal in all this rain? Okay, Justine, get into the left lane. I'm sure it's a left turn." The story continued writing itself. *She…Judy is happy in the garden. She has hours and hours of happiness before she gets the dreaded phone call.* Oh wait, here's the river. Didn't I cross it already? It must be the rain. I'm not at the diner yet. Am I in the right lane? *He'll die on the bridge, the bike sliding out from under him in heavy rain. Or hit head-on by a car driving the wrong way in the rain.* Wait, is this right? Did I miss the diner? Damn, is it across the river? I can't turn around here. *The thing about a motorcycle crash is that it would be fatal in weather like this. No lingering for years and years in a coma.*

Okay, now pay attention, remember to turn. God, this stretch is anonymous. What's that ringing sound? I hope I'm not low on gas. Where the hell is the damn turn? Here, here. Okay, there's the arrow to the mall. The diner's right in here. I bet I'm on time for a change. Despite the weather, I didn't have to back-track at all. Some of the others get so cranky if anyone shows up a little late. What is that ringing? Plenty of parking. Okay, where the hell is the diner? I'm sure I saw it as I turned in. Did I park at the wrong end of the mall? Where am I? Where the hell am I? These places all look the same.

She breathed in and breathed out. Don't panic. Start with what you know. We passed the turn of the century a while ago, so it must be… Where *do* I live? It's not Florida, there would be palm trees. Colorado? On a day like this you can't see the mountains. No, Danny was born there and he's not a baby any more. Not Ohio where the other one was born. Great art museum in Cleveland. Not Takoma Park though that was not so long ago. Not… how many places has Joe dragged me to? How the hell does he expect me to know where I am?

I'll sit here for a minute and wait until it comes to me. Judy—she comes in from the garden with that satisfying ache in every muscle. What if she died instead of Joe? Would it be Joe's last good day? No, he'd get over it, get invited to star in another role. In a few months some attractive, adventurous woman would snag him, wrap her arms around him on the Harley, go off on a cross-country tour of the sort he's always dreamed about... What was that sound, damn it, did I trigger some alarm in the car? Oh, it was the damn phone. "Hello? Hello?"

The phone rang a few more times; then it stopped. Technology. As useless as dust. Justine looked through the fogged window. Where the hell was she? How was she supposed to see where she was in the damn rain? It wasn't Florida, no palm trees. The phone rang again. "Hello? Hello?"

Nothing.

Okay, this was serious. She definitely couldn't remember where she lived. She knew her role, but not what theater she was playing this week. That was a good line, maybe she could work it into the story. But now, she'd go into that supermarket and hope her mind would get clear of this fog. It was just the damn rain. Maybe she'd have to ask someone. Surely, someone would know where she was going, or where she lived. She'd have to be clever. She didn't want Joe to know. She seemed to remember that he wouldn't like it. The phone rang as she slammed the car door. Justine shouted into it as she dashed for the store.

"New phone?" asked sympathetic voice. "You have to flip it open." She stared at the man she had nearly run into at the line of grocery carts.

"Like this." He demonstrated with his own phone.

"Oh, yeah, thanks. Technology isn't my field." She flipped open the phone but it wasn't ringing anymore. She held it out to the nice man.

"Here," he said, "Push the *call back* button like this and it will dial the person who just called."

"They think of everything, don't they?" She smiled her best smile. He was so nice, she wanted to ask him where she was going, but she couldn't think how to put it. He disappeared into the store as a voice came from the phone, "Mom? Mom! Where are you? Dad is frantic."

"Who is this?" she asked.

"Danny. It's Danny."

"Danny." Her tone didn't admit whether she knew him or not. "Gosh, how did you know where to find me?"

"Mom, it's a cell phone. It doesn't matter where you are. But where *are* you?"

"If it doesn't matter, how the hell should I know?" she asked. "You're the one who called me."

"Mom." His voice was careful now. She could tell it was careful but she didn't know what was wrong with him. "Is it Joe?" she asked. "I thought they'd be calling to let me know."

"Mom, I don't know what you're talking about. When you didn't answer Dad went to some diner looking for you. You weren't there."

"He's alive then? What hospital?"

"Mom, Dad is *not* in a hospital. You didn't call him like you were supposed to. You didn't answer his calls. He's trying to trace your route. Are you in a hospital?"

"Of course not. I'm here at the...um, place you buy stuff to eat. Do you need anything? I can pick up a few items for you, too, but I'm in a bit of a hurry."

"Mom, don't hang up. Mom, listen. I want you to tell me—hold on a second." She heard him talk to someone else, "Call Dad, tell him I have her on the cell phone. She sounds a little vague." Then he was talking to her again, "Mom, are you lost? What's the name of the store?" She hesitated. He added, "There must be a sign."

"Visa, MasterCard, American Express..."

"Good, Mom, good. Anything else?" It was that careful voice again. He was probably lying about Joe, trying not to upset her.

"Oh, here's the nice man. Maybe he can tell you...It's my son. I don't know how he knew where to find me, but he wants to talk to you."

The nice man looked like he wanted to run for his car, but he took the phone. She heard his half of the conversation as she listened for some hint about Joe's death. "No, I'm not in any writers' group. I just saw that she didn't know how to use her cell phone. I told her how to press call back. She's your mother? We, um, she's in front of the Food Lion." His eyes flicked at her and quickly away. He must have heard something about Joe, she thought.

"Brantley. Yes, across the river...Hmm, she looks okay. Calm. Just a little lost."

The nice man shot her another glance. He spoke into the phone, "I have to get home. I'll ask if she can wait in the grocery store until you get here...Okay, I'll tell them to be sure she doesn't leave. Food Lion. Brantley Creek Mall, just to the right, across the river."

Now he looked anxiously away from her. No doubt he didn't want her to see that he knew about Joe. She caught a few words, "Yes, yes, a red Corolla. I see it...looks okay...parked all right... Okay, I'll tell her that you're on your way."

The man led her to a bench near a window just inside the supermarket door. He told her that someone would come for her and then spoke to a clerk at the checkout counter. After he waved good-bye, Justine sat quietly. There wasn't anything she had to do except create a story, a play of words with roles that would make people clap as if they loved every minute. Let's see, *Judy and Jim. Those were her characters. Natalie, something about Natalie and her lover. Paul?* The thought made her laugh out loud. Sloppy Paul, not a likely choice for someone intelligent and sophisticated like Natalie. She tried to picture the two of them together. They would not be willed into words.

A woman brought her a pastry and a cup of coffee. Justine tried to tell her that she really didn't have time to eat, that they were waiting for her at the writers' breakfast, but the woman suggested there was some problem with her car, or her driving, or it was too late for the breakfast. It was odd that she used that same careful voice as Danny. Justine ate the pastry and drank the coffee. She wiped the napkin across her mouth, and then along the metal cross-piece of the window where the dust was piling up.

She saw all things at once. Herself dusting the window frame, the people in the store who looked at her and then quickly away. Joe, lying in the rain on the east-bound lane of the bridge. Danny, speaking to her in that careful tone because he didn't think she could bear it. He didn't know how strong she was.

How lost Judy would feel when she had pulled up every living thing from the garden and transplanted it drawing by drawing onto the walls of the cottage. She, Justine, the just and mete creator, would write a role of endurance for Judy so she could dig up every plant, rip out every weed without pause, fury giving strength to her intention. Then she'd create the garden again, drawing it into herself. She'd need a good supply of pencils: 6Bs, 4Bs, 2Bs. After that she, the wounded one, would paint—the words of the story of the last good day and the day after would wind among the vines and bushes and flowering plants in the colors of the dying season: burnt sienna, alizarin crimson lake, brown ochre, burnt umber, the cadmiums; greens, orange, red, scarlet, yellow; carmine lake, Gamboge lake, golden Borak red, vermillion. No blues. She distrusted blue. Maybe she had time to stop at the art store on the way home. She pictured seduction in the form of rows and rows of color tubes.

The dust on the window frame caught her attention again and she wiped at it with her napkin. Car lights came out of the rain and shone directly into her. She waited for the impact with distant interest, but the car turned and stopped at the curb. Danny looked out the window. And Joe…Joe was coming around from the other side. She ran for the door.

"Joe, Joe, they told me you died! I thought I'd never see you again. I thought my last good day had passed me by."

Joe wrapped her in his arms. "Oh, Just," he murmured into her neck. He was trembling or maybe it was her. He didn't assure her that it would be okay, not this time.

PERFECT INSTINCTS

Vanessa Orlando

WHEN THE FIRST LETTER COME, TONY GET SO EXCITED he keeped reading it and reading it, looking for words to make him whoop and holler, but after he finish, he sit on the curb and shake his head. The second day another one come but he don't tear it open quite so fast. That time, he sit on the curb and treat the process with more respect. Like the letter were holy and if he make a ceremony of opening it, the words would be different than what they was. There was a two-day quiet stretch, and then two more letters come. Both start the same as the others. Dear Applicant. Dear Applicant.

Tony don't get many letters, but them two words tell him all he need to know. Otherwise, they would say, "Dear Tony Zitarelli" or "Dear Mr. Zitarelli" or "Dear Anthony." But Dear Applicant? Why they even bother? Why don't they just send a paper that say, "Dear Shit-for-Brains, fuck you."

Becca Carruthers were the last person to give up. "Soon as Tony find a ship, he gonna do some smooth sailing," she keeped saying. And to Tony, she might as well have stripped to her skin and fucked him silly for all it meaned to him. Of course, she done that four times already, and she done it a whole lot more times if you count boys other than Tony. Everybody in East Hedge know Becca Carruthers spend too much time behind Sabitini's Subs and Deli, giving away a little of this and more of that. But then the earth go off course or something because Becca Carruthers decide real sudden to turn into a good girl and hold out for a white picket fence and an apron that don't get dirty. She tell Tony she ain't going behind Sabitini's Subs and Deli with him no more until he get a job—a good job—and make an honest woman of her, with a new name and a fat shiny ring. "Buy me a cow," she say, "and I'll buy you the milk."

Of course, she don't say nothing about going behind

Sabitini's Subs and Deli with anyone else. (Ain't no reason to join a convent while Tony get respectable.)

Tony hear her clear and loud, but he don't believe she serious. No one do. Becca Carruthers been one color stripe too long to change into poked dots now, but then she really do start holding out on him. By the end of one full month, Tony got a bad ache and a stack of Dear Applicant letters bulging out of his top right pocket so bad that he look swollen and lumpy. By the end of the second month, Tony got enough of a lump in the left pocket to even things out. Each letter make him mad, of course, but he get maddest of all when Becca "Turncoat" Carruthers tell him that no hell from high water were going to stop the letters from flowing in like a river. Tony seen her more than once walking toward Sabitini's with Joey Martin, whose pop was a muckety-fuck with East Hedge Sand and Gravel. It weren't fair that Muckety-Fuck Junior got the best piece of ass in town handed to him on a lunch platter just because his old man got a regular job.

"Who will it be today, ladies and gentlemen? Harvard? Yale? Place your bet right here."

Coach Harrison were inside the teacher's lounge and kids ain't suppose to hear anything that happen in there, but the door were open a jar's worth, and that's all the space Misfortune need to run in muck.

"Guess the total number of schools rejecting the big kid by Friday, and the person who comes the closest without going over walks away with the jackpot, which is now up to six dollars," Coach say.

"Do you know that boy actually applied to Brown? Brown!" Mrs. Garth said. "I wonder if they even bother to open a letter from East Hedge."

"Of course they do, Marge," Mr. Frank said. "Even the serious-minded people at Brown need a laugh now and then."

"I'm in for seven schools," someone said.

"Shit. Okay, then, I'll say eight."

"I'll say sixteen."

"Sixteen? Holy God, no. I'll go with nine. It can't be higher than that. Can it?"

"That's all we have time for now, ladies and gentlemen," Coach say. "The jackpot's up to ten dollars."

"How did he afford all the application fees?"

"And the postage?"

"The paper it was written on?"

Tony hear the big mocking ha-has, which were bad enough, but then he hear something lots worse. He hear Henry Scott sniggering from the stairwell. Now, Henry Scott were slight and short and had a bully mouth, and everyone know (or ought to) that being mean, small, and stupid is a dangerous combination, especially in East Hedge.

"They're talking about you, asshole," Henry say. "They're betting your whole fucked up life stays all fucked up forever!" Henry start laughing and holding his side, like laughing make his ribs hurt. "They're betting on you, fuckhead," he say. "They're betting on you!"

"Shut up," Tony yell. "Shut up, you goddamn little fucker."

Stupid Henry Scott got even stupider and shove Tony against the wall. "You're such a loser," he said. "Even a whore like Becca Carruthers won't fuck you no more. You can't go much lower than that, can you, Loooser?"

What come next ain't a big surprise.

Tony's first punch turn Henry Scott's nose into a bloated mound of clay, and Henry were honest-to-glory surprised. "You broke my nose, you fucking freak!"

When Tony seen blood dripping down Henry's chin, it's like his whole black-and-white world got color. Shit, it got Technicolor. Tony think maybe he discovered blood and invented the broken nose, and he get a little proud of himself. And everyone know that being strong, mad and proud is a dangerous combination, too.

Tony walk forward so that Henry got to shuffle back until he hit the wall. At first Tony just jab him in the chest, but when Henry try running, Tony grab tight.

"Leave me alone!" Henry wipe his nose, and the back of his hand come away with a wet streak of Technicolor pink. He start to sniffle a little, and in East Hedge (and lots of other places too), there ain't nothing sweeter than watching a bully turn coward before your eyes.

Other boys prone to blood sporting appear out of nowhere, like ghosts. They got no allegiance to Tony or Henry. They just mean boys, looking for entertainment. Tony understand that he got the spotted light, and he start punching Henry like there's some kind of prize at stake.

"Give it to him harder for Christ sakes."

"Don't let him get away with that pansy shit."

"Kill the cocksucker."

Then Tony hear Becca Carruthers yelling. "Use your knuckles, baby. Hit his fucking head with your fucking knuckles!"

Tony aim his knuckles at Henry's forehead, then hears a crack, like a whip against stone. Henry start to groan and sway like he drunk enough to pass out, and Tony's feeling like Superman and God all rolled into one. His sad, black-and-white world is disappearing behind splashes of blood set to the music of a sweet-sounding whimper.

"Hit 'em in the kidneys. Make him hurt! Make him goddamn sorry!"

Tony don't know why Becca Carruthers got a bloodlust all of a sudden but if it make her happy, he's willing to punch all night and all day and into next year.

"Like this?" Tony yell. "You want it like this?"

Henry's head ping pongs between Tony's fists and the concrete wall.

Becca Carruthers starts shrieking and clutching her own hair and vibrating from nose to toe, like she being electrocuted or something. She start chanting, "Do it to him, daddy. Do it! Do it! Do it to him, daddy. Do it! Do it!" Tony's arms move like pistons, and Becca Carruthers start yelling "Yes, yes, yes," like she being fucked better than anyone got a right to be fucked, and to Tony it all seems like sweet Jesus delivered because ain't no one in East Hedge going to laugh at Tony Zitarelli again.

Well, of course, Coach Henderson and Mrs. Garth and Mr. Frank and all them grown-ups run out in time, and all of them are yelling, "Boys! Boys!" as if both boys was fighting, instead of just one.

To tell the truth, Coach Henderson were the only one in East Hedge big enough to duck one of them punches—or take one, but Coach don't do nothing. He watch like he's in a trance, like he don't got the responsibility to do a goddamn thing. He whispering to hisself: "Left jab, right uppercut, left hook. The kid's got perfect instincts."

Coach don't even notice that the stupid boy's eyes is all rolled up in his head and that it don't take no talent at all to keep beating a boy already beat.

Tony get so tired he stop to rest. That's when stupid Henry Scott finally go down—and everyone in East Hedge can tell the difference between a live body in a heap and a dead one, and there weren't no question which one Henry Scott was.

Tony were soaked with sweat from scalp to knee, and panting hard when Becca run up like she ain't seen him in twenty years and clamp her legs round his hips. He too tired to hold on, though, and they fall together next to stupid Henry Scott, and Becca laugh like it's the funniest thing ever happened on God's stinking earth.

Coach Henderson and Mrs. Garth pinch the stupid boy's neck and wrist with half a heart, and then they look at each other with that locked-eye way grown-ups have when they don't want to say "shit" out loud.

"You fucked him up, baby! You fucked him up good."

"Becca Carruthers!" Mrs. Garth yell.

"I love you, baby, I love you." Becca actually goes for his fly right there in front of all God's children, but Mrs. Garth grab her by the arm and her hair too.

"Fucking bitch!" Becca try to break free and show everyone her ass is bad enough to be with Tony, but Mrs. Garth done grown a steel claw and she don't let go even though Becca biting and pulling and swearing a streak of blue.

Tony look at Coach Henderson and laugh. Coach want to laugh, too, you can tell, but he don't. Instead, Coach let out a big sigh and grips Tony's arm, but he do it gentle like. With respect. "Come on, son," he say.

Coach and Mrs. Garth walk them lovebirds down the hall, but all anyone hear is Becca Carruthers, yelling, "Will you do it for me again, baby? Will you?"

Nobody hear what Tony say.

Nobody have to.

FAMILY RECIPE

Lynn Stearns

JUNIE KEATING USED THE FIRST BABYSITTING MONEY SHE EARNED watching the Walker kids on Saturday night to buy a box of brownie mix on her way home from school. At home, she smiled to herself as she found the measuring cup and baking pan, and removed two eggs from the carton in the refrigerator. Her little brothers were going to be happy to see brownies for dessert, and there would be enough left for their lunch bags tomorrow.

Junie hoped she'd be able to continue earning a little money and helping out like this in the future. The Walker kids weren't any trouble and their parents seemed impressed that she'd brought her own bag of things to entertain them with. All three kids had warmed up to her right away, wanting to see what was in the bag, which was the point. She pulled out the yarn, crayons, and white cardboard squares from her mother's pantyhose. She demonstrated how to peel the paper off the crayons and sweep them across the cardboard on their sides—red, then orange, then yellow—so the colors blended. They cut the colored cardboard into leaf shapes and taped them to pieces of yarn tied to a hanger to make a leaf mobile. The kids were really proud of their work, and when their parents came home, Mrs. Walker told Junie, "I can see you have a good natural instinct with children. We'll call you again next time we need a sitter."

Junie was standing there with the eggs in her hands, about to put them on a clean dish towel so they wouldn't roll off the counter, when the back door slammed shut. Her mother was home from work early.

Cynthia Keating plopped her purse down on the table and looked at the eggs, then at Junie. "What do you think you're doing?"

"I was going to bake brownies." Junie started to explain how she'd bought the mix with her own money, but stopped when her mother shut her eyes and pinched the top of her nose.

"Get out the big green mixing bowl and the wooden spoon, and make sure you have all the ingredients before you start." She shook her head. "The one day I get home early, and here you are, making a mess. I sure hope we have everything you need because I'm in no mood to go out in that traffic again."

When Junie read the directions on the box in the store, she remembered seeing oil in the cupboard and eggs in the refrigerator that morning. Water was the only other thing she needed.

Cynthia slipped out of her tweed suit jacket and handed it to Junie. "It's time for you to help out once in a while, young lady, instead of adding to my burden, but if you're determined to bake brownies, at least do it right." She flicked her hand at her jacket, draped across Junie's arm. "Hang that up so it won't wrinkle while I look for my mother's recipe."

When Junie returned from the hall closet, Cynthia had found the yellowed paper, stuck between a couple of pages in her Southern Style cookbook. As she studied it, she told Junie to turn the oven on to three-fifty. "We'll need the unsweetened chocolate, vanilla extract, and a stick of butter from the refrigerator." She nodded to a chair. "Pull that over here to stand on and get the new bag of sugar off the top shelf. We don't have enough left in the canister, and real brownies take real sugar."

While Junie was getting out the ingredients, her mother pointed to the red box Junie had bought at the store. "I hope you saved the receipt because we're not using some mix that's been sitting on a store shelf for who knows how long." She started opening and shutting drawers, looking for her wooden spoon. "A box mix indeed. I can't understand why you have so much trouble catching on to the way things are supposed to be done." She finally found the spoon and turned her attention to the recipe.

"Bring that flour over here. It's in the big canister, and the baking powder. Get in the habit of double-checking. Make sure you use baking powder, not baking soda. I'm not always going to be handy to see that you do it right." Cynthia picked up the thick bar of chocolate and broke off two squares.

Junie tried to figure out how to say she knew how to follow a recipe and could take it from there without it sounding like she was sassing, but before she could, her mother yanked open the drawer under the oven. The pots and pans clattered as she pulled out the small sauce pan she was looking for.

"If it's one thing I know," she said as she set the pan on the stove and turned on the burner, "it's that I'm doing my part as a parent. The problem is, you're thick-headed, June." She dropped the chocolate squares into the pan and leaned over to check the burner. "You were born looking for the easy way out, like Grandma Keating on your father's side, and that whole bunch."

Junie knew what was coming next and braced herself.

"You look like all of them, too, with those weak green eyes and that red hair. People have been telling me you don't look a thing like me since the day you were born. Like it's something I should be blamed for. Believe me, that hair isn't my fault."

She spooned flour into the plastic measuring cup and held it up to the light and tapped it to make sure she had exactly the right amount. "Everybody gave Grandma Keating credit for being a good cook." Cynthia poured the flour and sugar into the bowl, and the baking powder, then cracked the eggs into the measuring cup. "Just because she had four boys and they all grew up to be big and strong doesn't mean it was because she knew anything about anything. Most people aren't aware of all the short cuts she took."

Junie watched her mother make a well in the dry ingredients and dump the eggs in, and a few drops of vanilla.

Cynthia passed her the teaspoon to put in the sink. "If Grandma was standing in this kitchen right now, she'd probably swear there was nothing wrong with using a box mix, but I wasn't raised by any short-cut method, and I'm not about to raise my daughter that way." She turned off the stove, and moved the pan of melted chocolate to a back burner. "You want to melt it, not cook it."

Junie nodded, relieved that her mother's eyebrows had finally gone down, though not as relieved as she would have been if she'd started talking about something else, like what a pretty autumn they were having. The maple tree in the back yard was completely covered with bright orange leaves. It looked like a picture on a magazine cover.

Cynthia tapped her spoon against the bowl. "Stop daydreaming and put the rest of that chocolate away. After I stir this in, it'll be time for the nuts."

Junie wrapped the unsweetened chocolate and put it on the shelf in the refrigerator. When she closed the door, her mother was pouring the melted chocolate into the rest of the mixture. "Pay attention now. Most brownie recipes call for half a cup of chopped walnuts, but my mother used a whole cup of pecans. Southerners substitute pecans whenever possible. They're a better nut."

Cynthia lifted the silverware tray from the drawer and reached into the back for two packages of pecans. Without warning, she tossed them onto the counter and whacked them with the wooden spoon, then rocked it on the bags, pressing her weight down as she did. She used her teeth to tear open the ends of the bags, and shook the nuts into the green mixing bowl. "You won't find fresh pecans growing in New England, where Grandma Keating's people were from, way up in Rhode Island." Cynthia looked at Junie. "I'd like to know when you ever heard of any good role models coming from there."

Junie leaned into the counter and waited, knowing she wasn't really expected to respond.

"Your father and uncles brag about how the house was always full of music and laughter when they were growing up. Whenever people describe their childhood that way, it usually means the mother didn't take her responsibilities seriously. I was only at Grandma Keating's a couple of times before she moved into the rest home. It didn't look so bad then, but that was after her children were all grown and on their own."

Cynthia stopped folding in the nuts and stared at the wall under the top cupboard like she was watching a scene on TV. "I can see her now, that pasty skin and orange mop of a head. They say she'd play the piano and people sang and played charades late into the night."

Cynthia turned back to Junie. "People know how to cook and how to raise children right in the South." She shook the spoon to make her point and globs of chocolate-coated nuts dropped off into the bowl. "Children need structure. That's why we have a strict bedtime and other rules around here," she said. "Get a couple of paper towels and watch me grease and flour the pan. Anybody who'd use a box mix probably doesn't know how to prepare the pan properly, either." Her eyes bulged with the thought that suddenly occurred to her. "You'd better get your mind off joining chorus next semester. See if you can't sign up for a cooking class instead. Let somebody else try to teach you how things are supposed to be done since you don't seem to want to learn from your own mother."

While she was tilting the pan and thumping the loose flour off the sides, Cynthia said that someday Junie might get that red hair of hers tamed. "And if you can get into a decent college and make something of yourself, and if you're lucky enough to find a young man who wants you to settle down and have a family with him, you might even have a daughter."

She stared at Junie for a minute, making sure she had her attention. "That's a lot of ifs, but you never can tell. Anyway, if you do, she may ask you how to make brownies someday, and then you'll be glad you had the kind of mother you had, appreciate all I've done to raise you children right." She nodded to the recipe. "When you're older and have proven to me that you have your act together, I'll pass this on to you. By then maybe you'll understand that being a mother isn't about using instant this and instant that, just sitting around laughing and singing and playing games with your children."

Junie forced herself to keep quiet, just waiting for her mother to finish.

"Being a parent, especially a mother, is about setting an example, doing things the right way without looking for a short cut. My mother certainly didn't put up with any nonsense from us, and look at how we turned out."

Junie thought about her mother's brother, Uncle Jack. He had lost his house in a poker game. Cynthia's sister, Aunt Simone, had been married, and divorced, four times. She referred to herself as a single mother, her six poodles as her children.

Cynthia held the green bowl at an angle and used the wooden spoon to scrape the batter from the sides and bottom, into the pan. "Keep the pot holders handy, and don't think you're going to leave this kitchen before you clean up your mess." She slid the pan of dark batter into the oven and as Junie went to the sink to get the sponge, her mother rapped the spoon against the bowl so hard Junie jumped. When she caught her breath, she checked to see if the glass had cracked.

"What's wrong with you?" her mother asked. "Your mind has been drifting the whole time I've been talking to you. You'd better pay attention, young lady, or there's no telling what kind of mother you'll turn out to be. It's not too soon to start thinking about that, you know."

Junie had been thinking about it. "I'm paying attention," she said, and when her mother was setting the oven timer, Junie flipped her wild, red hair off her shoulders and smiled.

THE MAN WITH THE PATCHWORK SOUL

Sherri Cook Woosley

ANAL SEX. RUSS COULDN'T STOP THINKING ABOUT IT. It wasn't that he wanted it, or even didn't want it. The problem was that he had developed a fear about his rear sphincter and its involuntary penetration. After serious thought, Russ decided he wasn't homophobic—after all, it wasn't only penises he was afraid would get in. Anything phallic-shaped was suspect. Watching a nature program, the rhinoceros made Russ shudder with thoughts of someone accidentally backing up onto the horn. Last week when corn-on-the-cob had been served with dinner, Russ's heart had gone into palpitations. This morning Russ had discovered that he had a new mannerism. When he felt scared or intimidated, which was not uncommon, Russ's hands automatically crept around his lower back to form a physical blockade against imminent intrusion.

From this behavior it might be surmised that Russ had been raped or even spent time in jail, but this was not true at all. Russ rented the upstairs of a townhouse in Baltimore City and worked at a fairly typical job in a small- to mid-sized marketing company. At thirty-one years old, having worked there for two years, Russ was above the entry-level position but below anything meaningful. He was not the mail boy, but did sometimes have to deliver interoffice mail when said mail boy had quit for a better job, called in sick, or was otherwise not immediately available for his duties. Russ was nominally assigned to the accounting department, but not allowed to touch any reports or crunch any numbers. Instead, he was sent to track down invoices, make sure expense reports were signed by the proper authority, and make the phone calls that no one else wanted to make. Russ did not consider this a satisfying career.

On this particular summer day Russ was going to be late for work. He knew he was going to be late, but there was very little he could do about it. His car was dead, quite dead, and the only surprise was that it had lasted this long. The little hatchback had been breaking down repeatedly for the past three months. The last time had been on Calvert Street, over near the Walters Art Museum, right where it became one lane because of the parked cars in the other. The hill had been too much for the car and every time it got about halfway up the engine would cut out and a miserable Russ would sit inside the car as it rolled back down to start all over again.

Unsure what to do—there were parked cars on the left side, a statue on the right side, angry drivers behind, and an insurmountable hill in front—Russ had finally just sat in his car listening to the car horns, curses, and angry voices. These noises gradually faded out as Russ began to create an elaborate daydream in which he was Sisyphus serving his interminable sentence in Hades. Instead of pushing a stone up the hill, he was burdened by this car.

A tap on the window made him jump. Looking out, Russ saw an African-American man wearing a stylish cap and a brown leather jacket. Russ closed his eyes, but the man rapped on the window again. Sphincter tightening, Russ rolled down the window politely.

"You gonna move or what?" The man didn't yell; he just sounded curious.

"I can't go up the hill." Russ squeaked. He tapped at the side of his glasses.

"You already call some Triple A?"

"I don't have a cell phone." Russ wondered if he should add "sir." This man seemed used to commanding respect.

The man sucked his teeth while another black man got out of the car behind Russ. This one was huge and wore sunglasses with a t-shirt that tried to stretch around his girth.

Russ closed his eyes again. He knew he wouldn't be able to poop for a week.

The man spoke to Russ again. "You backing up traffic all the way, far as you can see. This tangle made the radio news. They talking about traffic back to 395. There's no place to go, only forward, but you are forward, and you aren't going."

When Russ didn't respond, the man in the cap walked over to his robust companion. Russ overheard snatches of their conversation: "…just going to sit there…that is some damn…" and "stupidest cracker I ever seen."

After this conference the first man came back to the car window, still not hurrying. "We going to push you up the hill. Put the car in neutral and get over soon as you get to that corner up there."

Russ thrust his thumb up as a sign of "okay." The man in the cap shook his head in what was presumably disgust. Before Russ could feel embarrassment, his neck snapped forward as the car behind him hit the hatchback's bumper. The corpulent fellow shouted out the passenger side window. "Get off the brake, you moron! Put it in neutral!"

Quickly Russ switched gears and sat while his car was pushed up the hill with no problem. The car behind kept driving straight while Russ was able to turn off Calvert at the circle by the statue. On a flat street now, the car rolled forward and Russ turned the car off. Cars, finally released from deadlock, flew past where Russ had pulled over. He lost count of how many times he got the finger. When the rush seemed over Russ turned the key and the over-worked engine sputtered to life even as a loud metallic clank came from the rear of the car. Getting out, Russ looked at the bumper, lying battered and beaten on the cobblestones like an unwanted girl-friend. Finally he scraped it up off the pavement and tossed it onto the backseat.

Since then Russ had avoided all hills and as many places without handy-dandy pull-off shoulders as possible. However, this morning the car wouldn't even start—it seemed to have chosen suicide rather than spend another day with Russ. That meant Russ could either call a cab to get to work or ride the old bicycle. He didn't have the money to take a cab, certainly not as the main method of getting to work every morning. The problem with the bike, and the one Russ had been wrestling with as the hands swept around the face of his watch, was the bicycle seat. The seat fit onto a hollow metal tube, part of the frame of the bike. The seat could be moved up or down depending on the rider's height, but this also meant that the seat could be entirely removed from the tube. What, wondered Russ, was to stop the seat from flying off if he went over a bump? In other words, what was to keep the bike from sodomizing Russ? Not having been able to come up with an acceptable answer, Russ stood by the bicycle, despondent about being late for work.

He might have stood there indefinitely if Mrs. Santos hadn't rounded the corner on her morning walk. Mrs. Santos was the nosy old woman who rented the top half of her house to Russ. He thought she was Latina, but age made it difficult for him to tell. She kept tabs on the entire block and could tell you not only the general "scoop," but also the more inane details of the residents' lives. Russ was pretty sure she went through his rooms when he wasn't there. Perhaps that was why Mrs. Santos didn't care for Russ and didn't bother to hide her feelings.

For his part, Russ felt uncomfortable around the small, crotchety woman and her rapidly deteriorating dog, Toto. Named for the canine that accompanied Dorothy to Oz, this dog also seemed like it was in another world, but that was probably due to doggie narcotics prescribed for its nervous condition, allergy to wheat products, deafness, blindness in one eye, and general old age. Clumps of hair that randomly fell from the creature proved very distressing to Russ; looking at the dog made him nauseous. Mrs. Santos and Toto had almost reached Russ and he shifted his weight, unnerved by potential caustic remarks from the one and realized bald patches on the other.

Avoidance, however, was not going to suffice today. Mrs. Santos was too concerned about her financial investment. "You're not going to work today?" A suspicious once-over accompanied her words.

"I'm going." Russ mumbled, blinking his small eyes. It was difficult to tell the color behind his coke-bottle glasses. Russ's constantly slumping shoulders and his hangdog expression made him appear like a human Eeyore. Unlike Milne's grey donkey, however, Russ was an unbaked dough color, even during the middle of summer.

Mrs. Santos made a point of looking at her watch. "You're late."

Toto was also looking at Russ suspiciously with his one good eye.

Russ pointed to where his bicycle leaned against the house—maneuvering it out of the crowded shed in Mrs. Santos's cramped backyard was as far as he'd gotten this morning. "I have to ride in this morning."

"Eh?" She hadn't heard him because he'd spoken too softly. Russ pointed again and repeated his statement in a louder voice, which caused Toto to erupt in a fit of barking. Mrs. Santos looked at the rusty blue three-speed with the chipped reflector over the rear tire. If she had any doubts about the bike's trustworthiness, she said nothing. After all, rent was due next week.

Instead she queried, "Well, why don't you go?" She answered her own question. "Young people have no work ethic. It's an absolute shame. Mr. Santos worked every day until his death, God rest his soul." She made the sign of the cross with a pious expression on her face.

Russ looked at the bicycle, then at the dog, barking madly at a dandelion growing out of a crack in the sidewalk, then at Mrs. Santos, who was giving the impression that she wouldn't leave until she'd seen her tenant off to work. With a feeling of dread, Russ gripped the handlebars of the bike and walked it a couple feet down the sidewalk. When he glanced over his shoulder, the old woman and dog were still fixing their three eyes on him. Closing his own eyes, Russ threw his leg over the frame, set the pedals, and launched away from his landlady and towards work.

Arrival at the complex of office buildings found the bicycle seat still intact, but Russ utterly defeated by the midmorning heat. Two blocks before the office building where Russ worked the back tire had been punctured by one of the many shards of glass that littered south Baltimore. Russ's legs had pumped, but to no avail. His glasses were fogged up and kept slipping down his nose. He walked his battered bike towards the building, sweat stains spreading out from his armpits like grotesque mushrooms. His face was pulsing, hot and red. Now that he was a pedestrian his situation seemed even worse because there was no breeze to cool down his body. His upper thighs, unused to the exercise, were already protesting emphatically. Close to the building's entrance Russ let the bike fall to the concrete. He hadn't brought a chain to lock it up, a change of clothes, or even a drink. Russ stumbled towards the nearest bench and sat down gratefully.

He must have dozed off because Russ woke up to the sound of feminine laughter. He blinked his eyes. The sweat on his face had dried and the mushrooms that sprang up on his shirt under his armpits were beginning to fade. Russ saw Ana and Kris, two women who worked at the marketing company with him. Ana had worked there for almost a year and Russ found her haughty and distant. Kris, the new girl, was entirely different. She was beautiful and kind, friendly and smart. Russ looked longingly at the young woman. She was sitting on the concrete wall, smiling as she kicked her feet.

The sun picked out red highlights whenever she moved her head. Ana was standing next to her, saying something while she smoked a pungent clove cigarette. Russ curled his mouth. Smoking was gross. Kris didn't smoke. Therefore, by Aristotelian logic, Kris was not gross. Russ snickered at his own joke. He wasn't sure if he was using the formula correctly—he'd only gone to the first day of the Logics and Relation class at junior college.

More giggling attracted Russ's attention and it finally dawned on him that this was the opportunity the book had been talking about, the book with the yellowing pages and ripped cover that he'd bought for fifty cents from the library book sale. His heart started knocking in his chest, an engine about to break in an old car, and Russ clasped his right hand over it, unconsciously striking a pose to recite the country's pledge. Instead of pledging, though, Russ adjusted his glasses and mentally reviewed Step Two from the book. Be Bold, he said in a mantra underneath his breath as he walked forward, approaching the women. Step One was to decide whether you wanted to sleep with the woman or have a relationship and sleep with her. Russ had decided that the relationship option was best so there wouldn't be any unpleasantness afterwards in the work environment. Besides, he'd never really had a girlfriend. This choice took him to Steps Three through Seven, while if he'd wanted just sex he would only have had to read Steps Eight through Ten. Still, Russ didn't mind the extra reading if it meant he and Kris could be together. Step Two, necessary for either course, was to Be Bold.

Standing within arm's reach of Ana and Kris, Russ stopped and cleared his throat. They continued their conversation and Russ reached up to readjust his glasses impatiently. It was Kris who finally looked at him with a smile.

"Hey, Russ. Was that you taking a cat nap over there?"

"Uhm. Yes."

She winked and said, "Don't worry. We won't tell." Kris turned back to Ana, "Should we…"

Ana nodded yes as she stubbed out her cigarette and threw the butt away.

They were leaving, Russ realized frantically. "Wait!" he burst out. He reached out and grabbed Kris's arm. Ana and Kris looked at him with surprise. Be Bold, Be Bold, Be Bold, Be Bold, Russ thought. The moment turned awkward and headed for uncomfortable. Signs for disastrous began appearing before Russ said lamely, "I wanted to talk to you for a second."

Ana and Kris exchanged a look, then Ana shrugged and went inside while Kris took her place on the wall. *Good*, thought Russ about Ana, *you get out of here.*

Kris asked, "What's up?"

Russ cast about for anything to say. "My car broke down and I had to ride my bike in to work today. That's why I fell asleep."

She looked sympathetic. She was so beautiful when she was sympathetic. "That sucks, Russ. Couldn't you have taken the bus?"

Russ swallowed. "That's really smart, Kris." There, that was good. Step Five: Give a Compliment. "I guess that's what you would have done, living over in Canton and all."

Kris's eyes narrowed. "How did you know where I live?"

"Oh." Russ waved his hand like he was swatting flies. "You must have mentioned it to me one time." He didn't want to tell her that he'd looked at and copied down the address on her paycheck. After all, being the office scut did allow access to certain personal information. He'd also typed her address into Mapquest to get directions. He wanted to be prepared for when, one day, she invited him over. Going to her house would be much better than trying to bring someone back to his place under Mrs. Santos's watchful eyes.

"You know what? I've got to get back to work."

Russ didn't notice the sudden coolness in Kris's tone; he was busy thinking about how long it would take before she invited him over. Ever the gentleman, Russ walked her all the way to her office, even though she was walking kind of fast. When she went inside he heard Ana say, "So what did Stinky want? Seriously, he smelled…" Abruptly her voice cut out.

Face flaming, Russ backed away from the doorway and went down the hall to his cubicle. He wondered what was wrong with him. It was like everyone had a script and he hadn't gotten one; like *Groundhog Day* where everyone else had already had a chance to try out the consequences and could now breeze through while he was stuck making the best choices he could on limited knowledge. If life was a choose-your-own-adventure-book, he was the only one in the world who couldn't flip ahead to peek. Russ put his head down on his desk and let lethargy creep over his body.

Maybe that was it.

He had a body like everyone else, but maybe there was something wrong with his soul. He hadn't read very much of Plato's discussion of souls—that was from another junior college class that only saw Russ once—but he did recall that Plato said something about souls being assigned before birth. Then, depending on your soul, you knew what your profession should be, and there was a whole hierarchy. Maybe he didn't even have a full soul. What if there had been a shortage and his soul was made up of all the scraps and leftover pieces from everyone else's soul?

Russ sat up straight. He was worse than Sisyphus with the rock; he was The Man with the Patchwork Soul.

Russ took off his glasses and laid them upside down on his desk so he could think about the ramifications of all this. If he was right, and he suspected he was, then he'd been playing this life all wrong. He shouldn't, and couldn't, be held to the same standards as the people who were lucky enough to have a whole soul. He was handicapped. There were obviously some vital things missing from his patchwork; that explained why he was always accused of not having common sense. That piece of fabric belonged to someone else; it wasn't in his scrap. Charm, bravery, knowing what to say: all missing from his patchwork soul. Russ slapped his hand on his desk with excitement. If he hadn't been born with a whole soul, then he didn't have to follow the rules, right? After all, how could you be held to the rules of a game when you didn't get the handbook that was passed out at the beginning?

Feeling better than he had in a long time, Russ decided he would go talk to Kris again. Russ had just stood up when he saw Jamie walking in his direction. Everyone liked Jamie; he was a gregarious and popular fellow. Russ did not usually elicit Jamie's attention, so it was with some surprise that he saw Jamie stop and lean against his desk, propping his hip against the corner.

"Hey, Russ."

"Hey." Russ looked around, anywhere but at Jamie.

"Just so you know, Mr. Stickler has been looking for you since this morning."

Russ looked at his watch. It was almost one thirty in the

afternoon and he hadn't even turned on his computer yet.

"Oops, there he is. I'll talk to you later." Jamie slipped around the other side of the cubicle.

Russ was cornered, watching as his boss came closer and closer. A stereotypical manager type, Mr. Stickler wore a white button-down shirt and fat tie that did nothing to hide his middle-aged spread. The remaining hair on his head had a tendency to fly up as the hours of the day passed, while his tongue periodically flicked out like a lizard's to wet dry lips.

"Russ, good afternoon. You are just the man I wanted to see. Have you been hiding all morning?"

Russ tried to smile despite a growing urge to vomit.

"Why don't we step into my office for a moment?"

Silently Russ followed Mr. Stickler into the corner office and watched while the door was shut behind them.

"Why don't you have a seat, Russ?"

When they were seated and looking at each other across a large oak desk, a strange expression came over Mr. Stickler's face. He swiveled around in his chair and opened the window. With a fake laugh, he said, "Why don't we just let a little fresh air in?"

Russ waited.

"So, Russ. How is it going?"

Russ felt like he was about to be violated—his sphincter was already on the alert. Russ squeezed his butt cheeks together and looked around the office. An attack of some sort was definitely imminent.

"Well. I know this might be a little surprising, but the company is having a bit of restructuring. Think of it as our way of trying to stay as efficient as possible in order to compete in today's marketplace. You understand what I'm saying, don't you?"

Russ's stomach certainly understood; it was now doing flipflops.

"The powers that be," and Mr. Stickler spread his hands palms up to show that he was not one of those powers, "just can't rationalize your position at this time. There were a lot of factors that were looked at and these very painful decisions must be made." After a pause he leaned forward. "It's nothing personal, but really, falling asleep right in front of the building after being hours late is a poor advertisement for the company's image."

Russ waited.

"Daryl is right outside the door waiting for you with a cardboard box. You will go to your desk to pack your personal items and we will mail the last check."

Russ stood up and left.

RUSS WALKED SLOWLY down the hallway with his box. There hadn't really been anything to pack—certainly not with Daryl's eagle eyes pinned on him the whole time. His access card had been taken away, he hadn't been allowed to turn on the computer and print any personal emails or take any disks. Apparently everything done on the company computer technically belonged to the company. Russ was glad that he'd printed out and taken home the Mapquest information about Kris the day he'd gotten it. He also had a picture he'd stolen off the wall in human resources from a holiday party. With a sigh, Russ headed for the door.

Suddenly it seemed as if the gods, as capriciously as they'd been treating their Sisyphus, had finally decided to help. Russ caught a glint of auburn hair disappearing into the Ladies Room. He set his box down against a wall and stood there indecisively. Then, he saw Daryl at the other end of the hallway and Russ's breathing quickened. Step Two echoed in his mind: Be Bold. He paused at the restroom door, his last chance to talk to Kris, but then kept going. Talking was well and good for guys like Jamie, but Russ had to plan every move carefully. Knowing where she was meant he knew where she was not.

Nonchalantly Russ walked past the exit doors and turned into the stairwell. He sprinted, a man on a mission. Slowing down at the top, he glanced around before going to the office that Ana and Kris shared. He stood at the threshold to the empty room, unsure what to do next. He wanted to find something in her desk, look at her pictures, listen to her voicemail. Anything that would let him know Kris better, give them something in common, something for him to think about. He moved forward and sat in her cushy black chair. He deliberately changed the setting by pulling the lever, wondering if she would notice when she came back.

He glanced at her email Inbox, but none of the subject lines seemed personal, so he began to rifle through her top drawer.

Lipstick, hand cream, paper clips and hard candy scattered about, yellow post-it notes, a highlighter…He picked up the lipstick and took off the cap. He examined the color, imagined Kris putting it on her lips.

"What the hell are you doing!" Ana stood in the doorway holding a steaming cup of coffee, fury written across her Mediterranean features.

Russ panicked, standing up into the open drawer, sitting back down, mouth agape. He stammered, he didn't know what to say, and then suddenly he was talking. "Kris is fired. Mr. Stickler sent me up here to clean out her desk."

Ana shook her head in disbelief, but Russ was focused behind her shoulder on Daryl. The security officer was coming, looking into every cubicle and office. Frightened, Russ lunged forward and around the desk to get away. Surprised, Ana screamed and instinctively threw her hands up, letting go of the coffee. Yelping as the hot liquid burned him, Russ pushed Ana to the side, windmilling his arms frantically to get to the stairwell. The heavy hand on his shoulder stopped all momentum.

Russ was turned around slowly to face Daryl. All was quiet as employees came from cubicles near and far to see the spectacle. Head down, coffee dripping, Russ still noticed that Kris had come at some point and had her arm around Ana.

"Let's go."

Daryl kept his hand on Russ all the way down the stairs and out of the building.

Behind him Russ heard Ana yell, "You dirty pervert! You sicko!"

That night Russ lay on his lumpy couch with a beer balanced on his stomach. He'd been in this position since he'd finally made it home. He didn't even have the energy to look at the picture he'd stolen of Kris, taped to the back of the directions and serving as a bookmark in his book about how to interact with women. Russ took another long swallow of beer. What a nightmare this day had been. He had no idea how he was going to pay rent, his car was kaput, and he hadn't made any headway with Kris. And, of course, he couldn't go back to the company even to visit because crazy Ana had labeled him a pervert. Remembering her shocked expression when he'd lunged at her made Russ start to smile. Ana's mouth had flown open when he knocked the self-righteous bitch against the wall. Soon he was laughing. Then something strange happened. As he thought about how he was the cause of Ana's surprise, and even fear, Russ's fear of anal sex began to recede from the foremost part of his mind. Instead, an unfamiliar feeling of power began to run through him.

He finished off the beer and went into the kitchen to get another one. Plopping back down on the couch Russ opened the can and drank deeply. Then something else began to happen, something that hadn't happened in a very long time. As his fear of penetration metamorphosized into a fantasy of his being the cause of fear, there was a stirring down the left side of his pants leg. Russ unzipped his pants and stared in amazement at the beginning of an erection. With one hand around his erection and one hand around his beer, Russ laid back against the cushions of the couch. Shaking his head at the wonder of it all, Russ raised the can into the air. "To the Man with the Patchwork Soul," he solemnly intoned.

Then, curious, Russ stood, shedding his clothes and walking to the mirror in the bathroom. He turned this way and that, proud of his erection, mesmerized by its masculine power. Suddenly, a knock at the door made him jump, scrambling to grab a threadbare towel to cover his shrinking genitals, shutting the bathroom door automatically, and then opening it again to call out through the empty apartment, "Who is it?"

"It's Mrs. Santos. I didn't see your bike out front. I didn't know where you were."

"I'm right here, Mrs. Santos, please go away now."

"What's going on in there? Is someone else in there? I'm coming in."

"No!" Russ closed the bathroom door, trapped inside, listening for the key in the lock.

"Are you doing drugs?"

"I'm not doing drugs, Mrs. Santos! Please go away."

Instead there was the turn of a knob. Fear welled up inside Russ. "Mrs. Santos. Do. Not. Come. In. Here."

He slid down against the bathroom door as he imagined the old woman and her deformed dog probing his apartment with their terrible three eyes.

Finally Russ heard the door shut and footsteps descending the stairway. When he removed the towel and looked down, his tree had become an acorn. He jumped to his feet, face flushing, and ripped open the bathroom door, charging across the floor to the main door and yanking it open to stand naked at the top. "You dirty pervert!" the Man with the Patchwork Soul yelled down the stairs.

All the anger drained away as Russ closed the door, locking the flimsy deadbolt. His beer still sat on the scratched coffee table; his clothes were still piled on the floor. Russ shuffled back to the bathroom to get the threadbare towel, laying it across his lap as he sank back into the couch, reaching for his drink. Outside the sounds of a city evening were faint: car doors slamming, people calling, music from the restaurant around the corner. Russ once again reached, this time for the library book, and opened it to where Kris's picture served as a bookmark. He began reading, not concerned that he was starting in the middle because he'd read it so many times before, but knowing there must be something he'd missed.

The Dryad

Angela Render

A BIRD TWITTERED HAPPILY AS A STIFF, COOL BREEZE BLEW ACROSS *the rushing, rain-swollen river. Fresh earth and damp leaves smelled sweet after a cleansing rain. The sorrel gleamed under the lush canopy of the ancient trees. Debbie passed a grandmother redwood, the ancient's trunk emblazoned by an old lightning strike. Grandmother redwood's children ringed her roots in a lovely, complete fairy ring.*

Debbie's companion giggled from up ahead. "Come on."

Debbie lengthened her stride, enjoying the way her doeskin leggings swished with her stride. Her long, dark braids clattered softly as the wooden beads and shells shifted around her shoulders.

Debbie rounded an old auntie redwood and reached her favorite fishing spot. The rocky bank was no more than a sliver this morning, grudgingly permitted to show itself by the raging waters. Debbie set her hand-woven basket on the trail and stepped carefully over the edge of the bank to the rocks below. Her foot slipped.

Icy water gripped her like a giant fist chilling her instantly—shocking muscles to immobility.

"Etta!" her companion's scream pierced her ears just before the angry river sucked her under. Debbie forced her chilled muscles to work. She kicked and struggled against the river's fury. Around she swirled, over and under and down. The water pressed tighter and tighter against her chest—constricting…choking…

Debbie woke with a gasp. One breath. Two. She fumbled for the light as she concentrated on the simple act of breathing. Her heart pounded even as the familiar smells of her room helped clear the dream haze—new carpet, latex paint…a bit of fabric softener. Her room was exactly as she'd left it. Her old wooden desk was piled with clean, unfolded clothing as was the comfortable armchair. Suitcases and out-of-season clothes threatened to explode from the inadequate closet. The industrial bedside lamp warmly illuminated the bare, freshly painted taupe walls.

Debbie's skin still felt chilled from the dream—clammy—and her chest felt as if a tight band were wrapped around it. She rubbed her face and shook out her sandy-blonde hair. Every night since she'd been here, the same dream. She had no memory of any aquatic trauma and she was certain she'd never fallen in one of the rivers around here. The place details from the dream could be from nowhere else—the redwoods, the river with its water-polished agates were all uniquely Pacific north coast.

Debbie lay back against the pillows and settled the rose comforter around her bare shoulders. It got cold here at night, even in summer. As she composed herself for sleep, she knew it wouldn't come easily. The dream was just too real.

Maybe it was a metaphor for feeling smothered, prompted by her parents' recent split. Or maybe for feeling lost in this middle-of-nowhere refuge her mother had moved to. Ellen, her mother, had moved to the aptly-named "Lost Coast" only three months before. Debbie had joined her last week, on summer vacation from UCLA. Since then, they'd walked among the giant redwoods only twice. Instead, they'd both been working with break-neck industry to renovate Ellen's dilapidated Victorian home.

Debbie was at school when she received word that her parents were splitting up. She wasn't surprised by the news, but it still hurt. Then her mother called her to excitedly announce that she'd bought an old Victorian in northern California to "rescue."

"In San Francisco?" she'd asked.

"Ferndale."

"Napa Valley?"

"Six hours north of San Francisco," Ellen patiently explained.

Debbie was certain the divorce had driven her mom crazy.

When Debbie drove up the windy two-lane "highway" that was the only road into Humboldt County, she'd begun to see the appeal—especially after she touched her first redwood.

Then she saw the house. Surrounded by a quarter-acre of waist-high weeds, the little house peeked over the tops of some bushes growing around its foundation. After triple-checking the address, she reluctantly got out of the car and carefully picked her way across the front lawn—eyes wide and alert for slithering entities. She reached the porch steps without incident and looked up and up and up. The house loomed over her, much bigger than it had appeared from the road. Its scale had been completely lost to the overgrown vegetation around its perimeter. Bushes shouldn't grow tree-sized. Even the bright white blooms from the lilies looked her in the eye. Paint, yellow-grey with age, peeled away from the grey, sun-damaged Victorian gingerbread details.

The place was creepy enough to shoot a horror film in. Debbie felt the hair on the back of her neck stand up. She reached out to knock on the door. She jumped as the door flew open and her mother squealed a happy greeting. Then Debbie was wrapped in Ellen's wiry, crushing embrace. Bleached-blonde hair was hidden under a scarf and her mother's athletic body was buried under a baggy T-shirt and ripped jeans. Blue, almost-grey eyes snapped with warmth as Ellen ushered her inside.

Her mom had happily shown her only child around her mid-life crisis, expounding on the original detail and charm of the aging house. The second story bore evidence of Ellen's efficient labor in the form of two finished bedrooms.

Debbie must have fallen asleep again during her ruminations because she woke suddenly to another dismal grey morning. At first the misty days had been sort of a nice change from L.A., but only a week later, they were just cold and depressing. With a groan, she turned over and pulled the comforter over her head. The scent of strong coffee cut through the odors of renovation and stabbed into her brain. Annoyed, but aware that she wouldn't be falling back to sleep, Debbie dragged herself out of bed and donned her rattiest jeans and sweatshirt in preparation for another day of grime, dry-rot, and bent nails.

"Did you sleep okay, sweetie?" Ellen asked over the rim of her favorite kitty cat coffee mug.

"Coffee," Debbie answered and shuffled towards the elixir of consciousness, this time remembering to step over the jagged edge of the half-ripped up vinyl tile and sub-floors one and two. She dazedly prepared her drink and made her way to the table. She forgot about the floor, snagged the toe of her sneaker and nearly dumped the contents of her mug onto her mother.

"Shall we finish the demo on that today?" Ellen asked

brightly as Debbie made it to the safety of the breakfast table and perched on a stool.

Blasted morning people! Debbie thought irritably.

She helped herself to the English muffins there and shook her head. "I want a shower."

Ellen laughed and nodded. "That would be a nice change," she agreed.

There were two bathrooms in the house, but one was so disgusting as to be unusable and the other had only a tub.

They finished breakfast and made their way to the bathroom in question. The room itself looked as if someone had slammed it into the back of the building—sort of an in-house outhouse. Garbed in heavy gloves, masks, and goggles, the two started ripping down the mildew-soaked drywall. Four hours later, Ellen dropped her pry bar, affectionately named "old blue," onto the floor and declared, "It's dry rotted. Whole thing's got to come off."

Debbie straightened up and nodded agreement. The pine addition had even started to rot the redwood original wall where the timbers joined. "Reciprocating saw?" Debbie asked, partially eager, partially dreading using the unfamiliar tool.

"Looks like," Ellen agreed. Debbie detected an uneasiness in her mother. The saw in question remained in its box, untouched since its purchase months ago.

"I'll get it," Debbie volunteered. "Maybe you can fix lunch?"

"Sure can," Ellen agreed a little too readily.

Dread crept into Debbie's heart as she unwrapped the saw and fit a blade into the aperture with hands that trembled. A lump lodged in her throat. The hair on the back of her neck rose. She shuddered.

This was silly. She'd used power tools before and she was twenty-nine years old for Pete's sake! Resolutely, she hefted the tool.

She bent and plugged in the saw, then froze, heart pounding. She looked down. Instead of the small, blue saw, she held a huge, two-handled hand-saw that stretched across the room. Its jagged blade was sharp and chipped. Shavings of blood-red wood clung to its cold teeth. As she watched, listening to the rapid thud of her heart in her ears, a flake dropped from the edge and fluttered to land on the floor with a wet splat. Fear clawed at her throat, but she stood, paralyzed and unable to look away.

Heart pounding in her chest, she forced her frozen muscles to move. Debbie shook as she bent to examine the drop of blood on the floor.

Then it was gone.

Debbie blinked rabidly as she felt around the place the blood had been. Nothing. She looked at the now innocent-looking tool in her hand, its small, clean blade. No woodchips. No blood. She wiped the cold sweat from her forehead with her sleeve. It had been so real. As she calmed herself down, common sense reasserted itself. This was not a Victorian logging saw and she was not going to cut her leg off. What she was going to do was carve out the decay on this house like a dentist would to a diseased tooth.

Annoyed with herself for being afraid of a stupid saw, she stomped toward the bathroom. She turned on the saw. Nothing happened.

"What now?" she growled, frustration restoring some of her shaken wits.

She turned it off and traipsed back only to find the saw unplugged from the extension cord. Hadn't she plugged that in? She must be more tired than she thought. She shrugged and tied the cables into a half-knot before plugging in the saw again. That should hold it. She flipped the switch and the blade blazed to life. She turned it off and walked toward the bathroom. Every step became harder to take as fear filled her again. "Stupid," she chastised herself as she entered the room, but the feeling only got more intense. Sweat broke out on her face and arms. She flipped the switch. Nothing happened. Vexed, she stopped short of slamming the tool to the floor. She went back to check the connections only to find the extension cord plug lying on the floor below the outlet. Debbie looked at the cord. Its length lay in loose coils across the floor—too loose for her to have jerked it out of the wall.

"I'm tired. That's all," Debbie told herself, stripping off her gloves and throwing them to the floor. She rubbed her arms vigorously as a chill crept down her spine. She headed for the kitchen. A rare shaft of sunlight shone innocently through the large windows, burning off much of her apprehension. Still, this place was getting to her.

"I didn't hear much cutting," Ellen commented as Debbie grabbed a soda from the refrigerator.

Debbie popped the tab and sat down at the table. "Too hungry," she lied.

"You look tired," her mother observed as she brought over two turkey sandwiches and sat down.

"Nightmares," Debbie commented and took a bite of the sandwich. Her mom knew just how she liked them.

"What kind?" Ellen asked, leaning forward, suddenly serious.

"Drowning," Debbie said after a long drink of her soda. "Mom, this house gives me the creeps."

Ellen studied her a long moment before she put her sandwich down and said, "Me, too."

Debbie wasn't sure how long she stared at her mother before she blinked and asked, "Really?" She'd expected her to be offended.

Ellen nodded. "At first I thought it was because I was alone in a big house for the first time in twenty years, or because of that creepy guy at the hardware store who remembers every project I've ever started and asks about it. Then you came and I don't feel any different." Her mother sighed. "I keep dreaming that I'm a girl who slips into a cold river and drowns. Every night."

"Now you're weirding me out," Debbie interrupted. "You're not supposed to have my nightmare."

"Then there's the disappearing hand saws and garden tools, and my power tools keep breaking—when I can bring myself to use them, that is. That circular saw is the fourth. Thank god for warranties."

Debbie thought about the boy they'd hired to cut their grass. He'd broken his mower and never returned to finish the job. "Mom, do you think a house can want not to be renovated?" Debbie asked and immediately felt stupid for saying it.

Ellen let out a nervous laugh. "Three months ago, I'd have said that was ridiculous. Now I'm not so sure." Ellen took a long drink of her diet soda. "Still, I have a lot invested in this house. I have to finish the repairs before I can sell it and I can't afford to hire someone else to do it."

"So we'll just finish as fast as we can," Debbie stated with more confidence than she felt.

Ellen nodded and they ate quickly. After lunch they approached the bathroom together.

"All right," Debbie began, swallowing against the sudden

dryness in her mouth. "I'll saw. You watch the plugs."

"Okay," Ellen agreed.

Debbie donned her protective gloves and goggles with hands that shook. She willed her inexplicable nervousness away as she picked up the saw and entered the bathroom. Her steps were slow and resolute as if she were prisoner walking to her own execution. She flipped the switch and the tool roared to life. Debbie cut into the first beam.

Searing pain lanced across her ankles. Debbie opened her mouth to scream, but the sound caught woodenly in her throat. Images flashed through her mind and then she felt herself...

...*growing tall—strong. Debbie felt her arms stretch through the clouds as cool mist clung to her fingers and hair. She was majesty! She was life! Worms and insects tickled her toes where they stretched deep into the soft earth. Life flowed into her and she stretched her feet deeper. She tilted her face to the sun. Cold wind ruffled her hair and kissed her face, bringing the scent of the sea to her. Surrounded by her children, she delighted in the moment.*

Chop, chop, chop.

The screech of her firstborn vibrated through the ground like an unnatural earth tremor.

Zip-saw, zip-saw, zip-saw, chop, chop, chop.

Her daughter's screams tore through her. Unable to move, she was rooted to the earth, paralyzed and helpless to stop it.

Chop, CHOP! CHOP! CHOP!

Silence.

A sudden, hideous silence.

Then a long creak split the air, punctuated by the shrieks of her children as her firstborn fell and hit the ground with a sickening, snapping crash. For a moment, the earth shook; then there was silence again. Debbie's heart ached.

Something cut into her trunk. Again and again, the blows fell on her. Chipping away. Cutting, blazing, searing....

With a shriek of pure terror and pain, Debbie dropped the saw and fled. Only when she was safely outside where the bright sun could bake its way through her panic-hazed mind did she realize that her mother was outside with her. Ellen's blue eyes were wide with fright, her face streaked with tears. Debbie watched as a fresh tear trailed down her mother's cheek and dropped to the ground. Somehow, seeing unflappable Ellen this way was almost worse than the fright she'd just experienced. Mothers were supposed to be strong and collected and comforting. Debbie wrapped her arms around the trembling woman.

Ellen returned the embrace with crushing urgency. "My baby. Oh, my baby," she murmured. "I thought I'd lost you."

Debbie held her mother until the tears eased, then pushed away. "Come on," she said and turned to walk down the sidewalk.

"Where?" Ellen asked as she followed.

"Away from here." Debbie couldn't help the nervous laugh that escaped her.

They walked down the block, hand-in-hand, just like they did when Debbie was little. The contact was comforting.

"To think I always dreamed of fixing up an old house," Ellen sighed. "What am I going to do?"

"What? Twenty years of *This Old House* and Bob Villa and no tips for renovating a haunted house?" Debbie joked, suddenly feeling really silly. The day was lovely with a clear, blue sky and a bright warm sun. Out here, everything was perfectly normal.

Ellen laughed. "Maybe I should write in," she replied, giving Debbie's hand a squeeze.

They walked further, admiring the fully-restored Victorian homes in all their splendor. "You know, when I first looked at that house, I imagined it like one of these. A stately painted lady. Now I know why no one beat me to it."

An ancient man sat in a rocker on the porch of one especially elegant house. Its rounded turrets were covered in diamond shaped shingles and its intricate woodwork was painted in shades of green, red and gold. Debbie smiled at him pleasantly—reflexively.

"I see Etta finally put her foot down," he commented in a wheezy voice.

"Etta?" Debbie and Ellen demanded, stopping to stare at the man.

"Your dryad," he elaborated. He studied them a moment and broke into a rasping laugh that Debbie imagined might just be the end of him. "You didn't honestly think," wheeze, gasp, "You're the first people to," pant, cough, "run from that house screaming, do you?"

Debbie and Ellen exchanged stunned looks before Ellen finally found her tongue. "You knew about that thing and you didn't warn me?" she demanded.

He pointed a gnarled finger at her and said, "You wouldn't have believed me."

That stopped Ellen cold. He was right. They wouldn't have. "But I thought a dryad was supposed to be a helpful wood spirit," Debbie said, wracking her brain to try and recall anything she'd read on the subject.

"A spirit bonded to a specific tree," he corrected. His pale, creased face was dotted with age spots and his sparse, white hair fluttered in the light breeze. He waved his hand dismissively. "Now mind, this is what I've managed to piece together from talks with the previous owners and visits with the local native tribes, but I think Etta is the spirit of a Wiyot girl who drowned and was buried according to local custom, which was to plant a redwood sapling over the grave." He paused as a coughing fit took him. He drank a few sips from a water glass on the table nearby and went on. "The tribe would then perform some sort of ritual, inviting the spirit to inhabit the tree and live on. Redwoods can live a thousand years. That's virtual immortality. Unless a logger clear-cuts you, that is."

"So you're saying Etta's spirit didn't die with the tree?" Debbie asked dubiously. "She's haunting the house?"

"I'm saying she *is* the house," he paused with a significant look at each of them. "All these old redwood houses have a certain spirit to them, but yours is the only one that ever objected to a few changes."

"So what do we do?" Ellen asked. "Doesn't she realize that the house...it...she...is falling down?"

The man shrugged. "I suggest that you find a way to reassure her."

"Like what? Plant a tree?" demanded Debbie facetiously. Her reflexive laugh caught in her throat. That didn't sound half bad.

"Why not?" said Ellen, suddenly brightening. "The exterior needs work too and won't require power tools so much. Maybe an old fashioned hand grass cutter?" Nothing ever did keep Ellen down for long. Her cheerful enthusiasm could be annoying sometimes, but right now it was exactly what Debbie needed.

"Okay," Debbie agreed, letting her mother's eternal optimism and the rare dose of sunlight infect her.

They made their way back to the house. It all seemed so perfectly normal that Debbie again felt stupid. Slowly, they mounted the steps to the porch. The house loomed impossibly large over them and Debbie felt icy fingers tickle the back of her neck. Debbie and Ellen exchanged glances, then turned around and headed to Ellen's pick-up truck. A peace offering was definitely in order.

Two hours later, they returned from the local nursery, overwhelmed and excited by the variety and laden with a full load of plants. As one, they each picked up potted ferns. Ellen led the way toward the house.

As they approached, her mother slowed and held the hanging baskets of foliage aloft and called, "Etta?"

Debbie felt a laugh catch in her throat. Her mother was talking to the house? Then she remembered the terror of the vision she'd had and sobered abruptly.

"Etta, we brought you something," Ellen said and crept up the front steps. "We really don't mean you any harm, Etta. We want to help you."

As Ellen entered the house, Debbie mounted the steps and displayed her plants. "We want to take care of you, Etta," Debbie found herself saying. Strangely, it felt exactly right to speak to the house like this. While Debbie felt uneasy entering the house, she was no longer afraid.

Ellen set the plants down on the floor and straightened up. "We can hang these tonight. Let's get the rest unloaded from the truck."

Debbie nodded and followed her mother's example.

The next morning started abruptly and drizzly on the heels of another nightmare. Apparently Etta wasn't quite ready to trust them. They decided to brave the misting rain and work on getting the new plants into the ground.

"At least we won't have to water them in," Ellen commented.

Debbie didn't mind her mother's glass-half-full attitude so much this morning. In fact, the work was pleasantly cheery in a drippy sort of way, fun in a way Debbie hadn't experienced since she was small and mud pies were culinary delights. They both found themselves carrying on a three-way conversation with Etta and it didn't feel at all silly. In fact, Etta seemed to have a sense of humor and a definite opinion as to where the plants should go—the three redwood saplings in particular. They'd bought three because they weren't sure which kind of redwood Etta had been, so they got one of each.

The redwoods were the first things in the ground. The coast and dawn redwoods went in the back yard, while the giant sequoia was planted in front. They worked steadily, planting a border in the front yard and around the sapling, then moved to the back.

Late in the afternoon, Debbie stretched her aching muscles as she walked around the house to collect the last two flats of flowers. The hand grass-cutter had managed the weeds better than its gas-powered counterpart. The yard was going to look fantastic. She ducked past an overgrown holly bush. "Etta, do you think we can cut back these bushes?" Debbie asked. "We need to put a new coat of paint…umm, bark, on you and they're in the way. Not to mention their roots are undermining your foundation. I mean your roots." When Debbie felt a little uneasy, she continued, "I thought we might replace them with antique rose bushes." Debbie imagined a skirt of pink flowers ringing the house. "All those pretty…."

Debbie trailed off, noticing a group of teens hanging around on the sidewalk in front of the house. One boy rode a mountain bike much too small for him in lazy circles in the street. Muddy mountain bikes lay on their sides on the sidewalk and in her new planting beds.

Dressed in an array of scruffy, teen-aged fashions, they traipsed through all Ellen and Debbie's hard work with absent-minded negligence. But what set Debbie's temper on fire was the tall, dark-haired young man leaning indolently against the redwood sapling, heedless that the tiny tree was bending dangerously under his weight. Righteous indignation flooded Debbie's system.

"Hey!" Debbie shouted and rushed over to defend her plants. "What the fuck do you think you're doing? Get out of here!"

The boys stopped chatting and looked at her. The two standing in her pansies jumped onto the sidewalk with murmured apologies, but the dark-haired one straightened up, squared his shoulders and crossed his arms over his chest, trampling still more of her plants as he did. Debbie strode right up to him, fury flushing her face hot. He frowned down at her and that was when Debbie realized that, while younger than her, he was a head and shoulders taller and no lightweight in build.

"It's a public sidewalk," he sneered.

Her temper cooled and a little fear bit at her. She pressed on, "That is not a public tree and those aren't public flowers. Get the fuck off my property."

He took a menacing step toward her, "Make me."

Debbie stood her ground, but felt her heart lodge in her throat as fear pulled at her like a riptide. He was going to fight her over this? He'd kick her ass in a second. Where were all the garden tools? Why hadn't she brought her shovel with her?

As she stared him down, she felt the wind suddenly pick up. She heard it gust and saw two of the boys stagger. Her attacker's plaid flannel shirt whipped around him and he had to step back, though Debbie felt only a light touch of the wind and the sapling's flat, soft, coniferous leaves barely rustled. The wind gusted again and bike boy was knocked over. The other boys clutched their jackets as they were pushed back and away from Debbie.

Her attacker grunted as an invisible force slammed into him. He staggered away from Debbie. His mouth made an "O" and his eyes were wide. Debbie's hair barely ruffled.

"My ankle! My ankle!" screamed one of the boys, hopping from foot to foot as he tried to clutch first one then the other of his legs to him.

The dark-haired attacker's face drained of color and his eyes bugged out. His hand clutched his chest as he let out a shuddering gasp. His eyes were brown, Debbie noticed as sheer terror filled their dark depths. He let out a ragged scream and backed away from her. As soon as his feet hit the pavement, his body sagged, nearly collapsing to the ground. Another gust of wind and the boys fumbled for their bikes and half-ran half-rode away, their frightened screams carried back to Debbie on the dying breeze.

Debbie blinked, then a smile crept across her face. "Thanks, Etta," she said and then bent to examine the damage done to her plants.

DEBBIE STUFFED THE last suitcase into her car and paused to look back at the house. She felt a swelling of pride at what she and her mother had been able to accomplish over the summer. The exterior had been sanded, primed, and painted in shades of gold, white, tan, and green. The overgrown bushes were long gone and replaced with antique roses. The spindly twigs were festooned with pink flowers. They'd grow in thick and beautiful. Bedding plants lined the front walk and sidewalk and ringed the sequoia. Every plant grew strong, lush, and beautiful.

After the back-breaking job they'd done on the landscaping, both Debbie and her mother felt more comfortable in the house. The country kitchen was now a completed eat-in gourmet. After the kitchen, they'd tackled some of the dry-rot issues and hadn't felt more than a twinge from Etta.

As Debbie gazed at the house and grounds, Ellen came out the front door to see her off. Her mother looked trim and radiant as she approached and gave Debbie a fierce hug. "You're coming back for winter break?" she asked.

"You bet," Debbie replied, returning the hug. Debbie thought she'd never felt closer to her mother. "I still need to try out that shower."

"I'll have the tiling done well before then," Ellen promised.

Debbie pulled away and wiped a tear from her mother's cheek. "I'll drive safely and call when I get in," she promised, pre-empting her mother's parting words.

Ellen closed her mouth and laughed. "You better!"

"Good-bye, Etta!" Debbie called to the house. "See you in a couple of months!" She had a smile on her face as she got into her car and drove away. She felt a pang as the house grew small in the rearview mirror, but she was already planning how they'd refresh the faux-finishing on the grand staircase when next she visited. She'd miss the dreams, though. Etta sent nightly visions of peaceful trees swaying with the ever-present breeze, frond fingers stretched out in the warm sun. Debbie enjoyed dropping off to sleep with the gentle sound of a rushing river in her ears.

She couldn't wait to come back home to her mother's haunted house.

CHICKEN NECKING

Jennie L. Deitz

FINALLY, SOLITUDE.

A blue heron quietly swooped by, arching its large, powerful wings and trailing its long, stick legs behind it as Gwyn Smyth felt the muscles start to relax in the back of her neck. The end of the family pier on Broadwater Creek seemed to be the perfect place to sort through her emotions and work things out. A familiar place next to the water to help her regain a sense of balance, maybe even a new perspective on things.

The bright green reeds next to the pier rattled as the evening breeze picked up. Gwyn stretched her short legs out further so she could graze the surface of the cool water with her toes. Her eyes followed the heron's graceful flight. She wished she was flying alongside of it; she yearned for the feeling of being free, to go wherever she wished. Her fast-paced life as a journalist in the Windy City didn't seem appealing to her anymore.

It had been a really tough week; her emotions were raw and closer to the surface than they had been in a very long time She had always felt in control of her world, but her father's sudden death had left her unfocused. An only child, Gwyn didn't have any other siblings to lean on. She only had her cousin, Tim Cooper, who still lived in the small fishing village of Belle Haven. It was at the end of this very pier that she and Tim had spent their youthful summer evenings tying chicken necks to weighted ropes, dropping them into the water and netting a few more crabs to add to her father's catch for dinner.

Gwyn could think back, but it was difficult for her to think past today. Her job at the *Chicago Tribune* was not only states away, but worlds away. Her Blackberry, personal cell phone, pager, laptop, and digital recorder were back in the house and all turned off. She had even left her watch behind on the kitchen table.

It was the viewing at the funeral parlor that had really taken its toll on her. Seeing her father lying in that casket left her feeling empty and more alone than ever before. His craggy, weather-beaten face was painted up in sheer pinks, like one of her mother's water-color paintings of summer evenings on the Chesapeake Bay. It just didn't look like him. "And wasn't that the reason to have an open casket viewing in the first place?" she wondered. It was difficult to say good-bye to someone who wasn't recognizable.

Gwyn stood by the guest register to greet people as her father's friends filed by to express their condolences. Some of the individuals were still familiar to her. However, her visits home had become less and less frequent over the years. She had become a stranger, an outsider in her own home town.

As the room filled to near capacity, she began to feel claustrophobic. She just wanted to get out and go somewhere. Away from the corpse that didn't look like her father and away from all of these kind, well-meaning people. More importantly, away from all of the emotion pent up inside of her. She was relieved to see her cousin Tim come in the door and head straight for her.

"Gwyn, I'm sorry about your father," he said, looking down at her tired, pale face. He glanced over to the nearby casket and quickly turned his watery blue eyes back to her. He bit his lower lip, a nervous habit he'd always had growing up together on the creek.

Still dressed in his Department of Natural Resources Police uniform, Tim bent down to give her a big bear hug. He smelled of diesel, sweat, and faint cologne. He looked the same after all of these years, except for a little grey in his dark, wavy hair.

"Thanks Tim. Thanks for being here. It really means a lot to me," she said trying to stay composed in the crowded room. Gwyn had always looked up to Tim as a big brother. Faded recollections of their time growing up in this small water town came rushing back to her.

Summer days were spent together with her father on Waterbug, his draketail workboat, checking crab traps in the Chesapeake Bay, or in an old canoe exploring the marshy backwaters of Broadwater Creek. Summer nights were spent together catching fireflies and depositing their luminescent gems in an old Mason jar before setting them free the next morning, or sitting on the screened-in back porch and listening to her father's stories about the pirates who used to hide out in the Chesapeake Bay between raids on Europe-bound, Spanish ships laden with gold and other treasures from South America.

When school was in session, the cousins spent time on fair weather weekends with her father: harvesting oysters in the fall; fishing for striped bass and perch in the winter; and catching eels, catfish and early perch in the spring. When she and Tim weren't on the water, they would sometimes watch her mother stand at her easel, painting watercolor scenes of the area. At times, Tim would stay longer, confiding in her mother about things he couldn't or wouldn't reveal to Gwyn or members of his own family.

The memorial service at the church was followed by a wake at one of her father's favorite haunts, the Rusty Anchor. She was seated with many of his watermen friends, enjoying Fred Mercer's tale of going out on the water with her father only to discover that beavers had chewed holes in their nets. It was just like George Smyth would have wanted it. The laughter helped her relax and feel like one of them again.

Her father's small, white workboat with its graceful swept-back stern now rocked gently beside the pier. It joined the ranks of many other watermen's boats lining Broadwater Creek. Times were tough for those who still tried to earn a living from the Chesapeake Bay. Those boats that had not been refitted to charter fishing parties remained tied to piers like abandoned memories. They were now replaced on the water by expensive yachts and powerboats in this ev-er-developing waterfront community.

Gwyn looked out over the wide creek as small wave after small wave of shimmering water rolled past her and out to the Bay. The evening sun was setting behind the tree line. Its fading light cast a pale pink glow over the creek.

After her mother had passed away five years ago, Gwyn had tried to ready herself for the inevitable. But her father's death had come so quickly. No tell-tale signs or lingering illness like her mother. His strong frame belied reality. Either he didn't know about his illness or he didn't want to worry her.

An osprey called out to its mate with a sharp, frenzied chirp as it returned home from an unsuccessful fishing expedition. The large, brownish-black and white bird remained almost motionless in the air as it rode the wind current high above her. From a nest of sticks on a nearby telephone pole, another osprey answered its call. The bird folded its wings, dropped down with precision, and landed safely in the nest. Their home reminded her of a high-rise luxury condo complete with one of the best water views in the area.

"It's all about location," she murmured under her breath.

As the sun's last light touched the water, she decided to head back up to the house. Once inside, she checked her cell phone before going up to bed. The cell phone alerted her to several messages. All of them were from Tucker Owens, her mentor and senior editor at the newspaper.

"Gwyn, please know that we are here for you. The whole staff. Call us if we can do anything for you."

Click.

She noted the time. He left the message right after she had left the house to sit down on the pier.

The second message was very much the same.

"Gwyn, we are here for you if you need anything. I realize that your cell phone is off and you need time to collect your thoughts about your father. I just wanted you to know that I... miss you," Tucker said as his voice trailed off.

Click.

This was the first time that Tucker had verbally acknowledged his feelings for her. She was grateful for his concern, but it still made her feel uncomfortable. He was much older than Gwyn and, more importantly, married. Although she valued his mentorship, she was careful to always maintain a friendly, but professional, relationship with him at work.

The third message was more frantic. His voice cracked as he spoke.

"Gwyn, please, call me as soon as possible. I'm worried about you."

Click.

She glanced at the clock. It was too late to contact him now. She would have to wait until after tomorrow morning's rush at the newspaper to return his calls. She wondered what she would tell him. Her mind was in a whirl. She felt the pull of her surroundings, the rhythm of the water.

Gwyn's parents had not been rich by any means. But before the Bay's steady decline in the early '70s, they had managed to pay off their waterfront house in full and to save enough money to send her to the University of Maryland for an undergraduate degree in journalism.

She pondered the possibilities of leaving a major city for a small town and the lifestyle changes that would follow. Although Gwyn grew up on the water, she never did feel that Lake Michigan was her home, even after fifteen years. And she knew she wouldn't miss the bone-chilling winters and blustery winds.

Belle Haven was built on the blood, sweat, and tears of the local watermen, but its focus was changing. Art boutiques, coffee shops, and small, high-end seafood restaurants now intermingled with the old filling station, the two-room bed and breakfast inn, and the town's weekly newspaper headquarters. Many of the older people living on the waterfront had sold their properties for remarkable sums of money and moved south to a warmer climate to wait out their years. At the same time, many of the younger people like herself, who had abandoned the water way of life in favor of a guaranteed paycheck, were now returning to the area in pursuit of a slower lifestyle. The small town was growing and the new amenities could make the transition from city life easier for her.

The next morning she dialed Tucker's number from the back porch. He answered on the first ring.

"Hey Tucker, I got all of your messages last night," she said trying to sound upbeat.

"Gwyn, we're all worried about you, especially me. How are you managing down there?" he asked.

"I'm fine, really I am." She paused as the osprey called out to its mate again.

"What in the world was that?" Tucker shouted into the telephone.

She had to wait until the osprey finished its piercing chirp to continue the conversation.

"It's the local wildlife," she said chuckling at his startled state. "It's a bird. An osprey. A fish hawk."

"Oh," Tucker replied softly.

"Tucker, have you ever gone chicken necking?" she asked.

"No, what in the world is chicken necking?" Tucker sounded confused.

"It's a local tradition," she murmured into the cell phone. "I'll talk to you about it next week when I get back."

Worlds apart.

She heard his faraway voice in the background as he put down the receiver. "She's gone native on us," he said to someone in his office.

Gwyn turned off her cell phone, walked back inside the house, and laid it on the kitchen table. She pulled a mystery novel out of her bag and walked down to the end of the pier. Lowering herself onto one of the two white Adirondack chairs, she watched as the creek rippled back to the dock.

With the family property free and clear, a small amount of money left by her father's life insurance policy, and some of her own investments, she could actually move to Belle Haven and finish the mystery novel that she had been working on for years. A gentle breeze blew across her face and ruffled the pages of the book in her lap. A calmness settled over her as she realized that this was the natural way of things. There was a certain flow to her decision to come back and be part of this water community again. It was cyclical, just like life on the Bay.

It felt right to be home again.

Sherry Audette Morrow

MARSHA READ A SENTENCE, LOOKED UP, LOOKED BACK DOWN, read the same sentence over again. The girls were practicing in a different classroom, one with a window in the door. The light streaming through the panes of glass patterned the wooden floor of the hallway so that even when Marsha looked down at her magazine, diligently concentrating on the state of world affairs, she could catch the brilliance in the corner of her eye. Three steps to the right, just moving to the other chair a little further down the hall, and she would be able to see in.

Other parents, two moms and a dad, shamelessly crowded around the door, peering in, smiling broadly, sometimes laughing out loud, beaming proudly at the antics of their children. Marsha would never do that. Ballet was serious. The teacher was trying to work in there. Amy would be terribly distracted if she saw her mother looking in. *Besides,* Marsha thought, glancing at the parents over the edge of her magazine, *they look like a bunch of over-eager sheepdogs, tongues hanging out, tails wagging, waiting to jump all over their kids the minute they come out.* Why couldn't they be a little more professional?

She brushed her hair out of her eyes, went back to her reading. Communism was failing in Eastern Europe, governments were changing, women were becoming world leaders. The light on the floor flashed suddenly; someone must have passed in front of the door, a swift shadow and then light again. Marsha looked up. Was it Amy who had moved in front of the window? There was a space between the two mothers, big enough to see through, but Marsha was at the wrong angle. From the other chair, she would have a direct view.

It was only three feet away, that other chair, and it was cushioned. She would be more comfortable there. She would be able to relax and better concentrate on her article. She could quickly shift, no big deal.

Marsha gathered up her coat and Amy's, Amy's dance bag and her purse, Amy's backpack of schoolbooks, its strap looped over her arm. She held her finger in her place in the magazine and shuffled to the other chair, bent forward trying to balance everything. Her forearm began to ache from the weight of the schoolbooks in just that short trip; as she put everything down, the magazine slid to the floor with a loud rustling of pages. The other parents turned to look, and Marsha quickly bent to retrieve it, hiding her flushed face, trying to pretend she had been sitting in this seat all along.

Finally composed, magazine neatly on her lap, Marsha glanced up at the door. The father had moved squarely in front; there was no way to see in. Marsha's chest tightened, frustration setting in, and she took a deep breath. It was probably better this way. Two more rehearsals to sit through and she would be able to see the finished product at the recital on Friday evening. It would be better to be surprised at the beauty of the whole production. It would be better not to know what was coming beforehand.

The father moved away, walking to greet his wife as she emerged from the stairwell. Full sunlight streamed into the hallway from where he had been standing. Marsha could suddenly see a good quarter of the dance studio.

The studio looked the way it should, the way Marsha had imagined it would look: the polished, golden wood floor, the rows of silvery mirrors along the far wall, the tall, bare windows with exposed steam pipes running along the top of them, the two-leveled wooden barre running below. And pink and black clad children moving gracefully across the floor, delicate pink tights and ballet slippers, black, black leotards, hair swept up off downy necks. The rays of late-afternoon sunlight caught on the dust in the air and bathed them all in a golden, hazy glow.

Marsha narrowed her eyes to pick out Amy. The girls were running into position, freezing with feet together, arms poised. The teacher leaned over the record player, moving its arm into position to start the music again. Faintly, the music floated through the door. The girls began to dance. It was a complicated dance. Two girls moved forward, two came across. They had to stay even with their partners across the room, they had to freeze again into position, balanced on one knee, when their part was finished.

Marsha found Amy as she moved into view. She had her right foot forward instead of her left. She hesitated, surreptitiously glancing at her partner to see what she was doing. She quickly brought her hand to her face to push up the glasses slipping down her nose and wobbled dangerously as she knelt in her frozen position.

Marsha pulled her gaze down to the graph of auto sales colorfully pictured on the page opened on her lap. Her ears burned with embarrassment. She heard the music start again. They were going to go through it again. The other parents were going to see Amy wobble again. They were going to laugh again. She could not look. She would not look. She would spend the next two rehearsals waiting down in the parents' lounge instead of up here in the hall.

Finally, the music ended. There was rustling from inside the room and the moms and dads moved back as the door burst open. The girls exploded from inside, running to their parents, chattering excitedly as they pulled sweatpants, short swirling skirts, brightly colored sweaters over their leotards. Amy breathlessly reached for her bag to get her clothes as Marsha closed her magazine and started gathering stuff together.

"Did you see me, Mom?" Amy asked. "Did you see me dancing?" Amy's hair hung in wisps, escaping from her bun, falling across her face and down into her eyes. She straightened her glasses and pushed the hair out of her face in one motion. Marsha looked at her for a moment, forcing back the urge to straighten Amy's hair even more.

"No, I didn't," Marsha said, glancing quickly away. "I was reading my magazine. It's distracting to the teacher to have a bunch of parents staring in." Marsha looked back at Amy, feeling the heat in her face, hoping Amy wouldn't notice. "It'll be better to see the whole thing as a surprise at the recital. You don't want to ruin that surprise, do you?"

Amy sat and tied her shoe. She pursed her lips tightly. Her eyes, magnified behind the lenses, blinked rapidly. Marsha could see her disappointment in her stiff shoulders, her fierce concentration on the loop of her shoelace. She couldn't tell her the truth. She couldn't tell her how awful she was. Marsha sighed, her lips tight over her teeth, tight as Amy's.

"Come on, we have to get home and start dinner. Dad will be home soon." And they walked down the hall together, Marsha's hand gently against Amy's stiff little back, propelling her in the right direction.

MARSHA AND TOM sat on the sofa, he doing a crossword puzzle, she reading the evening newspapers. There was just too much to know, too much to read, no way to keep up. Marsha wearily turned the page and the newspaper crackled as she snapped it into place along its fold.

"I'm ready for my hugs and kisses." Amy stood before them, nightgown reaching to the floor. A button missing, Marsha noticed. She kissed Tom first and Marsha could smell her perfumed hair, clean from her bath, and her minty toothpaste breath. Then Amy leaned into Marsha, practically knocking her over in her enthusiasm.

"Hugs aren't supposed to hurt, Sweetie," said Marsha, holding her back, regaining her balance, feeling irritation rise as she held Amy's small body barely against her. "You're supposed to hug carefully. Now give me a kiss. We'll be up soon to make sure you're covered up." Amy carefully placed her pink lips against Marsha's cheek, a solemn, warm seal on Marsha's skin.

"I'm really worried about Friday," Marsha said after she was sure Amy was out of hearing.

Tom looked up. "Hmm?"

"I watched her today, at dance. She really isn't ready. She doesn't know all the steps."

"She's got a few more days to practice. She'll be fine." Tom went back to his puzzle. "Besides, they're only six. They'll be adorable. Who's going to care?"

THE WINDSHIELD WIPER swished rhythmically across the glass. From the radio, a deep, calm voice intoned the latest death statistics in Central America. The traffic light turned green and Marsha cautiously made her way across the slippery intersection onto the freeway on-ramp. The rehearsals were over. The recital was tomorrow. It would all soon be over. Amy bubbled with excitement.

"Miss Wright said we did really well today, and that we should get a lot of rest tonight. We have to have all our muscles ready for tomorrow."

Marsha glanced at her as she maneuvered into the right lane. Amy was pulling the hairpins from her bun. Her blonde hair corkscrewed from the elastic that held it high on her head. Her face was still a baby's, round and pink, her lips so ready to smile, her eyes so ready to sparkle. She had no idea what this was all about. Marsha's stomach tightened and suddenly she could taste the turkey sandwich she had eaten for lunch, bitter and partially digested, in the back of her throat. Why did they put little children through these things anyway? She gripped the steering wheel and peered through the windshield, swallowing hard and coughing to clear her mouth. The exit was just ahead. The green sign over the roadway, grey in the rain, read, "Baltimore-Exit Only," and the arrow pointed down the familiar road. But to the left, the "New York-Caution Left Exit" sign beckoned, bright and yellow.

"I want to invite my teacher from school." Amy said giddily. "She said she'd like to come. Can I invite her?"

"What?" The language Amy was speaking didn't seem like English. Marsha struggled to make sense of the sounds. "To see the recital? To see you dance?"

"She said she really likes that sort of thing." Amy's hair swung loose on her shoulders, angel-like, soft, curling at the ends.

"You've already asked her?" Marsha slowed the car as they approached their exit. Trying to listen to Amy, trying to follow the road, she had no control over either. The car slid onto the shoulder as she rounded the curve. Adrenaline quivering through her arms, Marsha pulled back onto the roadway, the driver behind blasting his horn as if it would blast Marsha right into oblivion. She wished it would.

"I just told her when it was, and where. I thought I should ask you first." Amy grinned hopefully at her. "She's gone to see other kids' recitals."

She should win the teacher of the year award. Marsha grimaced. To her left, the New York sign flashed out of view. Too late. It would have been the perfect weekend to get away. A woman's voice floated from the radio. Three more priests had been killed in El Salvador.

THE HALF-SIZE VIOLIN felt large and heavy in Marsha's seven-year-old hands. The bow slid across the strings, emitting a fingernails-against-blackboard screech. A little more rosin on the horsehair would help, she knew. She laid the violin down carefully and fumbled in her case for the little box. The amber cube blew up sticky, white dust as Marsha drew it briskly across the bow hairs. Sometimes she thought she could see bees in the translucent depths of the rosin. They were the right color, bees, and it seemed natural that they would be embedded in the honey-like rectangle. Besides, sometimes the violin sounded just like it had bees in it, buzzing and vibrating in her hand. Sometimes Marsha wondered why they didn't make paperweights out of rosin. They could put bees in them instead of butterflies and the rosin would stick to the paper, making sure it didn't go anywhere.

Marsha drew the bow across the E string once again. It was much better. The E let out a high, clear tone. She started her scales, sliding her small fingers into place to correct the pitches as she went up the string and then returned. The tone of the violin filled the room, warbling on the air, changing the air so that Marsha felt she breathed in the music. She started on her recital piece, "Au Clair de la Lune," pulling the bow firmly, pulling the notes from the violin.

She was on a stage in a huge concert hall. Millions of people in fancy clothes stared up at her in wonder. She smiled graciously at them as her music held them enthralled. It was as if they all held their breath as she played. They could not believe that anyone so young could have so much talent. She swept to the conclusion of the piece and the audience broke into thunderous applause. Someone handed her an armful of roses. The audience shouted for more.

"I think you should stop practicing now. The neighbors are going to complain and, besides, I have a headache." Marsha looked up at her mother standing in the doorway.

"But the recital's tomorrow night, Mom." Marsha held the violin in front of her like a shield. "I need to practice. I want to be the best." Marsha's mother stood with her arms folded across her chest.

"Well, Marsha." Her mother stared straight at her. "I think I should be honest with you. The way you're going, I don't think you will ever be the best. Adequate, but not the best." She hesitated. "Well, maybe adequate." She looked doubtful. "Look, you don't have to do the recital if you don't want to."

Her words hit Marsha like a slap, stinging, resounding, leaving an imprint. Marsha hung her head to hide her red face, to hide the tears reddening her eyes, and she slowly packed the instrument away.

MARSHA FOUND AN empty corner of the hallway and settled Amy and her bag of supplies into it. Little girls in tutus galloped up and down the hall, nervous energy splashing from them like ocean waves. Older girls sat carefully tying toe shoes and adjusting leotards. Marsha briskly brushed Amy's hair up in her hands and pulled it to the top of her head. As she tried to loop the elastic around, another mother, daughter in tow, knocked her arm. The elastic slipped on crookedly and Amy's hair lumped across her head. Marsha pulled her shoulders back, hearing them crack with tension as she loosened the hair and started again. The elastic on. The ponytail twisted around. The hairpins shoved into place. Marsha turned Amy around. Hair still escaped, blowing across Amy's forehead, dangling in front of her ears. A few more hairpins. It would have to do. The glasses were sliding down Amy's nose again. Marsha's neck ached. She would have to do.

"I'm really nervous, Mom," Amy said as she pushed up her glasses.

This was her chance. She could say it. *If you don't want to, you don't have to, Honey. You don't have to be humiliated in front of all these people.*

"Just stand up straight. Remember the steps. Smile. Don't touch your face, no matter what." Marsha took a deep breath. "You'll be fine."

The lie sat heavily just below her lungs. She could barely breathe, it was so large. "I have to go find Daddy now. Just do what your teacher tells you." She turned to go, then turned back. Amy stood there, small, so small, her eyes wide and glistening, her face white, her mouth smiling a small, excited smile. Marsha stepped back and kissed her stiffly, just barely brushing Amy's cheek. "Dance well, Sweetie."

Marsha quickly walked down the hall to the main doors of

the auditorium. She stood, searching the seats for Tom. The room was filling fast. The ceiling soared dizzyingly above her. The stage, washed in red and blue and orange lights, was huge and far away across the auditorium. The heat in the room caught in her lungs.

MARSHA SMOOTHED THE skirt of her white lace dress, which her mother had made for her seventh birthday the month before. It had made her feel like a princess when she wore it to her birthday party, the skirt swirling out like a ballerina's. Her hair had been swept up with a red velvet bow. It had been a magical dress.

This evening, though, the magic was gone. The heat from the stage lights reached backstage, raising small drops of moisture on Marsha's forehead and over her upper lip. Her damp hands left smudges on the lace. The lining of the dress had become a wrinkled mass at the back of her knees during the car ride to the school, and now it clung to her legs.

It would soon be her turn to perform.

Marsha listened to her friend Jenny playing her piece, "Frère Jacques." She sounded so good. Her notes were clear and firm; Jenny obviously had enough rosin on her bow. Marsha quickly glanced at her own bow. Had she forgotten to rosin? She couldn't remember. Jenny was finishing, no time to search for the little gold box. The teacher out on stage was announcing her name. Someone, the stage mother, had her hand on Marsha's back and was steering her out into the hot lights. The brightness was blinding. The teacher smiled at her from her seat at the piano at the side of the stage. The lights were white in Marsha's eyes.

Marsha balanced her music on the flimsy metal stand set up at the center of the stage and raised her violin to her chin. She nodded to the teacher to let her know she was ready. She raised her bow and glanced once more at the bright lights.

Despite the bright lights, she saw her mother.

Her mother sat at the side of the small auditorium, in the third row from the back, in a black corner. Marsha was amazed that she could see her in all that darkness. She sat in her black dress, the one with the long sleeves and the black, cut-glass buttons down the front. She had bought that dress for a funeral, Marsha remembered.

It was her white face that Marsha saw shining out in the darkness, white and stern and somehow ghostly, floating in all that black.

Marsha heard the piano introduction and began to play, her fingers moving from memory. She could not look at the music. She could not look anywhere but at her mother. She could see her as if she were standing directly in front of her, not yards away across the room. Marsha could see her grim mouth and her head shaking in disapproval.

And as Marsha played, she could hear everything her mother heard. The notes just slightly out of tune—she imperceptibly shifted her fingers to correct; the bow scraping on the strings, not enough rosin—she pressed firmly on the bow to get a clearer sound; the notes, half there, half lost because her fingers lay loose against the fingerboard—she pressed tighter, careful not to cramp her thumb against the neck of the violin. Still her mother shook her head in disgust.

The final repeat was coming. She would soon be done. She moved the bow firmly and rapidly across the strings, keeping time with the piano. The last few notes were coming. She could soon escape. She just had to get through the last notes.

And she was done.

And the audience was clapping and smiling; the music teacher was standing and clapping, smiling broadly, motioning Marsha to bow. But Marsha could only stand, cheeks flushed, mouth solemn, watching as her mother quietly got up from her seat and slipped out the rear exit.

TOM WAVED TO her from near the front of the auditorium. Marsha excused herself as she made her way down the crowded aisle. She avoided looking at Tom as she slid into the empty seat next to him and carefully placed her purse on the floor. Then she noticed that Tom's hand lay protectively across a sheaf of pale pink roses.

Her roses.

"For our prima donna." Tom smiled at her. "It wouldn't be a recital without flowers." Marsha reached to touch the roses in their bed of fern and baby's breath. The silky petals reminded her of Amy's soft, baby cheek. Her stomach tightened. "They're beautiful, Tom," she said. "You're always so thoughtful. She'll love them." Marsha could feel the tightness in her throat, the stiffness in her voice. She swallowed and looked away, pretending to survey the audience.

Amy's elementary teacher sat in the row ahead, just two seats over.

Marsha swiftly looked away, but she had already been seen. The school teacher smiled at her and leaned over to shake her hand.

"I love seeing what my students do outside of school," she gushed, "and Amy is such a sweetheart."

Marsha stared at the teacher open-mouthed, unable to speak. She's just doing this for fun, Marsha wanted to say. We send her to ballet to improve her posture. Nothing serious.

"I hope you enjoy it," she finally said. "We're really proud of her." Another lie. But the house lights dimmed and she was able to settle back into her seat. They could slip out as the lights came up later. She wouldn't have to speak to the teacher again.

Of course they would want to get backstage to congratulate Amy right away. Besides, she needed to get home in time for the evening news. Marsha slid down further in her seat. The hard wood of the seat pressed against her backbone. A headache gathered over her left eye.

The four- and five-year-olds came on first. They pranced across the stage as little teapots. They sang the song and tipped over at the end, giggling and glancing down at their teacher who mimed the dance with them at the foot of the stage. It wasn't even ballet, really. It was a chance to get up on stage, to move to the music, to get used to the lights, the nervousness, the overwhelming attention. They were actually pretty cute, bumping into each other and running back into place when they missed a step. Marsha glanced at Tom. He was relaxed. He was smiling. He was clapping along with the rest of the audience as the little girls curtsied at the end of their dance.

Maybe they could leave right after Amy's dance. It was such a waste of time to watch other peoples' kids perform.

The music began again, Amy's music, and Marsha's attention leapt to the stage. The ten girls ran lightly onto the stage and stood in position, feet one in front of the other, arms raised delicately over their heads. Amy stood right in front. She wasn't blocked by anyone. Marsha's heartbeat pounded in her ears. Everyone would see all her mistakes.

Marsha looked cautiously at Amy. She had taken off her glasses. Someone had redone her hair, spraying the loose strands up with hairspray and wrapping silk flowers around her bun. She stood with her hands perfectly curved, her neck stretched, long and graceful. She smiled, not a real smile, but a planned, sweet, professional smile. It was hard to see stumbling little Amy in this still, graceful child.

The music came to the downbeat and the girls slid into action. And Amy was suddenly not her child anymore. Without her glasses, Amy could only rely on her memory as she moved forward opposite her partner. Her memory was more precise than her eyes had ever been. Her back was straight, her smile was even, her eyes followed the graceful sweep of her hands. She moved and twirled and leaped, and finally knelt with perfect balance.

Marsha tried to look at the other girls to see how they were doing, but her gaze kept racing back to Amy. Marsha wanted to look at Tom, to see his reaction. She could feel him sitting up in his seat, leaning forward in concentration. But she could not miss a second of Amy. She could not miss a second of how beautiful Amy was.

The music crashed to a finish. The girls, Amy, curtsied deeply, bowing their heads down to the floor. Then they lightly jetéed offstage. Just as Amy disappeared from view, Marsha saw her smile break into her familiar, six-year-old, missing-toothed grin.

Marsha's heart beat wildly in her chest and she grabbed Tom's hand, kissing his knuckles.

"She did it, Tom!" she whispered. And she was good!

Amy's teacher leaned over.

"You must be very proud. I never knew Amy was so graceful," she said.

The music was coming up again. The seven-year-olds were running on. Marsha settled back. Amy had been very good.

THEY MISSED THE evening news. Tom and Marsha watched until all the performers had taken their final bows, then waited in the lobby until Amy emerged from backstage. She came out wearing her blue jeans pulled up over her leotard. Her hair was still up, the flowers still twined in her golden hair. Her face was brilliant with stage make-up.

Tom pressed the roses into her arms. "My princess!" he said as he picked her up and swung her around, pressing the roses between them.

"Daddy!" Amy cried gleefully. Marsha could smell the fragrance of crushed petals. Amy turned to Marsha.

"What did you think, Mom?" she asked. "Did you like it?"

But Tom was shouting, "Ice cream! We need ice cream to celebrate your glorious victory!"

THEY HAD STUFFED themselves with chocolate and strawberry and cherry vanilla. Tom joked and Amy laughed, and Marsha could not find the moment to tell Amy how wonderful she had been. There was too much noise, too many distractions. Then Amy fell asleep in the car on the way home. Tom carried her up to her bed and Marsha gently wiped the make-up from her face with a warm washcloth.

Now she picked up the evening paper. Would she ever be able to tell Amy? It wouldn't be the same tomorrow. Amy wouldn't be able to catch Marsha's excitement. Marsha probably couldn't catch it again herself. Already the evening was becoming hazy, muted, black and white.

Marsha smoothed out the front page of the paper on her lap. A grainy photograph spread across the top half of the page. They were tearing down the Berlin Wall. A mother and daughter, separated for forty-five years, hugged each other desperately over the rubble.

Marsha just had to cry.

Henna No. 25

Sally Whitney

BEHIND TALL, DARK OAK TREES, THE SKY WAS ABLAZE with red and orange and violet, the sun's last cry before sinking out of sight. "Ain't it beautiful?" Alice whispered so softly Carl could hardly hear her. Evening surrounded them on Alice's front porch, warm and sweet as only a June evening in Missouri can be. Through the still air, the whir of a lawn mower and the smell of fresh cut grass told of someone trying to finish a job before nightfall. Alice ate the meringue off her piece of lemon pie, and Carl blew smoke rings with a drag from his Winston cigarette.

"Don't you ever wish you could box something that beautiful and hide it under your bed?" Alice asked. She set the uneaten lemon filling and crust on a rusty metal table former renters had left on the porch along with the creaky glider. "Don't you wish you could pull something like that out every time you got sad and look at it till you felt better?"

Carl wasn't exactly sure what she was talking about, but he nodded anyway. That was one of the things he loved about Alice. She had lofty thoughts. It was hard to believe someone so beautiful could be so smart. When he first saw her at the roller rink he had been attracted to her slender thighs in black stretch leggings and her long blonde hair, shiny as turtle wax. Not until they had been going together several months did he realize what a brain she had. She saw connections everywhere. She even understood Woody Allen movies. "Can I get you some coffee?" Carl asked.

Alice frowned. He had broken her concentration on the wavy colors of the sunset. The violets were turning to blues and the reds to pinks. Alice was trying to find a pattern to the changes. There must be a reason why they happened that way. Beauty was never random. "Coffee's been keeping me awake at night lately. Even decaf. Must be some new chemical reaction in my body. Maybe an allergy."

"How about a beer, then? That'll help you sleep." While not a heavy drinker himself, Carl believed alcohol could cure a lot of maladies. The thought of beer made Alice's stomach heave. The only time beer was good was when the weather was very, very hot and the beer was very, very cold. Yet, she loved Carl for trying to please her. Usually he didn't have an inkling of an idea what she needed, but he tried. Like tonight, she was filled with a restlessness that twittered just under her skin. Carl would say she was horny and offer her passionate sex. Maybe this time he would be right. The colors in the sunset faded to grey wisps of cloud. "Well, if you don't want a beer, what do you want to do?" The lawn mower fell silent, allowing the bedtime noises of birds to take over. "We could go inside and watch the 'Wheel,' or ride over to the mall for a while."

"I don't know." Alice pushed against the floor with her foot, causing the old glider to sway and squeak. Durwood, a beagle-terrier who seemed to belong to the house, had been sleeping at the head of the steps leading into the yard. The shrill grind caused him to raise his head, look around with droopy eyes, and then, as if first realizing he was not alone, pad over to the glider and jump up beside Alice. "God, you stink!" Alice tried to shove away the dog, who was just settling in next to her. "I don't know what's wrong with this animal, but I've never smelled anything quite this bad."

Carl lit another cigarette off the one he was smoking. "So don't smell him."

Alice shook her head and stretched out her arms and legs. The restlessness poured into her fingers and toes. It was dark now. She could see only the outline of Carl's face, backlit by the streetlight. She walked over to the folding chair where he sat and wiggled her bottom into his lap. He exhaled a stream of smoke next to her ear. She stroked the side of his face lightly between his sideburn and chin. His bony shoulders twitched beneath his tee shirt. "I think the best thing for us to do tonight is get naked and take it from there," Alice said. She took the cigarette from between Carl's fingers and tossed it into the yard. He followed her past the glider where Durwood closed his eyes and sighed.

IN THE MORNING sun, Durwood's eyes were still closed. Alice went by to pat him as she left for work, but the heat increased his stench, causing her to shudder and hurry on. Her first customer was waiting for her when she arrived. It was a dye job, long and tedious, the hair coarse and grey, unreceptive to the color.

"I told that Mabel Larson..." The customer was talking a mile a minute to another beautician. Alice pulled her thickest comb through the snarled hair and then doused it all in the sink. The customer never stopped talking. The supposed recipient of her remarks grunted at appropriate times without taking her eyes off the layered look she was trimming. It was an art all beauticians learned eventually—how to act like you're listening when you're bored out of your mind. Alice amused herself sometimes watching the others practice it. There were five of them in the shop, not counting the manicurist, who only worked part time. They each had their own chairs, but there was nothing to give them privacy, no cloudy plastic partitions or anything like that. The shop's owner was too cheap to provide extras, and she insisted her employees provide pink uniforms for themselves. A bunch of sugar plum fairies, that's what we look like, Alice often thought, with our identical pink dresses and our white orthopedic shoes.

While she massaged her customer's scalp, Alice studied the grey roots, defiant in their own way, claiming their right to exist before being obscured forever. They made Alice uncomfortable. "Hey, Suzy," she said to stop thinking about the roots. "Did you go see Tom Cruise last night like you planned?" A short, plump woman with an old-fashioned pixie haircut looked up from the end papers and rods of a permanent wave.

"You bet!" A smile brightened Suzy's face. "He's my boy. I love seeing his face eight feet tall." She paused, rod in hand, and stared at Alice. "You know, Alice, don't mind me saying so, but you don't look good. You got them dark circles under your eyes. You and Carl been hitting the bars?"

Alice patted her face as if she could feel the shadows. The odor of fixing lotion ánd hair spray was intensifying; by afternoon it would be so strong the beauticians wouldn't notice it anymore. "You know Carl and I don't do that. Hell, we don't hardly go anywhere. It's just that I can't sleep at night. You know, I get to sleep all right, but I wake up at four o'clock, five o'clock, and I can't go back to sleep. It's like I got too much on my mind, or something."

"What you got to worry about?" Suzy wrapped a strand of hair in paper and twisted it around a rod. "You got a good job, a regular boyfriend, a good face and figure."

"I don't know." Alice finished rinsing and covered the offensive grey roots with a towel. The customer was still talking. From a box under her counter, Alice pulled out a new pair of disposable latex gloves. Just like a doctor, she thought as she stretched them over her hands. Just like a doctor. Inwardly, she smirked. *You ain't no doctor, girl.* Once upon a time, she had wanted to be a teacher, a teacher of little children learning to read, but she needed money in high school to buy clothes and make-up, so she started working afternoons at the beauty shop and somehow never left. She squirted Henna No. 25 from a tube into a cup and warmed it in the palms of her hands. When it was the right temperature, she stirred it with a paintbrush and removed the protective towel. Strand by strand, she painted the roots brown, an artist with a monotone canvas.

By five o'clock she had dyed three more heads, cut five, and washed hundreds, it seemed. On the way home, she hoped the sky would be as glorious later as it had been the night before. The thought of all that beauty started the restless rumblings in her gut once again. Durwood still slept on the glider. *Doesn't he ever move?* Alice wondered. She hung up the pink uniform, figuring it was good for one more day without washing. As she was putting on shorts and a shirt, she heard Carl on the front porch. "Hey, you smelly hound. Your mama home?"

"I am not his mama!" She met Carl at the door.

"I know, Punkin, but he thinks you are." Carl had obviously come straight from work. He still had on the grey shirt with his name embroidered over the pocket and the matching grey slacks. Alice thought it would make more sense to have gas station attendants wear black shirts and slacks so the oil and grease wouldn't show, but nobody asked her. "Look, I brought us some Kentucky Fried for dinner." Carl waved a bulging white sack in front of her face. Durwood caught a whiff of the spicy aroma and barked.

Alice waved Carl inside. "Come on in before that mutt thinks he's having dinner with us." After dinner, they went back out on the porch to watch for the sunset. Carl had his portable radio in his truck. He had taken it to work with him that day to try to catch the Royals' game.

"How about a little music?" He set the radio up on the rusty table. He tuned it through a few stations and finally settled on Vince Gill singing "Look at Us." The mournful melody struck Alice as odd accompaniment to the lyrics about a perfect relationship. "Want to dance?" Carl reached for her hand and twirled her in a small circle to the edge of the porch. Then he grabbed her around the waist and pulled her body close to his. He was warm and smelled of sweat and chicken. They swayed to the music. Alice imagined her neighbors watching and thinking, there goes that loony single woman doing something crazy again. They never danced on their porches. The only time they sat on their porches was to watch their children and keep them from running into the street.

The music changed into an upbeat rockabilly number, and Carl began to do a modified country clog. The heels of his boots made a solid thumping sound against the porch's old boards. Alice backed away, grinning at his flashing feet. He was such a sight. A grown-up little boy begging for attention. Durwood was startled by the sound of the dancing and the pounding music and began to howl. "Stop it!" Alice said, even though she was smiling. "Stop it!" This time the remark was directed at Carl.

"You mean me?" Carl pretended shock.

"Stop it or we'll have the whole neighborhood over here or calling the cops."

"So?" Carl wiped his forehead with his shirttail and unbuttoned the front of his shirt. "Sure is hot for June." He dropped onto the glider next to Durwood. "Why do you care what the neighbors think?" In the west, the first blazes of orange were beginning to stretch up from the horizon. Alice sat at the top of the steps, her back to Carl, and gazed into the sunset. It seemed so close, as if she could put her hand into the wispy colors and pull them back to her.

"Do you love me?" Alice's voice sounded far away.

"Of course I do." Carl leaned forward, unsure what she was getting at.

"Then what's going to happen to us?"

Carl walked across the porch to join her at the top of the steps. It made him nervous when she talked like this. He never knew if she meant tomorrow or ten years from now. Her breathing was deep and slow as he tried to think what to say next. "Well, some day we'll get married."

"And then what?"

"Have kids, I guess."

"And then what?"

Carl had the feeling that anything he said would be wrong. Instead of talking, he put his arms around her and tried to melt her against him, but she was rigid as a spike. They sat like that for a long time, watching the sky go from bright to brilliant. Just when Alice thought she was going to explode, Carl whispered, "Let's go to bed. That made you feel better last night."

"No!" Everything inside Alice was going off in sparks and crackles. "That didn't make me feel better. Nothing makes me feel better." The puzzled expression on Carl's face made him seem vulnerable. At another time, Alice might have pitied him, but at that moment she found him repulsive—weak, unresponsive, and repulsive. "Look, why don't you go on home now? I probably ought to be alone."

Carl shrugged, figuring this was one of her worst bouts of weirdness yet. Maybe she had PMS. In any case, he wasn't going to stay where he wasn't wanted. He picked up his radio and ruffled Durwood's sleepy head. Alice kissed him on the cheek and waved goodbye. As he walked toward his truck, Alice said, "Durwood, you are about the smelliest, most obnoxious dog I have ever had the displeasure of being associated with." Then she went into the house and closed the door without waving to Carl again.

ALICE WOKE UP about five o'clock the next morning. It was still dark out, but there was no moon and the stars were beginning to dim. She lay alone in her bed and pretended she was somebody else. She planned clothes that somebody else would wear and appointments she would keep. She tried to think like the somebody else, but the thoughts kept running away. At eight o'clock she put on her pink uniform and went to work. Every customer she had was fifteen minutes late or took twenty minutes longer than she should have. Alice finished her last blow dry at six-fifteen. Even the white orthopedic shoes weren't enough to save her feet. She kicked them off and drove home in her stockings, the air conditioning blowing full blast toward the floor.

The sight in her yard made her weary body sag, like a bag of sand had fallen into her lap. She eased the car into the driveway and sat watching, her hands and chin resting on the steering wheel. Carl was there, shirtless, exposing his milk-white skin and mole-covered back to the evening breeze. He had dumped the Coke cans out of her recycle tub and filled it with water, into which he had plunged Durwood, who apparently didn't like the situation at all. Carl had the dog in a chokehold with one arm, and with the other he was squirting him with what looked like dishwashing liquid. Durwood kept flopping his tail and hindquarters around in the tub, sloshing water and suds onto Carl's grey slacks.

Somewhere in the back of Alice's brain, a voice told her she really should find this funny, but all she could think about was that Carl looked so common. Or maybe not common, but incompetent. Or maybe not incompetent, but downright silly. She wanted to laugh, but it wasn't funny. She thought about driving out of the driveway and never coming back. Carl had already seen her, though, and it was her house. She threw up her hands in resignation and limped across the grass in her stocking feet. Carl waved at her with the bottle of dishwashing liquid. She was relieved to see as she got closer that it was dog shampoo. "So how are you going to rinse him?" she asked.

"With the hose over there. Hand it to me, will you?" Carl nodded toward Alice's green garden hose that she bought at a garage sale to water her zinnias. Trying to avoid getting splashed, Alice skirted around the edge of the yard, pulled the hose out of the bushes, and tossed it at Carl. "Hand it to me. I can't reach it from here." Carl still had Durwood in the chokehold and was stretching out his other hand toward the hose. His face glistened with sweat or water. He looked away from the dog for an instant and saw the disgust in Alice's eyes. Durwood turned in his grasp. He seized the slippery animal with both hands and muttered, "Never mind. I'll get it myself."

Alice made herself pick up the hose and walk it toward him. She turned the nozzle until a stream of cold water spewed out. "Get him out of the tub, and I'll hose him down," she said. Carl tried to lift Durwood, who kicked over the tub, sending soapy water creeping around Alice's feet. The cold sliminess almost made her cry. She turned the hose on the dog, dousing Carl in the process.

"That's enough!" Carl let Durwood go. The dog took off for the back yard with Alice squirting him as far as the water would reach. When he was out of range, she closed the nozzle and stared at Carl. He looked like a drowned rat.

"I'll get you a towel." Alice laid the hose on the ground and went into the house. When she came back, Carl had rinsed out the tub and put it back on the porch. He was rolling up the hose around his elbow. Alice handed him the towel. "I guess I should thank you, but he's not my dog."

"He hangs around here like he is."

"Yeah, but he don't belong here."

Carl hung the hose on the faucet under the porch and dried his hands and face with Alice's towel. "Guess I'll go home and get on some dry clothes." He handed the towel back to Alice.

Alice studied the familiar line of his jaw and curve of his eyes. Over his shoulder, the sun was dropping behind the oak trees.

"Carl," she said. "Don't come back."

Carl planted his hands on his hips and stood his ground.

"I mean it, Carl. It's over between us." Alice trembled even though the breeze had died down. The sun disappeared behind the trees.

"I won't give up that easy." Carl said. "I'll be back tomorrow, or next week."

"It's no use. It won't work. Nothing works. Go on now." She folded her arms across the water-spotted, wrinkled front of her dress.

"All right, I'll go. But it's not over yet." He walked in his squishy pants toward his truck.

Alice climbed the steps to the porch feeling every minute of the long day. She collapsed onto the glider and stretched her wet feet and legs out in front of her. From around the side of the house, Durwood found his way back into the yard and up onto the porch. With a small whine, he settled on the glider next to Alice. She looked down at his damp body. He still smelled bad.

POETRY

FRIDAY AFTERNOON ON CURRITUCK SOUND

Jane Frutchey

For Brianna

Today I sit on a weathered white bench,
welcoming scattered sunlight after
seven grey days of hurricanes
on Currituck Sound.
Eyes close—I listen.
Shallow waves swish in, swish out;
humid breezes rustle tall grasses along the shoreline,
sweep across my damp skin, thick salve on my soul.
I breathe in tidal perfume:
sand wet with yesterday's rain;
seaweed, green-black, acrid, pungent;
schools of minnows, silty, earthy.
A mother should not discount such simple bliss:
a walk along a pier,
rest by water's edge,
late-summer's sunlight,
azure afternoon sky,
sea-scented breeze.
Eyes open—I focus.
Sun-blanched slats, driftwood-colored pier
brace this seasoned bench that
holds me, holding you in my thoughts.
You are with me always—
in the arms of other mothers,
in the faces of other children.
In the distance, windows of a
blue-grey cottage, watchful eyes
overlooking this serene Sound.
Eyes close—I picture you.
Asleep in the arms of your father,
soft breath in, breath out

almost inaudible, like the waves' whisper-swish.
Often I watch you in the depths of sleep:
Sand-colored curls cascade over a
flannel blanket's white satin trim,
well-worn by tiny fists, pale pink, clenched, the
colors and curves of a sea-washed conch shell.
Fingers curled tight soon fan open,
like starfish tossed from the sea,
strewn on the beach, fragile, exposed.
Eyes open—I cannot linger.
I am drawn homeward, a vessel
moving through fog, led by a beacon of yellow-white
cottony light in the distance.
Beside you I kneel, watching your small back
rise then fall, breathing in as you breathe out.
Dimpled fingers, delicate starfish,
unfold to accept my kisses.

Exit Charlotte

Juliet M. Johnson

Luggage is carried by hand
I let mine go,
Though I usually carry it
A man looks mildly at
His crying five-year-old
"It's only temporary,"
 he says.
A woman crashes into me
In the bathroom tube,
Her sweatshirt balled up
Around her face
Like she's hiding, or crying
In a hurry to escape
A mother and daughter
With matching black pageboys
And white sandals.
Exit Charlotte
Plane in the sky
"Hi I'm Bob,"
 behind me.
Gate B15
Take the moving staircase
Concourse
Beeping car
He left his tickets on the plane.
Everyone's carrying
Southern accents
Like warm, fleshy taffy
In your underwear.
Who is Charlotte
Was she pretty
And terminally indecisive
Always leaving,

Barefoot in an aluminum building.
He can't get off here
It's too flat
Charlotte grins
Terminally Charlotte
Arching like a softball
Hurled into your eye
Opens up her ceiling
And gives herself to the sky.
She is unloaded
Bags all over the tarmac
Can't I get back on,
He begs
The people file off
But sir, this is your destination

WELL BEING

Susan Lesser

I stopped eating potato chips,
power walk every day, lost twelve pounds
over the summer, returned
to a size I hadn't seen for twenty years.
Anbula eats only breakfast, a pasty gruel,
trudges with buckets to the village well
two miles and back each day,
has worn the same kanga for ten years.
I mow grass and pull weeds;
she dreams of fertile fields, corn and grain,
to have her own well
and rains that come often.
I watch youngsters run on able legs, kicking
soccer balls, riding bikes;
Anbula's little boy scurries on bowed legs
after a skinny dog, ribs well-defined.
I sit with family and chant
words of thanks for endless blessings;
Anbula is grateful for the well being
so near, her boy strong and laughing.

Paulownia, The Tree

Liz Moser

Genus: Scrophularicaeae; species: Tomentosa (royal), Kawakamii (dragon)
Empress and Tramp.
Asian tradition
plants a tree for each girl child;
tree and girl child grow together
until she marries. Then the tree transforms
into the music of a happy life—a pipa lute or tansu chest.

Her silky wood, light as air,
is highly prized.
In the West
she is a weed tree:

after lilacs, before roses, her purple torches
hang above the railroad track, in vacant lots,
keeping company with

old men seeking shelter
from spring rain and wind.
They huddle in torn blankets at her feet.
Last year's opened seedpods hang in great grape bunches,
heart-shaped leaves erupt along her straggly branches;
she thrives,
tall and graceless, bark striated
as though scratched by felines
wandering in the perfumed night,
branch-end blossoms scoffing at the sky,
irreverent.

MÉLANGE

Liz Moser

My morning face is not my own.
It glowers at me from the bathroom mirror,
unadorned, still scarred
with sleep and idiosyncratic traits
inherited from members
of my family.
Today I am my aunt
on my father's side.
Her judgmental frown derides
my self-involvement, calls it navel-gazing—
why do I concern myself with shallow vanities,
her pursed lips ask; why am I
not more into the world of active charity?
Sometimes my mother's hooded eyes
and soft, sad face commiserate,
taking in my wrinkled cheeks and brows,
suggesting I accept this surface burden,
let my face show apprehension;
she is familiar with the mountains that I feel
I must ascend.
Sometimes I am my father—
chin out, hard-eyed, defiant; he never
lost that naughty boy,
do what I want, not what I should
expression.
Every now and then I am imperious—
my grandma, looking down
upon a world of smaller people,
noblesse oblige at best, more often
graciously accepting adulation.
As the day proceeds, I am them all
at once; my own distinctive traits are but
a mix, mélange, a boiled up stew
of heritage.

FATHER

Bonny Barry Sanders

Each morning I water the pepper tree
you planted for me before you returned
to your imperial oaks. The rusty watering can
drips on the hem of my bathrobe.
I remember the middle years when you gave me
names for birds and trees, took out
my splinters, corrected my stuttering, eased
my fears the way moonlight filtered
in my window through hemlock combs,
brushing away the edges of darkness.
Now I set the watering can on level ground.
Translucent leaves trace their shadows over rocks
the way the vague fossils of our days
engrave themselves in memory.
Light and shadow stir few early images—those years
rest dormant in my mind like the energy
inside winter trees. Your memory must claim
the me I can't remember or never knew.
You gave me my name, and
inside the sound of it, I must have felt safe.

THE GAME OF JACKS

Bonny Barry Sanders

Her mother taught her how
to throw the six-headed pins just right.
How to toss the ball
just high enough to pick up two at once
or eight or ten before it bounced. How to use
her fingers like pliers
and how to sweep all the jacks into the dustpan
of her small hand. Then she learned the calls
serious competitors use: no overs, splits,
Jack-in-the-box. She let the rhythm settle into her fingers
like a slow song. She mastered
the double bounce, eggs in the basket,
over the moon. On the flagstone walk, the smooth
shoe-sanded spots on the front porch, the polished kitchen floor,
a table top, or any secret niche,
she practiced the calls, the sweep of hand,
the toss of the ball—just high enough. Her fingers came to know
their purpose like a concert pianist
ready to perform. The day she was ready
to compete wore a different dress—that was the day
her mother stopped letting her win.

Mountain, Log, Salt and Stone

Laura Shovan

The mountain is taller than I,
halfway to the ceiling of our new living room.
This is how carpets are delivered,
piled in long, round rolls.
Put a penny in your mouth and you'll smell them:
acrid and heavy and new,
sour and exciting.
With my brother I skate over the wood floor in socks,
try to crash the mountain of carpets.
Climb it and we are king and queen of a log pile.
We cannot fell or budge them,
though their sandy undersides
mark geometrics on our knees.
These logs have no rot,
no rings to mark the fire or flood.
The disasters are all ahead of us.
When Dad is away we eat fast food,
French-fries at the new stone hearth.
In two years our brother –
the child my mother is carrying –
will bang his chin on this stone
and nearly sever his tongue with his teeth.
There will be blood on the rug,
the salty taste of it in the air.
But tonight the scent of salt and oil
is good. Furniture is scant.
We gather on the floor around the fire.
The young painter stands by the window.
He has stopped rolling the walls
and joined us for dinner.
My mother is somewhere in the room.
The painter watches her.
He has dark hair and the youthful,

slender form my father has outgrown.
I watch the way his mouth moves
when he looks away from my mother.
The muscles of his back are taut with longing.
Less than ten years in this country,
her accent still fits like an egg in her mouth.
He is not the first to mistake
her round, elegant vowels for virtue.
I want her to take offense, to fire him.
But she is as kind and inattentive to him
as she is to anyone. Angry for her sake,
I begin to love my mother
with a viciousness the painter can't know.
I pull her to sit with us by the fire,
meals spread on our knees,
and let the warm salt dissolve on her tongue,
until it burns there like a pungent kiss.

BROTHER

Laura Shovan

"Ahmed and Mohamed Ibrahim—who had been joined at the top of the head—were separated...after neurosurgeons finished dividing the boys' venous systems and brains."—CNN, October 13, 2003

When did I become aware of my brother?
I can feel him only if we
stretch our arms overhead at once,
our fingers touch.
From above my eyes, I hear
laughing, crying, words not my own.
An echo self? Are there two of me?
No. Not me exactly, but me.
We are a continuous line, a human palindrome,
my twin doing a headstand on my skull
where people imagine light bulbs or dark clouds reside
I have myself again, but not myself.
Has God melded us, or has he never unmelded?
Those dancing mitochondria swaying apart
have never stopped holding hands.
I have been given a word for the voice beyond my sight
and would like to face my brother.
I have never seen him, except at night
when I walk my feet up the crib slats
and he walks his feet up the other side.
If I raise my eyes almost to their lids
I can see—are they his toes?—moving.
And I have no sense of moving them.

CITY

B. Morrison

The corrugated siding
that shimmers in the sun
becomes the rippling sand
under the edge of the water.
The irregular layers
of the housing project
become the cliff's rocky face.
The tenement staircases
zigzag like rail fences,
and the factory windows
line up like rows of corn.
Stubbornly I make nature
from the wild tangle of streets,
see country patterns
in city's obstinate façades.
I'm a survivor,
the thin line
between a dream world
and a reality I can live in,
the persistent imagination,
the refusal to give in.

WANING MOON

Lalita Noronha

Even now I crave that heady sense,
blinding flash of lightning,
drum roll of thunder getting closer.
I have waited long,
buried passion like a sand crab,
my eyes lingering once, only once, too long.
They say time dims the moment
like a falling star you see,
or thought you saw.
Now what's left of love is not the moon
as once we knew,
round and full and pulsing, stars around its face.
Now I'm afraid to look at you,
afraid to let you look at me,
afraid we'll find a waning moon.

THIRTY-TWO YEARS

Lalita Noronha

Throat dry, I crave
half-forgotten moments,
that glass of iced water,
wedge of lemon floating,
a bowl of barley soup,
that cup of mint tea
you brought me
every now and then.
But always,
always at dawn,
I wait for those two cups of coffee,
hot and sweet,
we sipped together,
year after year,
just short of twelve thousand cups
in all.

Four Memories of Fear

Scott Frias

1
I remember being under water,
walking,
eyes pinned to the curves of an inlet that beckoned
like my mother's hands;
walking, because I could not swim,
breathing earth with my feet,
anchored by the will
to do
what I knew.

2
I remember the fierce lonely room
of divorce;
the absent furniture,
the cold, low bed.

3
I remember the row of sleepless cots
when the air war began;
faces staring out pin-holed canvas,
wondering if God filtered down in hair-thin beams,
every eye there
knowing,
or not knowing.

4
I remember sudden waking, the cold electric sweat,
the sharp inward breath,
staring into the night black air crib-ward,
the rise and rush with cadent paces slow
reaching,
feeling her tiny hands
for heat,
and the mouse-breath distance that separates us
from whatever lies beyond this.

Conditional

Scott Frias

the sweat of love. . .
would I could capture the essence of that phrase. . .
the mystery of that word, love confounds binding it in
beads of water, purging heat from our bodies like
confession.
is the father, there on the stand, trying desperately to convince the
judge of his worthiness,
is that the sweat of love?
and what hospital hour is not cursing god's
indiscriminate gestures, not yets, and whys?what love sweats amid
sterile white, there?
is it young, before prom door buttons?

fathers beaming after endless practice
sunk home in a single swing?
all the 'durance of trading a child, a metronome of car doors, 15
years,
begging for some levity from God
finding the casket swinging shut the dead heart. . .
none of your passions' sweat
no muscular pendulant bodies' lust
tears are the sweat of love
ever as miraculous a mother's sternness,
a stranger's art.
love
in droplets,
as pure as the first water.

MEMOIR

FEAR TO FREEDOM: MATURING AS A WRITER

Lauren Beth Eisenberg

A LIFETIME AGO, OR SO IT SEEMS LOOKING BACK AT THE 1970S, I was a young teenager who wanted nothing more than immersion in the arts. Yet, due to a series of complicated and sometimes tragic circumstances, I found myself a student at New York City's prestigious Stuyvesant High School, one of the most elite math and science high schools in the country. And I loved it.

My tenth grade English teacher was a humorless elderly lady with dyed red hair and blue glasses, which we recognized as better than blue hair and red glasses. We read *A Tale of Two Cities* and other classic works, all treated with a trace of boredom. I opted to take creative writing in lieu of standard English the following year. I'd had a long and troubled relationship with writing, but I knew I had a knack for it, and I was hungry for a class with a title that began with the word "creative." Besides, nearly every girl at Stuyvesant—though admittedly few in number—was in love with Mr. McCourt's Irish brogue. That alone was enough incentive to take his class.

Had I any doubts about the role of creativity in Mr. McCourt's class—or about his sense of humor—they were quickly dispelled. Our class, he informed us, would be working on a class project. This project would be similar to a literary magazine, except the stack of stories would be stuffed, unbound, into brown paper lunch bags, and we would celebrate the completion of this project with a potluck picnic in the park across the street from the school. But his message was serious: Life is unfolding around you, providing more raw material than any one person could possibly process. Use it as the basis to weave magic from your words.

On a grey day early in October, Mr. McCourt sat on his desk facing the class. In his lilting accent, he began to read a poem submitted by a student for a recent assignment. The poem was entitled,

"Love Is." Each line was a cutesy phrase that started with the words "Love is." The poem concluded: "Love is merely you."

He put the paper down on the desk beside him and looked out at the class. "We are not in the business of writing greeting cards," he informed us. "Don't write things that are cute or conform to some kind of template."

This episode launched Frank McCourt's explanation of writing with passion: "Find a topic you care about. Tell why you care. Make your audience care. Always maintain the role of the storyteller." He leaned across the desk with an impish smile. "And trust the reader with your feelings."

Whoa. Trust the reader? My rule for writing personal material was simple: Don't share. Worse, I had established a pattern of write and destroy, taking all my writings about my father, who had died, and discarding them down the incinerator chute one at a time. But now I wanted to write again, to see if I could still remember enough about my father to make him real. But my goal was interrupted by a new topic.

THE ALARM CLOCK jolted me awake. I turned on the radio, careful as always not to wake Mom or my sister, half-listening as I dressed in the pre-dawn silence of the apartment. "The headlines at the top of the hour…"

"C'mon," I muttered, "You know I don't care about the news. Just give me the weather forecast."

The newscaster ignored my words. "…Congress established the National Center on Child Abuse and Neglect via the Child Abuse Prevention and Treatment Act, covering four categories of child maltreatment: physical abuse, sexual abuse, emotional abuse, and child neglect including medical neglect—refusal of or delay in seeking health care as a willful act not dictated by poverty or cultural factors." One leg in my dungarees, I dropped onto the bed, staring at the radio in disbelief.

I purchased a copy of the *New York Times* on my walk to the subway station. BILL ON CHILD ABUSE IS SIGNED BY NIXON the headline announced, the text confirming what I suspected from the radio broadcast—medical neglect was now a jailable offense. Through all my untreated injuries since Dad died—the broken bones, the displaced kneecap—I never thought of Mom as abusive. That's just the way things were in our family. Yet now the government had put a name on it and promised to fund sixty million dollars over three years to address the problem. The notion that society needed such an organization frightened me. This act of Congress raised awareness of "shhh—don't tell" family secrets, causing people to wonder what goes on behind closed doors in other people's homes, and the silent few to question the normalcy of dominance relationships in our own troubled families. Long-buried feelings began to erupt, and I wanted to stuff them back in their box where I couldn't see them.

The policeman snaps handcuffs around Mom's wrists. He leads her out the door of our apartment, down the catwalk to the elevators. Neighbors watch from their windows. "Give her back," I scream. "I promise I'll be good if you just let her come back."

Shaken from my dream, I hunched over my desk in the darkness of my bedroom, chin resting on my hands as I watched the second hand snap to each successive tick mark on the clock. I reached into the top drawer, knowing the article was there. I didn't need to read it anymore. I knew what it said. "Liar," I hissed at nobody in particular. I wandered back to bed.

"Mom, my wrist is broken," I plead with her. "Look at my wrist, not my face. I'll paint tears on my cheeks if only it will make a difference. Mom, help me, please. I'm failing all my tests. I can't write. Don't you see?" I sit on a cold metal stool outside Mom's jail cell. Tears of blood spill down my face.

I awoke, shaking. "No more dreams," I whispered to the darkness. "Please, no more dreams."

Every day I bought a newspaper on the way to school, numbly scanning it for what I needed to know and could not bear to see. The articles in the *New York Times* were devastating: a mother and father withheld insulin from their diabetic son, causing his death; a stepfather beat an eighteen-month-old child to death because the little boy refused to sleep in a cardboard box; parents beat their thirteen-month-old son to death after he had been placed in foster care and then returned to his natural parents by court order. Parents were beating their children until they hemorrhaged, neglecting them to starvation. Children were dying at the hands of their own parents. The pain of these children was so real, so tangible. I wanted to gather them up in my arms and make them safe...but I also wanted to hide, not to see or know that such atrocities existed, that they occurred on a regular basis to children, innocents.

I began to write, to tell the story of the battle raging inside of me ever since the newscast about child abuse and neglect, perhaps since the beginning of time. My initial reaction to the newscast was acknowledgement of a dark secret, attaching the words "abuse" and "neglect" to our home life, my sister's and mine. It was both a relief and a shameful stigma, this admission that what we suffered at home was neither normal nor acceptable. Yet, I remained passive and compliant in my relationship with Mom.

Now, seething with silent rage at my mother for years of emotional and medical neglect, I could not forgive myself either, for turning into a person who could speak emotional truth only to a piece of paper. And still, I got up every day, went to school, ate lunch with my friends. I smiled, laughed, nodded and responded at the appropriate times, but I was no longer fully engaged. My mind was measuring myself against newspaper articles. Accounts of children who either died or were unlucky enough to survive and be passed on to foster parents who mistreated them even worse. Children who were hurt and then given back to their real parents because some decision-maker with no understanding of danger thought it safe to throw them back to the wolves.

I suffered alongside the faceless, often nameless, children in the stories, asking myself if I was justified in considering my own life traumatic, knowing that the severity of my home life paled in the shadow of the newspaper children. Yet, in the end it did not matter how egregious by comparison the offenses were—or were not—in my childhood. My reaction to my circumstances, the way in which I hid all my feelings, often from myself as well, spoke volumes for my suffering.

The battle raged on. The wounded warrior continued to spill tears of blood onto the page. *I am strong. I am weak. I weep for the children. I weep for nobody.*

I didn't dare share these writings with anyone, not even Mr. McCourt, skirting the issue with lyrical descriptive pieces or tongue-in-cheek satires that earned Mr. McCourt's approving comments scribbled across the top of the page.

I stood alone in the tiny room in the vestibule near the elevator in our apartment building. Newspapers were piled high in the sink, the stench of everyone else's trash wafting through the enclosure. Drawing a deep breath, I opened the incinerator door, closed my eyes, and dumped all my writings down the chute.

THE SCHOOL YEAR neared completion. Muggy June air infiltrated the classroom. I continued to write—and destroy—my best works.

Mr. McCourt stared at the class, his eyes boring into me, or so I imagined. Abruptly, he turned his back to us, writing two large Fs on the blackboard. The student behind me leaned forward and whispered, "Our grades?" A half-smile teased the corners of Mr. McCourt's lips as he drew an arrow from one F to the other. This, he explained, was his equation for academic success: FEAR to FREEDOM.

I earned excellent grades from Mr. McCourt, but I never mastered his equation. I don't think he ever knew. It never occurred to me that our paths would cross again.

In college, I discovered journalism, and the relief of detached writing. I no longer filled notebook after notebook with my innermost fears, the greatest of which was that people would see the real me—the vulnerable me—on the permanence of the pages.

My writings for English composition classes were articulate and descriptive, but never approached the raw emotion that made me destroy my writings not once, but twice, during my teens. When writing about the 1963 Birmingham, Alabama church bombing for freshman English, I wrote a tender tribute to the four young girls who were murdered. I never mentioned that my interest in historical cases of racial violence stemmed from my own experience as a victim of racial violence in junior high school, an incident in which a metal can opener was used to gouge a gaping hole in the back of my head. My success in protecting my physical writings stemmed from the violation of one of Frank McCourt's writing principles: tell the audience why you care. It was the only way I could make my peace with the written word.

Later on, in 1995, I was a frustrated artist and musician, earning a good living designing and writing software for ballistic missile defense, knowing in my heart of hearts that I was no kind of engineer. To fulfill my creative needs, I embarked on an enormous genealogy study that would end up taking my mind to places I could not imagine. Suddenly, the young girl whose memories were so painful that she repeatedly destroyed the stories describing them had grown into the family memory-keeper.

Immersed in the plight of Eastern European Jews, my eyes shone with a fire that startled my friends and family. But I wanted something more. The research satisfied the academic facets of scholar-artist, but where was the art? The idea of writing a family history book took on a life of its own, the work unraveling like a personal detective story. Vignettes emerged reconstructed from my research, complemented by my journey of discovery. Upon the death of my great-grandfather, my great-grandmother supposedly proclaimed to the assembled mourners, "Our family is like a book. One of the covers has been torn off. Don't let the pages scatter like leaves in the autumn wind."

"*Autumn Leaves*," I answered, in response to everyone's queries regarding the name of my book-in-progress. It was *beshert*, Yiddish for "meant to be."

Four hundred pages conveyed my sadness at the terribly difficult life of my ancestors in nineteenth century Russian Poland: infant mortality often claiming half or more of the children in a family; the harsh fact that most children never knew their grandparents; the frequent marriages of young girls to middle-aged widowers they had never met; the persistent feeling that they merely existed, trudging from one day to the next without any real pleasure, praying to awaken the next morning to find all their children still alive. This story honored the great vision of my ancestors who were bold enough to put the religious persecution of Eastern Europe behind them and build new lives for themselves, and those who paid the ultimate sacrifice at Hitler's hand.

But the emotional payload of my search spilled into the writing, and I found myself naked on the permanence of the pages. The familiar fear returned. I didn't want others to see that part of me. How could a topic such as a family history grow so far beyond a sterile retelling of who-what-where-when without me even noticing, without me being able to corral it and define its proper boundaries?

I rewrote *Autumn Leaves*, sanitizing it, giving it more distance, making it safe for public consumption. The revised book told my family background from the perspective of nobody in particular. My ancestors were just people on paper. The Holocaust was merely an event in history.

"Tell the audience why you care," Frank McCourt had taught us at Stuyvesant, a lesson that had stayed with me, dormant. More than twenty years ago, long before his Pulitzer Prize-winning memoir *Angela's Ashes*, Mr. McCourt instilled in me a love of writing that lingered through adulthood, and the promise of what I could achieve with the written word if only I could conquer my fears. Reverting to the original *Autumn Leaves*, I sent the manuscript to Frank McCourt's address listed in the New York City phone book, receiving in return the ultimate praise from the ultimate master. "I am in awe of your achievement," he wrote me. "The book is massive: scholarly, intriguing, passionate."

I sent *Autumn Leaves* to a bookbinder for private publication, bound in a hardback cover bearing a drawing I designed myself. It was the first artwork I had done since...I could not remember. I fell in love with *Autumn Leaves* over and over again, my magnum opus, my one true writing success. I bared my soul, but I did not destroy my work, and I was not hurt by it.

Frank McCourt autographed my copy of *Angela's Ashes*, mailing it back to me inscribed with the following words: "With respect, admiration and affection for a scholar and a sublime human being." We exchanged several letters in the years that followed. He told me that he toured a great deal, speaking to various groups, giving readings from his book, but always the little voice in his head kept saying, "Get back to work!"

Then a family crisis drove me out of the leisurely pleasure of personal correspondence, and, in fact, all writing. I continued to follow Frank McCourt's writing career. I read *'Tis*, and recognized the Stuyvesant of my youth in certain passages of the book. But my own pen was silent.

Six years later, when the dust of my divorce had settled, I knew it was time to finally address what I had learned in creative writing class all those years ago: Frank McCourt's motto, FEAR to FREEDOM. I had told my family's tale; now I needed to tell mine.

Once again, I began to write. The story spilled from me nearly unbidden. I was unable to turn off the words. Sometimes I wrote because it felt good to write, and sometimes I wrote because it felt bad not to write. The book began as a catharsis and turned into a self-inflicted wound. The writing was easy. The thinking was terrifying. I had opened Pandora's Box. My life lay scattered about me in broken pieces and I needed to put them back together.

Where was this freedom Frank McCourt spoke about?

I wrote to my old teacher: "In the past year, I have re-entered the realm of personal writing following a six year hiatus, during which the bulk of my personal research and writings were lost in a family crisis. My return to writing has been both painful and liberating. You played a significant role in my development as a writer; an undercurrent of my story is my difficult—passionate and heartbreaking—relationship with writing over the years. Thank you for always being an inspiration to me in my writing, through the memory of your teaching and through your own wonderful books."

My memoir continues to grow and change, and I along with it, progressing beyond the quote from *Angela's Ashes* that reads, "The happy childhood is hardly worth your while," to the quote from *Teacher Man* that reads, "Sing your song, dance your dance, tell your tale." Frank McCourt is a character in my book as much as writing itself is a character in my book. I have followed his advice to the best of my ability. Choose a topic you care about. Tell why you care. Make your audience care. Always maintain the role of the storyteller. And trust the reader with your feelings.

In an interview with the *Stuyvesant Standard*, Frank McCourt likened writing to a wayward child; no matter how many stories you tell, some remain so private they require containment—or at least an attempt to contain them. I know what he means. Still, I've learned that you can close Pandora's Box and seal it, but the contents escape the box, like tiny daggers. Bending down, I pick one up, gingerly turning it over in my hands, examining it from different angles, nicking my skin in a few places. I set this shard back in the box, not bothering to seal it anymore. Soapy water washes away the blood. I apply Band-Aids as necessary, and walk away.

PROBABLE CAUSE

Sherry Bosley

I FEAR THAT SOMEWHERE ON THE EASTERN SHORE OF MARYLAND, there's a man to whom I owe an apology. His stepdaughter was murdered and there's a possibility that I allowed the killer to get away free.

In February, with eight years on the job, I was given five cases that were considered stalled, stale, and the other unspoken word—unsolvable. Instead of leaving them in the file drawers with "No additional information developed" tag lines for local news hounds to shuffle through during the freedom of information forage, the local Maryland State Police barracks commander gave them to me so he could advise inquiring minds that the cases were instead "under review by headquarters."

Reconstructing crimes after years of dormant activity is one of the most difficult tasks an investigator can take on. Reading mounds of reports and witness statements is compounded by reviewing crime scene photographs that might have been taken with instamatics or disposable cameras if a department does not have a forensics team. Often investigative reports are written by officers in small municipalities who, too often, have been transferred, or worse, have left the job.

My first case was actually clear to the original investigators—the suspect was the husband but there was no evidence. Seven years had added a few girlfriends who were willing to offer some insight into his abusive nature and a fresh team of interviewers finally got a break. My second case was the basic "Follow the Money" trail—the money had recently run out and the suspect had started another scam to lure a victim—luckily we got there first.

My third case was the one that haunts me. It was that of a raped and murdered child.

Tamara Wise was fourteen years old when her partially clad

body was discovered in a wooded area near the Sassafras River in Galena, on Maryland's Eastern Shore. She had failed to come home from school on a day when her family was moving from a house in Sullivan Park to a house on Main Street. She had walked to school that morning and was to ride the bus home, for the first time, in the afternoon. Initially her mother thought Tammy had forgotten and gone back to the old house. After looking for her in the small residential area for several hours, she suspected her daughter must have run away.

Anything else was unimaginable.

But like so many of the nightmares that occur even when the lights are on, the unimaginable was captured on 35mm stills. When her body was found two weeks later—twisted and matted with dead brown leaves, a balled-up sock stuffed behind tape that had silenced her probable pleas for mercy—her mother knew only that Tammy had not been able to outrun whatever monster had chased her.

The case file bulged with photos, haunting in their Crime Lab starkness. A small pack of the lead investigator's color instamatic photos were also rubber-banded together, but the colors seemed to have drained and faded, making them appear like amateur watercolored copies.

Looking at any old case requires an investigator to gain perspective. This isn't a trained skill so much as a logical process of separating detail from fact and circumstance. For me, what immediately stood out were her panties.

In the locals' photographs, the "first on the scene" photographs, six frames had her striped bikini underwear—her only clothing—below her knees, and then six frames showed the panties nearer to her waist. The black and white crime lab photos had her panties in the position of the second set of the local photos, with lividity clearly evident on her right side.

I called our MSP barrack in Centreville to obtain background on the local investigators and to get a global perspective of the case itself. I like to make my first contact over the phone because it tends to bring out the "feet propped up on the desk" type of answers, and that was what I got.

"Oh, yeah. Sam Edward's stepdaughter. That was a hell of a thing. There are still some reward posters left at some of the legions and halls around town. So, what are you going to do with all of that paperwork they shipped up to the Puzzle Palace?"

I gave the conciliatory chuckle and asked if he had been on the scene.

"I was down there. Hell, you know how that goes in a small town. Everyone has their scanner on and there was a run to get down to the river. As soon as the call came out that a body had been found we all knew who it was." He paused and I imagined him leaning back in one of those old oak office chairs they seemed to hoard on the shore. "Damn hard to see a little girl like that. Just turns your stomach that some son-of-a-bitch would hurt a kid that way."

I took my eyes from the photos. "Do you remember anything about the clothes?"

"Her clothes were found by a pile of tree limbs…as I recall they told us her underwear was half-off when they found her, and they took photographs of that, but then they had everyone coming out there, the family and all, so they pulled them up a bit. I think that's how it was. Not something that might happen in the city there but it would here. Anyway that was Harold Bain's decision, but I might have done the same. He left the town PD but I think someone told me he's with Newark now, if you want me to try to get you a number."

I told him that would be helpful and shuffled through some of the photos I still had on my desk until I came to the ones of her clothing, stacked among the leaves and logs. "It just seems odd that after moving her body the killer would attempt to put her underwear back on," I said.

"Well, the sick bastard probably wanted to cover up what he had done to her. Probably hoped no one would find her for a while."

I uh-huhed my acceptance of his theory and didn't voice my doubts. If the killer had really wanted to hide the crime he could have buried the body or covered it with readily available leaves and branches, which would certainly have prolonged the discovery. I hung up after telling him I would stop by his office when I went down to look at the area in a few days.

The case file had extensive background reports on the victim. There were two points that seemed pivotal. The first was that Tamara had signed out of school ten minutes early that day, though she had not mentioned that she would be doing so to her friends or her mother. Those ten minutes were the key to her death.

The second point was that she was excited to have her two best friends come to see the new house after dinner. They were both adamant about this fact. She'd invited them to help her put away her clothes and hang posters in the new vaulted bedroom. If true, this would indicate that whatever was connected to the ten minute early departure was not perceived as detaining or dangerous to Tamara.

ONE PROBLEM WITH cold cases is that even the dust has been swept away by the time I get them. Some things never change, however, such as the quality of school lunches and the punctuality of the end of the school day. With this in mind, the high school was my first stop when I made my first trip to Galena.

The school parking lot was filled with pick-up trucks, Mustangs, and a few late model Chevys—cars manufactured after Tamara Wise died. The buses lined the sidewalk like bright chalk marks on a blackboard. I glanced at my watch. Two o'clock. Fifteen minutes before dismissal. Five minutes before Tamara Wise walked out of the front entrance, supposedly.

I watched a few students exit the school, weaving between buses to walk to the student parking lot. A parent emerged carrying a backpack, but without a child beside her, walked to the street and disappeared into a large black SUV with tinted windows. A blue-jeaned boy walked between the buses to the street in front of the school, where a tan Dodge Caravan waited to ferry him off. The bell rang as the SUV and Caravan pulled from the curb and kids swarmed from the school like bees leaving a bothered nest.

Perhaps it was the expression on the Caravan mother's face as she glanced at the chaos behind her—a look of relief that she was ahead of the train of yellow that would soon be pulling out onto the roadways—that brought an image of Tamara to my mind. Shiny brown hair swinging across her shoulders as she scooted through the line of buses, across the grass to someone waiting. Someone who also didn't want to be caught up in the dismissal traffic? Someone who waited outside the boundaries of safety for his prey to come to him? Interviews had produced no eyewitnesses to Tamara leaving school that day but it seemed probable that, as I had just witnessed, most would have been focused on their own plan of escape.

TAMARA'S MOTHER HAD remarried after the death of Tamara's father. Both the mother and stepfather were with at least eight friends, assisting with the move, on the afternoon that Tamara disappeared.

Stephanie Edwards was a small woman with the kind of skin you see on L'Oreal ads in magazines. I had expected lines to have been engraved along her eyes and lips, lines deepened by years of waiting, and watching, and wondering. But I was wrong. Her smooth features were broken only by the greenness of her eyes—a hard, clear green, like those Chatham emeralds manufactured in some remote laboratory.

I had come to Galena with some facts and a theory. The killer had murdered Tamara in a brutal but telling manner, stacking her clothes in a neat pile. Profilers have confirmed that this typically means the killer knows and cares about the victim. The killer also took the victim to a remote location where there was little possibility of detection; still, he gagged her, possibly indicating that her cries and screams would be very disturbing to him. He had kept her alive for a period of time and did not act in any apparent haste. The killer had also attempted to put the underwear back on the body, again a clear indication of concern for her dignity upon detection. These facts seemed to indicate that the killer may have loved the victim or would suffer emotionally upon discovery of her death.

"It's been such a long time. It seems like a dream sometimes." Mrs. Edwards looked into the living room through the kitchen doorway at a row of pictures on a bookcase by the window. "Sometimes I take her picture and hold it in my hand for a while because she seems like a dream I had. Like the other house was never real…I don't know. She never lived here, not even one night. Don't that seem odd?"

I nodded, letting her talk, noting the firmness of her voice, the steadiness of her hand as she raised the Corelle mug to her mouth.

"Seems like it's just God's will or something, the way it all happened."

I struggled not to vocalize my skepticism that God had

partaken in what I had witnessed through the still shots hanging across my desk in Jessup.

"Mrs. Edwards, I know this is difficult for you. I know that you have been through this many times before and have probably thought about this every day since it happened, but has there ever been *anyone* that you thought might have done this to your daughter?"

"No." She spoke sharply as she stood and turned her green vision away. "I can't imagine anyone I know that would do such....I have told myself the only thing that makes sense. It must have been a stranger, someone who moved on."

She turned to face me and leaned back against the front of the counter that was lined with little canister houses holding sugar and flour. "What can we make from it now? It's done and over and we can't change it. Nothing—nothing can bring her back."

There was a slight break in her voice, or maybe just a pause. I balanced her words with the fact that there was no bleakness to her eyes.

TAMARA'S ROOM HAD remained boxed and unassembled at the new house until her body had been discovered, and then the grocery cartons had been confiscated and taken to the lab for processing. I wanted to see her diary, read the words she had actually written prior to her death, listen for the voice that had been quieted. I found the right carton in the Property Held room at Headquarters and obtained the small volume after completing the chain of custody log.

The last entry was made four days before her death.

I know the new house is going to be nice but I will miss it here. I can still remember Daddy here. He made the bookshelf and we have to leave it 'cause it's nailed to the wall and the new people say that means it is built-in.

The other entries seemed uneventful. There were no coded initials, no mention of boyfriends, or enemies; a seemingly typical reflection of a young girl's life.

I spent six hours reading and re-reading the diary. Someone who knew her and "loved" her had killed her. She may have written about that person. I skimmed the pages, trying to find something that was one or two bumps above the line for an ordinary teenage girl. Then I found it.

Four months prior to Tamara's disappearance she had written:

Uncle Bill took us to the movies today since mom and Sam are still at the beach. Sometimes I hate to hear all of those people chewing popcorn in the dark—it sounds like bugs munching cornstalks and it gets on my nerves. Mandy couldn't stay over last night because it was her mom's birthday.

I remembered being annoyed with a date once and having that same feeling, as if being with a complete moron increased the sound of chewing. So was Tamara annoyed because her friend couldn't stay over, annoyed at the movie choice, or annoyed with Uncle Bill? Was the slope in the written word "Uncle" translated as sarcasm? Did the absence of the mention of a boy, whether real, or longed for, seem unusual in such a regular life? Didn't girls still pine over the boys they didn't have with as much passion as the ones they did?

"Uncle Bill" was now thirty-eight-year-old William Gallion, Stephanie Edwards's younger brother. He had been interviewed two days after her body was found, which resulted in a one-paragraph statement on a CIR form that read: "Gallion had not talked to his niece for several weeks prior to her death and was not aware of her habits or plans. Subject could not offer any information to further the investigation of this case."

I thumbed through the main case file box for the information that hummed in my memory. One of the other investigators had tried to retrace Tamara's life the week before her disappearance. Two days prior to the move, the family had gone out to dinner at a local eatery with "friends and Bill Gallion because the kitchen was packed up." Surely, Bill wouldn't have forgotten the last night he had seen his niece alive, merely two days before her death? Even with the body being discovered two weeks later those were not the details people tended to get mixed up. Relatives always relive those last moments and wonder if there was any sign, a premonition of the tragedy to come.

He agreed to meet me without asking any questions other than where.

Gallion looked smaller than he actually was, a fact I quickly attributed to his hands, which were soft and thin with rounded fingers that gave the impression that they rarely curved around anything other than a coffee mug or a bottle of Rolling Rock beer.

He opened the conversation, which only confirmed that he never played chess or watched old Perry Mason reruns.

"Steph told me you had been hired to dig all this up again."

He fingered the napkin under his coffee spoon and stared out the window of the local diner where we'd agreed to meet.

"Mr. Gallion, it is always a comfort to the families of murder victims to know that their cases are never *really* closed, that they remain open until the day they are solved. This is just part of the process. The case has now been referred to the Intelligence Division where we are reviewing all the documents, reports, and looking for areas that may have been overlooked, or need additional pursuit. And," I paused here for a moment longer than really necessary, "cases like this are my job and my team has a very high clearance rate."

One of the good things about my job was that at this point in the investigation it was hard to muddy the waters. I decided to toss a few rocks in the pond and see what floated to the surface. I opened my notebook and skimmed a page of notes.

"So, you used to pick Tamara up from the school on occasion."

"No." He frowned at the coffee cup and flicked a quick look at me and then returned his gaze to the silver stirrer. "I can't remember ever doing that."

It was all a gamble at this point. If I pushed too far, too soon, he could retreat behind the protection of a lawyer's letterhead, and if I backed away, I could miss the only opportunity of getting information while he was not prepared.

Of course, it was also possible that I was completely wrong about the order in which I had arranged my suspect list.

"One of the benefits of going back to a case after a period of time is that witnesses," I emphasized the word for him and caught the quick cessation of his hand, "often remember things they might have previously discarded as a useless bit of information. And sometimes, months later, a few people will be sitting around talking and someone will say something that will jar a memory."

I looked down at the spiral pad again, knowing Gallion's attention would be drawn to it also. I had gathered from the MVA records the make, model, and registration information of the vehicle that he'd owned at the time Tamara had disappeared.

"That's what happened here actually. One of the mothers of a classmate remembered seeing your van at school sometime during the week that Tamara disappeared. In fact, no one ever saw anyone other than you pick her up from school, since she could walk the few blocks to her old house."

"That was a week before she passed on." Bill looked even smaller then, his body sat deep into the red vinyl seat, his face flushed to a coordinating color that my grandmother would have called persimmon. He held my gaze this time until I broke it, and I broke it slowly, knowing he could sense the hardness that had settled into my core.

So much changed in that one blip of a second. Neither of us said anything for a moment. We didn't have to. It was as if each of us had to return to our corners to wait for the sound of the bell. What I knew in that second was intangible; it couldn't be taught in a criminal justice class or used to obtain a search warrant, but it was true nevertheless.

I was sitting across from the killer, and he knew that I recognized him.

My advantage was that, though I had little to go on, he didn't know how much I could or couldn't prove. His advantage was the same: I didn't have much and I could prove even less.

It was diction really. "Before she passed on," he'd said. Surely the choice wording of every killer who blames the death of his victim on her inability to do what he required her to do to prevent death. In his mind, he was guiltless, since the victim probably continued to scream while tortured and he was forced to shove her sock down her throat to shut her up. Yes, the victim had "passed on," not been "murdered" or "killed"—a murderer's passive choice of verbs.

And I had the confession of the eyes. The one brief instant when his eyes affirmed what might be impossible to ever prove, and mine had responded with words that would never be permitted in an open court room but translated to any equivalent of: *You worthless piece of shit.*

We sat for a moment longer before I took control again and closed the notebook with as much snap as possible for a slim piece of cardboard and 86 sheets of lined paper.

"She wasn't like everyone thought. She had a lot of problems, and I tried to help her without hurting my sister." It could have been the beginning of a confession, and I guess he must have thought so also because he added quickly, "She didn't want to move, although she really liked her stepdad. I...I was just trying to help her adjust a little. I don't think any of that is connected to, you know, what happened."

I thought about her stepfather, the one person who seemed to truly grieve for a girl he had embraced and accepted as his own daughter. I didn't meet him until five years after the incident, but I doubted he'd had that grey haze over his skin before grief and bitterness entered his life. He had struggled to talk, as if his throat was permanently dry, and his eyes had a watery coating like he was over a hundred years old. He had closed them briefly when I asked, carefully, if he had any suspicions about who had contributed to Tamara's death. Wrinkles seemed to have formed across the faded blue surfaces as he answered, "Maybe we all did. Maybe we all did."

I wouldn't accept what Gallion said at face value so I decided to stop with the pebbles and drop a boulder in the water.

"Do you think the weekend you babysat your niece for your sister contributed to her 'passing on'?"

I had the satisfaction of seeing the color drain from his face, but neither of us said a word after that. It was as if we acknowledged the rules of the game and the parts we were playing. After he left, I sat in the booth for while, pouring coffee without cream; I was too tired to even taste the dark brew at my lips.

It was the part of the job that I liked the least, when you had to sit back and be realistic about the facts and the odds. Legally I had nothing to take to the State's Attorney. And there wasn't a high probability of obtaining any hard evidence. There were no eyewitnesses. The weather had erased whatever physical evidence there was in the two weeks Tamara's body had merged with the elements. There was no semen for DNA.

We had to be "creative" in the investigative process.

Interviews would start in town where investigators from the Centreville barracks would ask people specifically if they had seen a van matching Gallion's on the day that Tamara Wise disappeared. This would spark conversation in town and might turn up some information. It would definitely make life a bit uncomfortable for Gallion.

A FEW DAYS after his interview, I made the two-hour drive to Bill Gallion's house. Investigators from the barracks had started interviewing a few people close to Tammy and asking what they knew about her relationship with her uncle. Those simple words, her relationship with her uncle, had taken about six hours to reach Stephanie Edwards, and it had taken her about two seconds to call my office and leave a scorching, venomous message on my voice mail.

Now it was four in the morning as I drove past a hundred deer crossing signs without really noticing if they proffered the truth. Although I tried to keep an open mind, I was personally making an early morning trash run on Gallion's house. In 1995, personal shredders were not so commonplace and people felt comfortable discarding anything and everything in the garbage, even when they knew the police were "looking at them." I released a sigh when I saw Gallion's Rubbermaid trashcans at the side of the driveway.

Later, I dumped the garbage on a plastic sheet on the floor of my attic office. With rubber gloves I sorted Dinty Moore Beef Stew containers, Campbell's Soup cans, and Swanson Hearty Dinner cartons from a week's worth of mail. Gallion seemed to be on the same junk mail list that I was on, although he had a few additions.

There were out-of-date issues of *Children's World* and *Wooden Soldier*, mail order catalogues for children's clothing. The kids in the ads ranged from infants to young teenage girls, with numerous pages featuring elaborate, yet innocent, underwear layouts with models wearing mostly white, little bows here and there.

A Limited Too catalogue featured all teen models and was from the previous winter's sales. Gallion seemed to have been house-cleaning. Pages eleven and twelve were stuck together with a substance that had hardened and looked a bit like watered down Elmer's glue. I sank back on the vinyl floor with an odd mixture of relief and revulsion. Unless Gallion had a car model hobby I suspected the crime lab might be able to give me the probable cause I needed for a search warrant.

That afternoon at three o'clock I called Gallion's house,

knowing he was still at work, so I could leave a message on his answering machine. I wanted him to have something to mull over, to listen to a few times, to perhaps work up a sweat about over the weekend.

"Mr. Gallion, there have been some developments in the case and we need to see you at Centreville barracks first thing Monday morning. I'll expect to see you at nine A.M. If there is a problem with that…" I paused a moment in my monologue for effect. "I can have someone come out to pick you up."

I took the weekend off, comfortable in the knowledge that the Investigation Division was watching Gallion's movements over the weekend and not being too covert about it, either. While we were doing a State version of good-cop/bad-cop on Monday, there would be a search warrant on the rancher.

THE PARKING LOT was as deserted as court day when I arrived Monday morning.

Marty didn't make me suffer long.

"Gallion's dead. A fatal early this morning on Route 301. He pulled in front of a tractor trailer with a preliminary guesstimate blood alcohol level of .28."

I sank onto the padded chair that was reserved for trooper applicants.

"Was he just drunk, or did he do it on purpose?"

Marty sighed and rolled his chair back a few inches. "I almost called you, but I figured you'd race down here like a bat-out-of-hell and I'd have another fatal." He picked up an empty coffee cup and then sat it back down. "Just like everything else, we're not sure about anything. Hamilton was on him last night—he wasn't driving erratic but he'd been in the bar for a couple of hours. Hamilton said he slowed at the intersection for a minute, and then gunned it. He could have timed it just right, or else been too drunk to know what he was doing."

For a moment I felt like I had been hit in the chest with a .357 slug while wearing my body armour; there would be no blood, but a lot of bruising.

"Are they still serving the warrant?"

"Yeah, they're there now." He paused, "I figured we'd go out there and see if anything turns up."

THE HOUSE WAS neater than I expected. The kitchen shelves were filled with old Tupperware containers that stored cereal and flour and other staples that were not so easily identified. Other than a small TV, the only entertainment piece was a new Dell computer on a desk in the master bedroom. The hard-drive would be dissected at the Crime Lab and Gallion's online history would eventually be mapped out.

There were some magazines in the bedroom similar to what I had expected, and a few that I didn't know existed, or maybe I just hoped didn't. Some of the foreign issues contained English tag lines for Young Love and Tender Buds. There were kids in them that appeared to be as young as seven, but most were just entering puberty.

I went back to the kitchen and looked through what appeared to be several days of unopened mail. There was an empty envelope with Stephanie Edwards's return address in the left corner.

The living room looked like the least used room in the house. My attention was drawn however, to the only personal photo in the room. It was a photograph of Tamara Wise, wearing a red sweater, a tiny pearl necklace, and a soft smile that spread from her near-perfect teeth to her clear, bright eyes.

The framed picture was one of two items in the room that didn't have a thin coat of dust covering them. A small rosary with worn, cold stones sat next to the portrait. I picked it up for a moment and ran the beads through my fingers.

Bless me father, for I have sinned.

As we were leaving, Sam Edwards pulled his commercial truck next to Marty's unmarked patrol car. He sat in the open window, looking at his brother-in law's house, before turning to me.

"So. Is the case still open?"

I swallowed, but met his gaze steadily.

"Yes. Murder cases remain open until they're solved. We might get a break," I looked back at the house, "but I'm not sure it will be enough."

He nodded his head in a motion that suggested there was pain somewhere in his body, and then nodded again in a manner that I'd seen in men who were given a life sentence. Then he turned and drove up to the house. A few days later, Marty sent me a copy of the obituary from the local paper. William Gallion had been buried next to his niece at St. Luke's cemetery, free from earthly prosecution and pardoned for his sins for eternity.

Two YEARS AFTER Gallion's death, I was doing some background work on a money laundering case near Galena and I stopped by the cemetery on my way back north. Although I had removed the crime photos from my office, I could not forget the face of the young girl with the trusting smile. Both graves were decorated with identical plastic flower arrangements, which I speculated came from Stephanie, mother and sister. I stood at the base of Tamara's grave and sent a silent prayer for peace sewn with a thread of apology. As I looked down, I noticed the spot where I stood was worn just a bit, unlike the ground at the next grave—someone stood at this spot often.

I imagined that perhaps in another five or ten years, another investigator might pick up the case and try to find some resolution. He would interview the mother who wanted to keep a dream more than she wanted to find the truth. He would interview the stepfather who was left to grieve, seemingly alone, in the maze of denials and wanting to forgets.

I said a silent prayer for all that had been lost and aloud a verse from an Emerson poem I almost remembered.

I left a single yellow rose near the bare spot at the bottom of the grave.

The names, locations, and circumstances have been changed to protect the innocent, and unfortunately, the guilty.

SAYING THANK YOU

Chris Bancells

I EXPECTED A LOT OF THINGS WHEN I WENT TO COOPERSTOWN, New York for the Hall of Fame induction of Tony Gwynn and Cal Ripken, Jr. I expected to tour the Baseball Hall of Fame. I expected to get lost among tens of thousands of Baltimore fans with orange eights emblazoned across their bodies. I expected at least a few San Diego fans to show up. I expected to meet, or at least see, a handful of baseball legends all gathered together. What I remember the most, though, was the one thing I never expected to see.

When I went to Cooperstown, I certainly did not expect to see my dad cry.

For more than two decades now, my dad has been an athletic trainer for the Baltimore Orioles, and that gave me a childhood that most kids would kill to have lived. Shoot, after what I saw in Cooperstown, I think there are plenty of adults who would have done a lot more than that for the chance to trade lives. In the day to day, however, it wasn't nearly as glamorous as it might sound. We lived in a modest suburban house and, thanks to the nature of a baseball schedule, I spent more time talking to my dad through a phone line than across the dinner table. I never begrudged him that, though, because his job also meant I got to spend endless hours at the ballpark and in the clubhouse, hanging out with him and the players he treated. Of all the ankles he taped, the most constant, the most influential, and, later, simply the most important belonged to Cal.

My first memory of Cal is that of height. Six-foot-four is tall by any standard, but when you're three years old he might as well be a giant. That's appropriate, I suppose, given the role he would go on to play for the Orioles and the sport. To me though, he was just Cal, or "Junior" since his dad was still around. Cal was my dad's friend who was always in the training room and who would sometimes, after games, take me to his locker and sit me in a trash bag full of popcorn. I was completely clueless about where this would all lead.

As I got older and went to school, I started to gather that the way I was growing up wasn't exactly the norm. None of my friends could go to the store and buy cardboard pictures of their dad's coworkers, for instance. I didn't talk about it a whole lot, never bragged about what I had done over the weekend at the ballpark, because it wasn't the way I was raised. My dad preached humility and hard work. He told me that, yes, he had a cool job with famous people, but it was still a job and they were still people with lives and feelings. To my growing eyes, Cal was the embodiment of everything my dad was telling me. Watching the two of them I saw reality in what is all too often an unreal situation. They came to work every day, always trying to be better, but never taking it for granted. That was the life I came to understand, came to believe in, by growing up with two men I respected, two men who were my heroes.

So when it came time for Cal to be inducted, as the whole baseball world knew he would, I fully expected my parents to get invited to the ceremony. I thought my wife and I, and maybe my two younger siblings, might tag along, find a room somewhere and watch from a distance. Apparently, my plans had been made for me. When the invitation came, all of our names were on it; we were all going.

In retrospect, there was no other way for Cal's induction to play out; it was always going to be one of the biggest moments in Orioles history. The Hall of Fame is only about a six hour drive from Baltimore and, let's face it, there hasn't been much for O's fans to get excited about these past few years. Even knowing all of that, I wasn't prepared for the orange and black fervor that was turned north in the last week of July 2007. I suppose six Ripkenless years of watching the Os struggle in vain to reach the .500 mark left people hungry for a reason to cheer. Even those who had given up following the team turned out with well-loved shirts bought during better times in Charm City.

That Sunday afternoon was one of those times you can feel history being made, when it seems like the whole world has paused to take notice. Tony Gwynn spoke well of those who helped him in his twenty-year career with the San Diego Padres and brought home that it wasn't talent but diligence that carried him to the Hall. He was honest and forthright and everything I had come to expect, from both him and Cal. But when Cal took the podium you could feel the whole crowd shift and sit up a little taller.

It wasn't just that the crowd was mostly Orioles fans. Cal had saved baseball. After the players went on strike in 1994, canceling the World Series, it was the drama of watching Cal break Lou Gehrig's consecutive game streak the following year that helped fans get over their sense of betrayal. For the people watching, for the people of Baltimore, Cal's induction had been looked forward to as a moment as certain as breathing, and it was not disappointing.

Cal spoke eloquently and elegantly about the people, game and city he had given his life to. The passion with which he talked about and to his family was tangible, working its way into even the most professional hearts watching. One of the classiest moments in the speech was when he thanked and saluted the fans, raising them to his level. He pointed to The Streak, saying, "I always looked at it as just showing up for work every day. As I look out on this audience, I see thousands of people who do the same, teachers, police officers, mothers, fathers, business people, and many others."

That's why people love him. That's why there can be no better hero in a blue-collar town like Baltimore. He accomplished something that had never been done before, never approached by any of his peers, and he took the greatness of that and draped it across the shoulders of everyone there. Nobility like that is an achievement in and of itself.

It was just after this that it happened. What had been a powerful and moving speech suddenly also became personal for me, my family, and my dad.

It was a simple thing to do, saying, "Thank you." Under the circumstances, though, it was positively heart-stopping. In one short sentence, Cal acknowledged twenty years of plane rides, taped ankles, ice bags, and inside jokes. He made my dad, and all athletic trainers for that matter, relevant to all those people who only had eyes for "8." It was a tip of the cap to every person behind the stadium scenes and a way of saying that if the Iron Man needs help, we all do. Other men might have wanted more, but in Cal's voice and in the tears that his words brought to my dad's eyes, I understood that what had passed between them, what I had seen during all those hours in the training room, could never be summed up with words. It could only have been said the way it was: simply and with heart.

We didn't get to talk to Cal before we left Cooperstown. He was swept away with Tony for more press conferences and handshakes. That was probably just as well, since I think we were all overwhelmed by the entire event. The speech has become a moment in time, like so many others I have gathered, that I will never forget. Day to day I forget countless things—dates, times, directions—but now I'm beginning to wonder if that isn't so I will always have space for the big moments, moments for which I will always be grateful.

If we had gotten the chance to talk to Cal afterwards, I would have wanted to say more than just two words. I would have tried to explain what I thought it meant to Baltimore that he had always been honest and hard working. I would have searched for a way to explain what it meant for me to have grown up knowing him, and how he and my Dad had shaped me into who I am. Had I gotten to talk to him, though, I have a feeling none of those thoughts would have found their way into words, and I would have been left simply saying, "Thank you."

HALF-CROWN

Al Karasa

B RIAN, MY RACE DRIVING COACH FOR THE DAY, IS SITTING in my car, behind the wheel, checking out the fit before he drives it. It's track time.

"Is that a foreign coin?" he asks, pointing at the half-crown inserted in the steering wheel hub.

"Yeah. It's a half-crown. British. 1950."

Remembering my grey hair, I wonder if he thinks that was the year of my first car. It wasn't. The significance of the half-crown is a little more vague than that.

Father always supported my ventures and never, so far as I remember, discouraged me in anything I set out to explore even when he must certainly have thought me to be foolish. He might have brought facts to my attention, but criticism usually stopped there. I know now that when it was given, his criticism was a gift. But one of his most memorable gifts to me was his acknowledge-ment of my erstwhile fear of horses and a later acceptance of my love of cars.

I may have been four. Whether it was my birthday or some other occasion, I now don't recall, but he presented me with a beau-tiful black and chestnut rocking horse of at least eight hands, a full two hands taller than I. No hobbyhorse, this was rounded and carved in exquisite hardwood, with a mane of real horsehair, a tasseled tail, and a fine leather saddle. It was big. It was magnificent.

He lifted me into the saddle...and it moved! I had never seen the world from such a lofty vantage point. It was scary. The whole room rocked! A sudden realization struck me like a ton of bricks: I'm gonna fall off! FALL OFF! Learn to ride it? Get on and off without help? By myself? Not on your life!

Subsequent tries to coerce me to mount my spirited steed were to no avail. There was naught to be done save returning it from whence it came. What disappointment my father might have suffered escapes me, but the relief I felt when at last it was gone still dwells in the treasure trove of childhood memories. What replaced that beautiful wooden horse, however, lives with me today in hard substance. What replaced it was a car.

Modeled after road racers of the time, it had open wheels with real rubber tires, low cut sides with no doors, a small, racecar type windscreen, a fine wood steering wheel, and power delivered to rear wheels via belts and rotating pedals. It had no brakes. But no matter, there were no hills. My father had not yet owned a car, and here I was with mine. That was something! Silver-grey paint sparkled like ice in the living room lights. I sat in the seat where he had tied a small cushion. I couldn't wait till tomorrow. Couldn't wait to get it outside and try it.

Paved walkways, meandering among my mother's flowerbeds and family orchards, were the "roads" that tested my skill behind the wheel of my magnificent new toy. No...this was better than that. This was no toy. This was a sports car! A racing car! Meant to go FAST! Even at age four, I knew that. The walkways and pedal power only went so far. But the street, just there behind the fence, now that was different.

The hill was short, but it was steep. I didn't know what would happen, but I had to find out. And find out I did. The wind of speed brought tears to my eyes. Pedals spun faster than my feet could follow. My shins were black and blue long before the car stopped. And it stopped of its own accord, brakes or no brakes.

I was elated. My inner smile did not fade until I had pushed my new racecar all the way back up the hill. But I had been seen. Never again was I to repeat this adventure on the threat of losing my magnificent new toy.

A half century later, and again I have a silver-grey sports car. It's bigger, with doors and fenders, even brakes! Brian turns the key and we're greeted with an angry snarl. A bark rasps out the cold exhaust. Brian smiles. He likes the sound. He plays the throttle gently, warming up the now awakened silver screamer.

The butterflies are there, but I feel no fear. I've done this many times.

In a minute we are flying down the first straight, his expert touch just letting the car have its head before control is lost in Turn One, but not enough for that to happen. The next one is a right turn, downhill and very fast, before the slow and cumbersome Turn Three is there to greet us. Brakes glow red with heat here, but keep us on track for the long straight following and its exhilarating speed. This one is uphill and the car earns its keep. The engine sings!

We smile and take the pleasure the car gives. It's the reward for driving well. It is also a rush to be driven this way, to drive this way. Like the rush that first time, on the street behind the fence. Sheer joy! Some things never change.

But I had to wait.

First there was war. Only then 1950, the year on the half-crown. The year I first saw a sports car, a real one. A British roadster. The year I knew I would own one. The seed Father planted truly germinated then. But it would be yet more years before the sprout saw the light of day, years filled with wondering what it was like to drive a real sports car on the other side of the fence. Oh, there were cars I drove and rode in through those years, but they did not belong to me and they were not sports cars at heart.

Only at college age could I aspire to car ownership. My choice was easy. My first car was a sports car. I put up with all its quirks and its complaints, its nervous urge to go. And I did it for a very long time because of its forgiving nature when my skill behind the wheel fell short of its capabilities. But it grew old faster than I. When the time came for another, it gave way to cars without a soul. They were utilities. Appliances. Nothing more. There were no sports cars.

Then they returned!

And now I'm back where I started. The car I have today, with its half-crown stuck in the wheel, is no utilitarian appliance. This one is a brazen, damn-it-all contrivance without compromise. When pushed by unskilled hands this one will bite. But now my skill is equal to the task it was intended for. It is meant for speed, for racing, for driving on the other side of the fence, where the pure eroticism of driving dwells just as it did when I was four.

TULIPS ON TRIAL

Rosemary Mild

WHEN YOU PLANT TULIP BULBS IN OCTOBER, YOU take a lot on faith. Will they reward you with gorgeous blooms in the spring? Or will the squirrels get there first, burrowing in, digging up the bulbs and feasting on them?

In Severna Park, Maryland, eight miles north of Annapolis, this endeavor was akin to buying a lottery ticket. My husband and I are not clever gardeners. Nevertheless, my fragile hopes ran high in October 2000, when we diligently planted fifty bulbs in the modest flower bed fronting our house.

We had bought our pack of bulbs in Aalsmeer, in the Netherlands, home of the largest flower auction in the world. But these were not your ordinary bulbs. Our precious tulips came fraught with symbolism and represented a grievous journey. We bought them a week before traveling to Kamp Zeist, southeast of Amsterdam. We were headed there to attend the trial of two terrorists: Abdel Basset al-Megrahi and Lamen Khalifa Fhimah, two top-level Libyan intelligence agents. They had been indicted by the United States and Great Britain in 1991 for planting a bomb on Pan Am Flight 103.

The 747 exploded over Lockerbie, Scotland, on December 21, 1988, carrying the most important person in the world to me: my daughter, Miriam Luby Wolfe. She was twenty years old and my only child. Miriam was a junior majoring in musical theater at Syracuse University, on her way home after a glorious semester studying with the Syracuse group in London. My remarkable daughter had many talents: acting, singing, dancing, teaching, writing and directing. Thirty-five Syracuse students died aboard Flight 103. Until September 11, 2001, it was the worst terrorist act against the United States in our country's history. All 259 people on board—including 183 Americans—were killed, as were 11 Lockerbie residents on the ground.

In the Aalsmeer gift shop, as I waited to pay for our bulbs, my thoughts drove me down two avenues: the romance of buying tulips in Holland, and their emotional context on the eve of the trial. These captivating flowers would be more than a souvenir of our trip. They would stand, year after year, as a memorial to Miriam.

So stubbornly had I fixed on these profound implications that I neglected to ask the gift shop ladies just where it is that you plant tulip bulbs. In the shade? In full sun?

Larry and I learned the answer by default. Across the street from our house, the sunny side, our neighbors' tulips sprouted early and bloomed weeks before ours. Oh, dear. Tulips belong in full sun. We, on the north side, get only half-sun. Sometimes only quarter-sun. In the winter, snow sits on our front lawn longer than on anyone else's in the neighborhood.

But in mid-April, 2001, the first bud popped open. I leaned over it and stared in dismay. So skinny, so anemic. Would they all be like that? Did tulip blossoms get larger, more robust each day? Or, if they were born underdeveloped, did they stay pathetic, unable to catch up? Amazingly enough, each day new blooms greeted me. And with each one, I rushed back into the house and announced the status to Larry. "We have seven, dear. Come look!" I shouted. "We're up to twelve!" I cheered. I counted the blooms obsessively at least once a day. Sometimes twice.

Our fifty brave bulbs gave birth to sixty-four blooms. And they all progressed from their anemia to a hearty cup shape. Not earth-shattering, not prize-winning, but respectable. I took pictures, many long shots, then close-ups, to capture their extraordinary beauty: a blaze of yellow bursting inside a scarlet cup; a white star nestling in velvety purple. Each day as I bounded out of the house for the morning paper, I greeted our tulips as if they'd be with me forever.

THE TRIAL OF the two Libyans took place in the Netherlands before a Scottish court at Kamp Zeist, a former American Air Force base. The United Nations had negotiated this unusual arrangement with Libyan leader Moammar Gadhafi, who demanded that the trial be held in a neutral country. A concrete building at Kamp Zeist was transformed into a modern courthouse with a special secluded lounge for the victims' families. We attended the trial—already in its sixth month—for a week in October 2000, along with twelve other Pan Am family members. Before leaving for Europe, I cried for days, filled with anxiety over the prospect of facing the murderers of my daughter. But Larry and I realized there would be a cathartic benefit to seeing the murderers in the flesh and showing our support for their prosecution.

As our minibus approached the courthouse, we saw formidable but reassuring security. High chain-link fences with barbed wire. Scottish guards in blue, white and black uniforms with Kevlar vests and automatic weapons. Entering the courtroom for the first time sent a chill down my spine. A massive, floor-to-ceiling bulletproof glass wall separated the spectators from the court itself. Just beyond the glass, on the left, the defendants sat in an elevated box flanked by two guards. Directly below them, the defense team occupied two rows of tables and chairs. Facing them along the right wall was the Crown's prosecution team, including several U.S. State Department advisers. The three presiding judges, plus one alternate, occupied the "bench," a massive raised dais under the Scottish court crest.

I stared at the two men accused of mass murder, the men who had destroyed the life of my beautiful Miriam. A wave of fear shot through me. Not because they looked like monsters, not because I felt physically threatened. But because they looked so ordinary. Author Hannah Arendt, writing about Nazi war criminal Adolph Eichmann, described "the banality of evil." I had not understood the concept before, but now I did.

The spectator side of the glass wall held upholstered theater-style chairs and headphones for translations. We family members were seated in the large center section near the front. The physical closeness of these twelve warm, loving people—strangers to Larry and me before the trial—gave me strength. We shared so much, belonging to an involuntary club as victims of terrorism. We shared memories of our loved ones; the pain of our altered lives; and our feelings toward the accused, the splintered and sometimes biased media, and the sway of the trial itself.

At the back of the courtroom sat a group of observers of varying ethnic origins, representing the United Nations War Crimes Commission. The defendants' families and supporters, numbering only a few, occupied the smaller section on the left. My eyes unwillingly met the angry gaze of a large swarthy woman wearing the traditional Arab woman's black head scarf: Megrahi's wife. Her outfit, a long print skirt and jacket, could have come from Sears or J.C. Penney. She sat with their two children, perhaps preteens, who fidgeted in their chairs. A stream of heavy emotions tugged at me. The defendants have families? Loved ones? How could men so zealously evil, deliberately killing innocents, even babies, have genuine feelings? Doesn't ice water run in their veins?

We were warned to use only the restrooms in our family lounge, not the general one for trial visitors out in the corridor, because we might find ourselves in a confrontation.

It is widely believed that Scotland is one of the most pro-defendant countries in the world. The *Washington Post* reported that a special chef would prepare meals for the two defendants. The court also granted them a prayer room and exercise room. Did Oklahoma City bombers Timothy McVeigh and Terry McNichols—or any other mass murderer in an American prison—ever receive such luxuries?

ON JANUARY 31, 2001, the three Scottish judges pronounced Megrahi "Guilty!" and sentenced him to twenty years before he would be eligible for parole: the longest sentence allowed under Scottish law. Pan Am family members expressed outrage and frustration. They were quick to point out that only twenty years meant Megrahi would serve less than one month for each of the 270 victims. Adding to our dismay, Fhimah was declared "Not Guilty." The prosecution could not directly link him to the purchase of the timer circuit board that triggered the bomb. All the evidence linking Fhimah to the bomb was considered circumstantial. We felt sick to read that he flew home to a hero's welcome.

Nevertheless, a small measure of gratitude swept over Larry and me. At least we got one conviction. Evil had not won out entirely. Most of the families felt as we did. Nothing would bring our children back, but after twelve years, the verdict gave us some measure of justice.

Our sense of gratitude didn't last long. Megrahi launched his appeal immediately after his conviction. But first came a hearing to decide whether the appeal should even be allowed to go forward. Back at home, Larry and I followed the nine-month trial on a secure website—established just for the Flight 103 families by the U. S. Department of Justice Office for Victims of Crime. Every day, as we printed out summaries of the hearing, I anguished over every shred of the defense's arguments.

On October 15, 2001, the five new Scottish judges announced their decision. I was horrified. "It's only a month after 9-11!" I ranted to Larry. "How can they allow the appeal to go forward?" I paced the kitchen floor, my voice strident. "The trial lasted nine months, and the Libyans had eleven years to prepare their case. Why is Megrahi being given such leeway? It's shameful!" My husband had no answer. He was just as upset as I.

The appeal trial lasted thirteen months. As we read the summaries each day, Larry remained coolly confident that each new piece of "evidence" produced in such volume by the defense was flimsy. I agreed with him intellectually, but my stomach knotted up with dread. What if the conviction were overturned? What if no one were made to pay for Miriam's death?

On March 14, 2002, at 5:30 A.M. Eastern Standard Time, the five Scottish judges announced their verdict: "We have concluded that none of the grounds of the appeal is well founded. The appeal will accordingly be refused. This brings proceedings to an end."

At the time, Larry and I were spending the winter in Hawaii. Holding our breath, our eyes transfixed on CNN at 12:30 A.M., we heard the verdict. Appeal denied. We did not whoop and cheer. No. We fell into each other's arms and cried.

A sense of relief flooded me. I could breathe again. But I still felt a lurking reserve—until much later that day, when I logged onto the *New York Times* online and read that Megrahi "was flown to Scotland late tonight to begin his sentence there." That single line somehow liberated me, released me. It was the first tangible news, something I could grasp and clutch and cling to. Megrahi is now physically caged in a Victorian-era prison in Glasgow. According to Reuter's news service, Barlinnie has borne the reputation (until recently) as Scotland's toughest jail, administered under "Dickensian conditions." Yes! The bomber is being punished for his unspeakable act of terror, the mass murder of 270 innocent victims.

Megrahi, the former security chief of Libyan Arab Airlines in Malta, is of course only one man. Although Fhimah was acquitted, the U.S. government believes he, too, was guilty. And it is universally known that the two men did not act on their own, that the order to bomb Pan Am 103 came from Gadhafi himself. For many years, Libya was on our State Department's list of countries that sponsor terrorism.

Considering the nearly insurmountable odds of collecting evidence, the conviction of Megrahi seems almost miraculous. The plane exploded at 31,000 feet. Debris was scattered over 845 square miles. Combing the countryside in the rain, sleet, mud and wind of the Scottish winter, investigators and private citizens collected personal effects. It took the combined heroic efforts of investigators from Scotland, Britain, Interpol, our FBI and CIA, and volunteers from the saintly town of Lockerbie to locate components of the bomb and thus determine how it was smuggled aboard the airplane. They found a brown Samsonite suitcase that, according to Flight 103 baggage records, had been unaccompanied by a passenger.

Though Federal Aviation Administration regulations demand that any unaccompanied piece of luggage be hand-searched, when the suitcase was loaded onto Flight 103 (bound for Heathrow and then JFK) in Frankfurt, Germany, Pan Am's security personnel merely x-rayed the suitcase.

If they had hand-searched it, they would have discovered a Toshiba cassette-recorder and the bomb hidden inside it.

A group of Flight 103 families has since filed a civil suit against Libya. The civil action, not yet completely settled, included this cornerstone condition: that Moammar Gadhafi, as head of the Libyan government, take public responsibility for the bombing and renounce his state-sponsored terrorism. In 2003, under pressure from the United States, Great Britain and the United Nations, he renounced his country's terrorism and agreed to dismantle his nuclear weapons program. In 2005, at last, he admitted responsibility for the bombing of Flight 103.

We returned home from Hawaii in time for our darling tulips to perform for their second season. As we wheeled our luggage up the walk, I cheered. "Larry, they're coming up!"

Well, sort of. A few scrawny leaves greeted us. In the next few weeks, I expected them to burst forth with buds and blooms even stronger and healthier than the first year's. I expected them to join Larry and me in celebrating and symbolizing our victory.

But April and May came and went. In our entire flower bed, only twelve clumps of leaves appeared. Twelve clumps. Not one tulip! There the leaves stood: lonely, straggly, disheartened. Some weren't even standing. They were lying down, pale and yellowing, without the strength to even make an effort. And surrounding them, I discovered dents in the soil. Dents and deep holes. Many holes.

Larry studied the dents and holes in the dirt. "Hmm," he said. "Must be the squirrels." I nodded, too disappointed even to agree aloud.

But after a day of letting it all sink in, I could visualize what must have happened. Our resident squirrels undoubtedly followed the Libyans' trial and appeal. In my mind's eye, I could see them gathered in a huddle, their plumed tales quivering.

"Listen up, fellas and gals," the head honcho squirrel said. "The trial's over. The appeal's over. Let's eat!"

Yes, indeed.

My daughter had a joyful personality, and her optimism sustains me every hour of my life. In one of her journals, returned to me by the Scottish Police, Miriam kept an account of her exhilarating three-day trip to Wales. Sitting on a hillside, gazing at Kidwelly Castle, she wrote: "The sky was bluer today, the sun was yellower today, and the whole of the earth seemed to be rejoicing in its own perfection!"

It's time to take my cue from Miriam. Instead of brooding about spring blooms and what will come up or not come up, I think of our precious Dutch bulbs and pack them away in a corner of my memory. I smile at the squirrels prancing along our red maple branches. My decision is made. I jump in my car and head for Frank's Nursery. I hear they have exquisite silk tulips.

Bay Betrothal

Elizabeth Ayres

O CEAN WAVES ARE HORSES WITH FOAMING MOUTHS, ridden by witches wielding reins of seaweed. So say the Mapuche people of Chile, and who should know better? On a map, their land looks like a long thin blade of seagrass flung shoreward by the vast Pacific. Waves could be an angry Na-maka-o-kaha'i, Hawaiian goddess of the sea. Or a capricious Neptune, prodding at the surface with his trident to make a spot of trouble for some sailors.

Such stories came to me yesterday as I paced a shell-strewn beach, plucking at words, trying to describe to myself the look of sunlight on the Bay's wind-ruffled water. Gleam, glitter, sparkle? No, jewels are too inert. Dance, laugh, play? That's better, more alive, but what about awe and reverence for something totally beyond, utterly other? Something I can never hope to possess or control, can only aspire to meet, greet, encounter. That's when I felt it, a primal need to populate those mysterious waves with beings divine or demonic, and like the surf so sibilant at my feet, half-remembered legends lapped the edges of my mind.

Later, I perched atop a log of silvering driftwood. Amidst a flurry of scricks and clicks, a tern coaxed its fledgling to a piling just off shore. She skimmed the glistening ripples, swooped up, fell down straight as a plumb bob, disappeared with a splash and then reap-peared in a skyward zoom, fish secured in her beak. With a flurry of shrieks and screams, a young girl ran to, then from, to and from, to and from the water where it shimmied onto sand. Her father grabbed her, hoisted her up onto his back, and the mother took a snapshot of the pair. A white-haired couple plodded along, their white-haired dog racing ahead in a flurry of barks and yips, chasing a lone, white gull.

Zest of Chesapeake, above, and below? From my sea-sculpted seat I pictured some of our Bay's more exotic denizens.

The exuberant bristles and paddle-shaped feet of the clam worm. The prickly bumps of starfish skeleton, poking out through the skin of radiant starfish arms. And, needing neither witch rider nor seaweed reins, our very own *hippocampus erectus*, the lined seahorse.

Could a more improbable creature be imagined? A horse's head, a kangaroo's pouch, a fish's fins, a lizard's eyes, a dinosaur's bony plates, a monkey's prehensile tail, a chameleon's wardrobe and wafting, skin-like appendages that imitate algae to fool predators. They have no teeth, no stomach, and scarf up four thousand brine shrimp a day. Seahorses mate for life, and only males get pregnant. Every morning of their wedded life, the blissful couple embraces by linking tails, twirling around, changing colors, then dancing off in opposite directions.

A friend just gave me a magazine that is celebrating the beginning of summer by offering a guide to the pleasures of the season. I looked up the word in the dictionary. "Pleasure" means "the enjoyment of what is good," and I thought, wow, those seahorses are onto something. How about getting up every morning and meeting the day with a zestful swirl, a colorful, impassioned twirl? We are similarly improbable creatures; spirits wed to clay, divine sparks flung on the wood of this world in hopes of a fine, bright conflagration, or maybe it's a joyous dance our maker had in mind?

As I left the beach yesterday, a pair of swans alighted on the tidal pool. Partners for life, they say, although sometimes swans cheat, reneging on their commitment to each other. I said a little prayer to bolster my own commitment to fishing terns and shrieking children, old folks, dogs, gulls. Light playing tag with the sparkling water. Waves laughing themselves onto shore. All the sweet and yes, the sour this day, this life shall offer. We are very, very good together.

FLYING WITH A GHOST

Ami Spencer

I WATCHED CHILDREN PLAYING IN THE CRAMPED CONCOURSE, trying to run but tripping over feet, bags, themselves. Their freedom made me smile and I wished for their energy at such an early hour. There were men in pressed suits and starched white shirts, checking their PDAs and rifling through their briefcases. A woman sat across from me lost in the book she was reading. I stared out the wall of windows into the dull darkness giving way to morning light. A magazine lay in my lap, open but ignored, as I waited anxiously to board my flight to Minneapolis. While I was excited to see my best friend, it had been more than a year since I'd been on a plane and I wasn't looking forward to the flight.

Having taken my fair share of cross-country and cross-continent trips for both work and fun, flying has always been something I do solely out of necessity, simply a way to get where I'm going. You see, I hate to fly—but not for the reasons you might suspect. I'm not afraid that the engines will stop working and we'll plunge into the sea, or that we'll be hijacked, or that the pilots are under the influence of some drug or another. My fear isn't about Mother Nature or mechanical failure. For me, the trouble with flying has always been this: I used to be too big for the space that each passenger is allotted on a plane. My entire flying history has been tainted by the size I once was.

My large body once overflowed my assigned space. My arms overlapped those of the other passengers in my row. My thighs rubbed against a stranger's and robbed her of her personal space. I felt sorry for my fellow travelers, sorry that they couldn't be at ease beside me. I quickly discovered that leaning into the aisle—unless a lavatory user or flight attendant passed by—was much more comfortable. It was better than being crammed between a window and the barrier of air I tried to create between myself and the person next to me, or being sausaged between two unsuspecting travelers who would suffer because of my size.

Once in my chair, I dreaded any hint of pressure below my waist. I loathed the experience of getting up, inconveniencing those nearest the aisle, and bumbling toward the closet of a bathroom, all the while knocking sleeping passengers with my baggy arms and bumping them with my ample behind. It terrified me. And I would have to do it again on the way back, after cramming myself into the tiny toilet and emptying my bladder. I avoided the unbearable experience with a simple prescription: No fluids for two hours before take-off and empty twice before boarding.

While I suspected this trip would be different after some recent weight loss, I wasn't taking any chances. I had carefully chosen my aisle seat, and I would follow my usual toileting routine. When I returned to the waiting area after my final trip to the restroom and settled back into my chair, I heard a discussion taking place behind my back between four college students—two young men and two young women.

I flipped through my magazine, barely listening but catching bits and pieces of their conversation—who had which classes and professors the next semester; who else would be on their trip to Costa Rica. Then I heard one young man with a gravelly morning voice pipe up and I listened more closely. "Well, that's why they decreased the weight of the luggage you can take. Because people have gotten so heavy," he said.

Another student, a young woman with a high, whiney voice, spoke up with disgust. "I know! America is getting so fat." I cringed as though she had reached out to strike me.

I immediately wanted to disappear into the faux-leather of my chair. In my mind, I knew that they weren't talking about me—not the person they could see anyway—but still I slouched in my seat attempting to hide a heavier ghost of myself. Though my back was to them, I ducked my head hoping they couldn't see the flush of embarrassment and anger that crept up my face. The students continued with their conversation as I glanced around to see who else might be overhearing these thoughtless words, who else might be offended and hurt by them. No one seemed to notice but me. I tried to shake it off with a quick glance over my shoulder and a tuck of my hair behind my ear. I cleared my throat and returned to my magazine, scanning the pages of emaciated models wearing the newest fashion trends. My overactive insecurities were getting the best of me again.

A third student, this time a young woman with a kinder, softer voice, said, "I heard they were supposed to be making adjustments and stuff so that those people aren't so uncomfortable. Like making the seats bigger and the aisles wider."

"Well I heard huge people have to pay for two seats now, to try to reduce the weight on planes," the young man replied. He actually used the word huge. I wanted to scream. Who did this guy think he was? The fat police?

"So when you make your reservation, you have to enter your weight or something? I didn't have to do that," said the soft-voiced woman, firmly challenging the young man's statement. I silently cheered her on. I even considered turning to smile at her, but caught myself before I did. My heart beat a bit faster and I could feel the flush rising in my face again. The din of the crowd around me threatened to drown out the conversation, so I listened more closely, turning my body a bit so that I could hear them better.

"Yeah," the young man said, "but maybe it's only for some flights right now."

The soft-voiced woman interjected again. "Well that's not fair. I'd be pissed if I had to pay double just because I weighed more."

I attempted to peek over my shoulder to get a good look at this friend of mine without letting the group know I was eavesdropping, but I only caught a glimpse out of the corner of my eye before another male voice, deeper and firmer than the first young man's, entered the conversation. "As far as I'm concerned," he said, "that's not always something people can control. I mean, people's bodies are made to be a certain size. They can't help it. It's, like, in their genes and stuff."

He must know someone, I thought to myself, someone who's dealt with these insults and struggles. Someone like me.

If one of them had looked at me at that moment, I doubt they would have had any clue why their words should affect me. On the outside, I looked like an average-sized woman. In fact, for the first time in more than a decade, I am an average-sized woman. Little did they know that inside my shrinking suit of flesh was a permanently fat version of myself.

The kind words of the second young man fell on deaf ears. The whiney woman chose that moment to toss her two cents in. "Well, I don't think it's fair that I can't bring as much stuff with me as I want to. I mean, I shouldn't be punished for someone else being fat." She giggled a bit, but her disgusted tone belied the serious sentiment behind her words. Would anyone notice if I hit her over the head with my bag?

The first young man laughed and then suggested a solution. "They should put a total combined weight limit on them. Like you and your bags can't weigh more than three hundred pounds, so if you weigh three-fifty, you have to lose fifty pounds in order to fly and a hundred if you want to bring a fifty pound bag with you." At least he could add and subtract. Some of the others laughed at his logic, although I couldn't be sure if it was out of amusement or discomfort. Maybe a bit of both.

Someone eventually changed the subject, or their conversation drifted on to another topic. But I was left there in the wake of all they had said.

When the flight attendants called my section, I boarded the plane with my carry-on bag, stuffed to the maximum capacity with reading material, my iPod, and a bag of snacks—carrots, an apple, and low-fat cheese. Though my flight anxiety was building, I smiled at the attendants and wished them a good morning as I passed. I slipped into the row that I chose months before and stowed my bags by my feet with minimal effort. I settled into the aisle seat that used to cause me indescribable discomfort and watched the others board. When my row-mates arrived, I moved easily into the aisle for them and then slid back without any difficulty.

I was ready, out of habit rather than necessity, to remain seated for as much of the flight as possible. Once everyone was comfortably where they belonged, I adjusted the air nozzle above me to blow on my face and leaned back, trying to relax. The flight attendants directed our attention to the safety pamphlets in the pockets of the seats in front of us and the safety video began. I tuned it all out and closed my eyes.

A short while after take-off, the drink cart jostled me from my nap, and a flight attendant offered, "Soft drink, coffee, tea, or water?" in a sugary voice. I knew I shouldn't drink anything, and I was already feeling some bladder pressure; I always have to pee when I wake up. Still, I was extremely thirsty. I hesitated for a moment, and then requested a diet soda. She passed it to me with a cup of ice and a bag of pretzels and as she pushed the cart past me to the next row, it occurred to me that my legs were crossed comfortably in front of me. The young woman next to me had plenty of room, even when I wasn't hugging my arms tightly to my sides as I was so accustomed to doing. I was resting without care in a tight space.

Still, even in the midst of this realization, my chest tightened and my stomach churned at the thought of heading to the back of the plane to release the pressure now screaming at me from my bladder. I finished off my snack slowly, delaying the inevitable. I eventually pushed through the fear, glancing over my shoulder to count the rows I'd need to traverse. Sixteen, give or take a couple. I took a deep breath, slowly lifted the latch on my lap belt and stood without once grazing the traveler to my left.

This surprised me, but I continued to move. I carefully, slowly made my way past rows seventeen and eighteen, avoiding bodies that encroached upon the aisle as I once did. I smiled at a large man in seat 23D and he smiled back, a moment of understanding and kinship passing between us. We are veterans of the same battles, he and I.

When I finally reached the lavatory, it wasn't as teeny and threatening as I remembered it. I closed the door and locked it without incident. I was able to turn around (I did it twice just to prove it to myself) and sit down on the toilet without any adjustment or squeezing.

Back in my seat, I breathed a sigh of relief and settled myself once again. It was not me those students were referring to in the waiting area for Gate C3, I realized, but a ghost of me that still visits now and then. She reminds me of where I have been and how far I have come. She nudges me with compassion for those whose size continues to be an obstacle too frightening to face alone.

And just in case I ever forget what it felt like to wear those extra layers of flesh, she makes me have to pee on an airplane.

AUTHORS' BIOGRAPHIES

ELIZABETH AYRES • **BAY BETROTHAL**

Elizabeth Ayres is a poet, essayist and writing teacher. Her books include *Writing the Wave* (how-to) and *Know the Way* (poetry). She's currently completing *American Dreamscape: Encounters with the Wonder of Earth, Sea and Sky*. Founder of the Elizabeth Ayres Center for Creative Writing (www.creativewritingcenter.com), Ms. Ayres has recently returned to St. Mary's County, where she grew up. She performs her essays every Saturday night from 6:00 to 6:30 on internet radio: www.wryr.org.

CHRIS BANCELLS • **SAYING THANK YOU**

Chris Bancells is a writer and teacher who lives in Bel Air, MD with his wife (his inspiration) and his dog (his comic relief). He is a regular columnist for the online magazine Blogcritics.org and his work can also be read at www.runningbowline.com.

SHERRY BOSLEY • **PROBABLE CAUSE**

Sherry Bosley holds an MFA in Creative Nonfiction from Goucher College. She has won numerous writing awards including one from the *Atlantic Monthly*. Bosley is a retired police officer from the Maryland State Police and is currently teaching English and Journalism. She lives in Bel Air with her husband, son, and daughter.

AUSTIN S. CAMACHO • **THE LOST DAUGHTER CAPER**

Austin S. Camacho is the author of four detective novels in the Hannibal Jones series and two adventure novels featuring jewel thief Felicity O'Brien and mercenary soldier Morgan Stark. Camacho is a past president of the Maryland Writers' Association and teaches writing at Anne Arundel Community College. A public affairs specialist for the Defense Department, Camacho lives in Springfield, Virginia with his lovely wife Denise and Princess the Wonder Cat.

JENNIE L. DEITZ • **CHICKEN NECKING**

Jennie L. Deitz is a freelance writer specializing in travel and human interest stories. She also works as a part-time publicist for local authors. She has published articles in the *National Geographic*

Traveler Magazine, Bay Weekly, Reunions Magazine, and the *Twin Beaches Business Journal.* She currently is working on her first thriller novel about a new domestic intelligence agency in the United States.

LAUREN BETH EISENBERG • FEAR TO FREEDOM: MATURING AS A WRITER

Lauren Beth Eisenberg is coordinator of the MWA Creative Non-fiction Critique Group. Her works include *Autumn Leaves,* a family history; *Shards,* her memoir-in-progress; *Excess Baggage,* a story about growing up, letting go, expectations, and biases; *Beyond Stick Figures,* a sassy look at life and the quest for artistic recognition; and *Better Than No Man,* a novel about domestic abuse in post-Katrina Biloxi. She has spoken at the 2007 Maryland Writers' Conference on "Daring to Write."

SCOTT E. FRIAS • FOUR MEMORIES OF FEAR • CONDITIONAL

Baltimore writer, father, military officer, UMBC English department graduate. Long time lover of words, sung or spoken, so long as with passion.

JANE FRUTCHEY • FRIDAY AFTERNOON ON CURRITUCK SOUND

Jane Frutchey's work earned awards in MWA's 2005 Short Works Contest and Missouri Saturday Writers 2005 Poetry Contest. Jane's articles, essays, and poems have been featured in the *Baltimore Sun, Maryland Life, Mason-Dixon Arrive, Tradition, Baltimore Dog, Women on a Wire, September 11: Maryland Voices, Cuivre River Anthology,* and *Spot of Grace: Remarkable Stories About How You Do Make a Difference.* She is author of *Seven Steps to Starting and Running an Editorial Consulting Business.*

ERIC D. GOODMAN • CICADAS

Eric D. Goodman is a full-time writer and editor. He's been featured in a number of publications, including *The Washington Post, Baltimore Review, Writers Weekly, Slow Trains, Arabesques Review, Scribble, JMWW, On Stage Magazine, Travel Insights,* and *Coloquio.* Eric has read his fiction on NPR, as well as at book festivals, galleries, and events. His first children's book, *The Flightless Goose,* flies into book-stores in 2008. Visit Eric online at www.writeful.blogspot.com.

JULIET M. JOHNSON • BIG, HOPEFUL LOOPS • EXIT CHARLOTTE

Juliet M. Johnson won the MWA One-Act Play Award (1999). Her plays have been produced by The Baltimore Playwright's Festival, Mobtown Players, SoHo Repertory, and the Samuel French Short Play Festival. Prose publications include numerous magazines, three anthologies, and her new motherhood book, *Somebody's Always Hungry*. She lives (transplanted from Maryland) in Los Angeles with her family. Check out her website: www.somebodysalwayshungry.com.

FRANK S. JOSEPH • OUR LADY OF THE HELICOPTER

Frank S. Joseph's story "Our Lady of the Helicopter" won second place in the 2002 MWA Writing Contest. His first novel, *To Love Mercy*, also an MWA contest winner (2003, second place, Mainstream Fiction), was published in 2006 by Mid-Atlantic Highlands. It has won six awards and is in its second printing. Frank lives in Chevy Chase, MD.

AL KARASA • HALF-CROWN

Al Karasa is an eclectic writer in subjects ranging from maritime fiction to heraldic sciences. His books include *Sidney's Pub* (2007), *Firehead's Malice* (2003), *Drive Smart!* (2001), and *Sherridan's Rain* (1995). His work has been seen in national magazines for over twenty-five years. He was a columnist at *MCA Magazine* and was locally featured in *Maryland Life* and *Chesapeake Bay*. For more about Al Karasa and his work, visit www.alsbooks.com.

SUSAN LESSER • WELL BEING

Susan, now retired from a varied career, lives and writes in rural Harford County, surrounded by nature, gardens and pets. She is past editor of *Manorborn* and *Poems of Place*, both published by the Harford Poetry and Literary Society. Her poems have appeared in *Penumbra*, *Poetry Midwest*, *Wordhouse*, *Avocet*, *Darkling* and others.

GARY L. LESTER • THE LAST DRUMMER

Gary L. Lester spends most of his time on planet Earth with his wife Linda and three sons. He won his first writing award at the age of seventeen. His writings include skits and comedies and numerous short stories. His novel, *Ursula the Yellow*, won first place Fantasy in the Maryland Writers' Association novel contest. You can visit his blog at www.earthundalles.blogspot.com.

SONIA L. LINEBAUGH • THE LAST GOOD DAY

Sonia L. Linebaugh creates her fiction and nonfiction stories on the shores of the Chesapeake Bay. Her nonfiction book, *At the Feet of Mother Meera: The Lessons of Silence*, was published in 2004.

ROSEMARY MILD • TULIPS ON TRIAL

Rosemary Mild is the author of *Miriam's Gift: A Mother's Blessings—Then and Now*, a tribute to her daughter killed in the terrorist bombing of Pan Am 103 over Lockerbie, Scotland. Rosemary's articles have appeared in the *Washington Post, Baltimore Sun, Washington Woman* and elsewhere. She and her husband, Larry, co-author the Paco and Molly mysteries: *Boston Scream Pie* (coming in 2008), *Hot Grudge Sunday*, and *Locks and Cream Cheese*. Visit the Milds at www.magicile.com.

B. MORRISON • CITY

B. Morrison writes poetry, fiction and nonfiction. *Here at Least*, her recent collection of poetry, is now available from Cottey House Press, and *Right of Way: Introduction to Identity and Privilege Management* will be released in Fall 2008. The award-winning writer lives in Baltimore, Maryland. Visit her website, www.bmorrison.com, for information about upcoming appearances and her Monday morning book blog (www.bmorrison.com/blog).

Sherry Audette Morrow • Imprints

Sherry Audette Morrow is a writer, editor, graphic designer, and publisher. She is the founding editor of *Scribble* magazine. Her work has appeared in publications in the U.S. and Canada, including locally in *Baltimore* magazine, *Chesapeake Life* magazine, *Scribble* magazine, and *Lite* literary newspaper. She is currently working on two novels.

Liz Moser • Paulownia, The Tree • Mélange

Liz Moser's poetry, fiction, memoirs and book reviews are well represented in national and regional journals and magazines. She published a chapbook, *Spirit Pond and Other Maine Poems* (Goose River Press, 2004) and, with three other women, a collection of poetry, *Leavings* (Bay River Press, 2005). She received a 2003 F. Scott Fitzgerald Literary Conference fiction award and the *Potomac Review's* 2002 Poetry Prize. She has been an Editor of the *Baltimore Review* since 2003.

Lalita Noronha • Shanti's Choice • Waning Moon • Thirty-Two Years

Born in India, Lalita Noronha has a Ph.D. in Microbiology and is a science teacher, writer, poet, and fiction editor for *The Baltimore Review*. Published in over forty journals and anthologies, her awards include the Maryland Literary Arts Award twice, Maryland Individual Artist Award, and the National League of American Pen Women Award, among others. She is the author of a short story collection, *Where Monsoons Cry*. Her website is www.lalitanoronha.com.

Vanessa Orlando • Perfect Instincts

Vanessa Orlando is the two-time recipient of the Maryland Writers' Association Short Fiction Prize. Her award-winning short story, "When Sara Looks Up," was made into a short film by Columbia College Chicago. Her work appears in two recent anthologies: *Enhanced Gravity: More Fiction by Washington Area Women* (Paycock Press) and *Mind Trips Unlimited* (Scribes Valley Publishing). She lives in Crofton with her husband, three dogs and two cats.

ANGELA RENDER • THE DRYAD

Angela Render has articles published on Smithsonian.com. Her historical fiction, *Forged By Lightning: A Novel of Hannibal and Scipio* (ISBN 978-1-4416-8002-9) was published in 2002. She has a column in *Writers' Journal* called "Computer Business," and she teaches writers how to build a marketing platform at the Writer's Center in Bethesda, Maryland. Her companion workbook, *Marketing for Authors: A Practical Workbook* was published in June of 2008. Visit her website at www.angelarender.com.

BONNY BARRY SANDERS • FATHER • THE GAME OF JACKS

Bonny Barry Sanders' first book of poems, *Touching Shadows*, was published by Val Verde Press. She is working on a second collection. Her poems, book reviews, and essays have appeared in *Birmingham Poetry Review*, *Blueline*, *Chattahoochee Review*, the *Christian Science Monitor*, *Connecticut Review*, *Florida Review*, *Hayden's Ferry Review*, *Louisiana Review*, *Negative Capability*, *South Dakota Review*, *South Carolina Review*, and others. Her historical novel, *Kiss Me Good-bye*, was released by White Mane Publishing early in 2007.

LAURA SHOVAN • MOUNTAIN, LOG, SALT AND STONE • BROTHER

Laura Shovan is a poet in the Maryland State Arts Council's Artist in Education program. A graduate of NYU's Dramatic Writing Program, her poetry has appeared in *Global City Review*, *Lips*, the *Jewish Women's Literary Annual*, *Poets Online*, *Little Patuxent Review* and the *Paterson Literary Review*. Shovan's poems have twice won honorable mention in the Allen Ginsberg Poetry Awards. She is also a freelance journalist and children's author.

AMI SPENCER • FLYING WITH A GHOST

Ami Spencer had her first experiences with writing and dieting in a small town in northern NY. She currently lives in Baltimore, MD and works as a technical writer while building her freelance writing business. Ami has published articles in various local, regional and online publications, including *AAA Carolinas GO Magazine*, *Radiant*, *Baltimore City Paper* and the *Potomac Review*. To get to know her and view some of her work, visit www.amispencer.com.

LYNN STEARNS • FAMILY RECIPE

Lynn Stearns leads "Story Construction" workshops at the Writer's Center in Bethesda and serves as an associate fiction editor for *Potomac Review*. She edited two volumes of *Stories From the Attic*, collections of poems, personal essays, and stories by Maryland senior citizens. Her work has appeared in more than fifty publications, most recently in the anthologies *Not What I Expected* and *Tapestries*.

MARY STOJAK • CLEAR LAKE

Mary has devoted a large part of her life to music and is now trying to not follow the Federal Government Printing Office guidelines regarding the placement of commas.

SALLY WHITNEY • HENNA NO. 25

Sally Whitney's short stories have appeared in literary and commercial magazines including *Buffalo Spree, Catalyst, Common Ground, Innisfree, Potpourri, Kansas City Voices* and *Pearl*, and anthologies including *Grow Old Along With Me—The Best Is Yet to Be*, published by Papier-Mache Press in Watsonville, California. The audiocassette version of *Grow Old Along With Me* was a 1997 Grammy Award finalist in the Spoken Word or Nonmusical Album category.

SHERRI COOK WOOSLEY • THE MAN WITH THE PATCHWORK SOUL

Sherri Cook Woosley earned her M.A. in English Literature from University of Maryland. She joined the Maryland Writers' Association three years ago and has since published short fiction at zonemom.com and in the spring '06 edition of *Mount Zion Literary Review*. Currently she writes a monthly column titled "Crankypants" for a MOPS (mothers of preschoolers) newsletter and is a contest judge for www.coffeehousefiction.com.

REPRINT INFORMATION

"Bay Betrothal" by Elizabeth Ayres. Originally published in *Bay Weekly*, volume 15, issue 21, 2007. Reprinted by permission of the author.

"Brother" by Laura Shovan. Originally published in *Little Patuxent Review*, issue 4, 2008. Reprinted by permission of the author.

"Family Recipe" by Lynn Stearns. Originally published in *Scribble*, volume 3, issue 1, 1999. Reprinted by permission of the author.

"Four Memories of Fear" by Scott Frias. Originally published in *City Paper's Annual Poetry Contest*, 2003 and Austin International *Poetry Festival Anthology*, 2004. Reprinted by permission of the author.

"Henna No. 25" by Sally Whitney. Originally published in *Kansas City Voices*, volume 3, 2005. Reprinted by permission of the author.

"Mountain, Log, Salt and Stone" by Laura Shovan. Originally published in the *Jewish Women's Literary Annual*, volume 6, 2004. Reprinted by permission of the author.

"Paulownia, The Tree" by Liz Moser. Originally published in *The Baltimore Sun*, June 29, 2008. Reprinted by permission of the author.

"Saying Thank You" by Chris Bancells. A longer version of this essay has appeared on the author's website, www.runningbowline.com. Reprinted by permission of the author.

"Tulips on Trial" by Rosemary Mild. Originally published in *Scribble*, volume 6, issue 1, 2006. Reprinted by permission of the author.

"Our Lady of the Helicopter" by Frank S. Joseph. Originally published in *Scribble*, volume 5, issue 2, 2005. Reprinted by permission of the author.

Membership Application

Membership in the Maryland Writers' Association is renewable annually. Contact the Membership Director for more information.

To join, either print and fill out the application below and mail it along with your annual dues of $35.00 (made out to MWA) to:

Maryland Writers' Association
PO Box 142
Annapolis, MD 21404

Or, submit your application online and pay your annual dues via PayPal.

Please allow up to 6 weeks for processing.

☐ I would like to join the Maryland Writers' Association. My dues for 12 months are enclosed.

Name _____

Address _____

_____

_____

_____

Home phone _____

Work phone _____

Fax number _____

E-mail addres: _____

My area of interest/writing specialty is:

_____

_____

My published works (if any) are:

_____

_____

_____

☐ Would you like to join a critique group?
☐ Would you like to help with the Writers' Conference?
☐ Would you like to receive Pen In Hand by e-mail only?

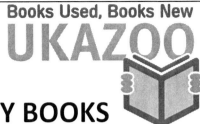

Printed in the United States
204898BV00005B/19-39/P

9 780982 003206